THE SPACE BETWEEN

A Novel
by Jordan Marlowe

For those who have ever wanted more, but feared what it might cost.

And for those who dared anyway.

This book would not exist without the encouragement and patience of my partner, Lauren, who reminded me daily that stories are worth telling, even when they're hard to write.

To my friends and early readers, thank you for holding me accountable and believing in this story from the beginning.

And to every reader who picks up this book, thank you. You are why I write.

Prologue

Every marriage has its secrets.

Some are small — a white lie about where the money went, a hidden annoyance never voiced aloud. Others are larger, heavy truths buried beneath routine and compromise, truths that no one dares speak for fear of what might happen if they were unearthed.

Kayla had always believed she knew where the lines were in her own marriage. She and Quinn loved each other deeply, built a life together, raised a child, paid the bills, endured the monotony of errands and late-night arguments about whose turn it was to do the dishes. Their love was ordinary in the best of ways. Safe. Predictable.

But safe is not the same as fulfilled.

It began quietly, almost innocently — curiosity disguised as conversation. A passing comment. A joke that lingered too long. The spark of possibility where there had once only been routine. Kayla wasn't looking to upend her life, not consciously. Yet the thought, once born, refused to be buried. What if marriage didn't have to mean limits? What if desire didn't have to be denied?

Quinn, for his part, had never imagined himself the type of man to question fidelity. He prided himself on being steady, on being the anchor in their partnership. But anchors can grow heavy, and in his quiet moments, when Kayla wasn't looking, he felt the same pull of what-ifs. What if there was more to love than the familiar? What if sharing didn't mean losing?

They never set out to invite strangers into their home, their bed, their hearts. They never planned to test the fragile boundaries between love and lust, between devotion and desire. But life rarely follows the plans we write for it.

It was supposed to be an experiment. A controlled risk. One night to

scratch an itch they didn't fully understand.
Instead, it became the unraveling of everything they thought they knew.

Because once you cross a line — once you open the door to what lies on the other side — you can't pretend you never saw it. You can't pretend you don't crave more.

For Kayla and Quinn, the question was no longer whether they loved each other. That was certain. The question became: could love survive the hunger for something more?

And what happens when the third person you let in isn't a stranger at all... but someone much closer than either of them expected?

Preface

The Space Between was born from a question I couldn't shake: what if love didn't fit the neat boxes we were told it must? What if longing and loyalty could coexist, messy and complicated, without canceling each other out?

This story is not my story, but it is informed by real human questions about intimacy, desire, and the courage to confront what we want most.

1

The morning sun filtered through the blinds, casting soft golden streaks across the Harris family's cozy, lived-in kitchen. The scent of freshly brewed coffee mingled with the warm aroma of pancakes on the griddle, a quiet but comforting start to another weekday morning. Kayla stood by the counter, gently stirring a pot of oatmeal while periodically glancing over her shoulder at their six-year-old son, Zeke, who sat at the kitchen table kicking his legs excitedly against the wooden chair.

Quinn entered the kitchen, still groggy from sleep, his tie draped loosely around his neck. He stepped behind Kayla and wrapped his arms around her waist, pressing a lazy kiss to her shoulder. She smiled, leaning back against him, momentarily closing her eyes at the familiar comfort of his embrace.

"Good morning," he murmured into her neck, his voice low and gravelly.

"Morning," she replied, tilting her head slightly as his lips grazed her skin. "Coffee's ready."

He sighed in relief, stepping away just long enough to grab a mug and pour himself a generous amount, taking a slow sip as he watched Zeke fiddle with his spoon. The boy was making faces at his reflection in the cereal milk, giggling to himself.

"Zeke, eat your breakfast before it gets soggy," Kayla called, placing a small bowl of oatmeal next to his cereal. "You've got soccer practice after school today, remember?"

Zeke nodded enthusiastically. "I can't wait. Coach says I might be the fastest boy on the team this year."

Quinn chuckled as he leaned against the counter. "That's because you're always running around like you have rocket boosters in your... shoes," he joked, correcting himself after receiving a glare from Kayla.

Zeke grinned proudly, scooping up a spoonful of oatmeal and slurping it loudly. Kayla gave him a playful side-eye before shaking her head with a smile. These little moments — these everyday interactions — were what made their family whole. Their life was predictable, simple, and yet filled with love in ways that made the chaos of parenting worth it.

Once breakfast was finished, the morning rush commenced. Quinn helped Zeke into his sneakers while Kayla packed his lunch, moving effortlessly through their well-rehearsed routine. It had been like this for years, with weekday mornings filled with the comforting repetition of shared responsibilities and stolen moments of affection.

Before long, it was time for Quinn to drop Zeke off at school before heading to work. Kayla kissed her son on the forehead, smoothing down a stray curl before straightening his backpack.

"Be good today, ok?" she said.

"I will, Mom."

Quinn patted Zeke's head and guided him toward the door, turning back for a moment. "See you tonight."

Kayla met his gaze, something soft lingering in the way they looked at each other. "Sounds good."

And just like that, they were off — Quinn and Zeke disappearing down the driveway as Kayla exhaled, finally taking a moment to breathe in the quiet stillness of the house.

2

Their days blurred together nowadays, indistinguishable from the ones before them. Mornings started the same way — Kayla's alarm buzzing at 6:30 a.m., a reminder that she had to start the day before she even felt ready. She would roll over, trying to steal a few extra minutes beneath the warm covers before sighing and pushing herself up. On the other edge of the bed, Quinn was already shifting, groggily reaching for his phone to check emails before his feet even hit the floor.

By the time Kayla was in the kitchen making coffee, Zeke was bounding down the hallway, already filled with the energy she longed for. She would greet him with a sleepy smile, tousling his wild morning hair before setting a bowl of cereal or oatmeal in front of him. Some mornings, Quinn would join them, half-awake, drinking his coffee while absently scrolling through his phone. Other mornings, he would be rushing out the door, muttering something about an early meeting or a last-minute deadline.

Then the day would truly begin. Drop-offs, commutes, meetings, emails, calls... Kayla's job wasn't bad — it was steady, reliable, the kind of position people considered a blessing. But it was also predictable and repetitive. Each day brought the same stack of tasks, the same polite small talk with coworkers, the same countdown until she could leave and return home. The hours passed like a slow drip from a leaky faucet, steady and unremarkable.

Evenings were the highlight of her day, but even they had become predictable. On a normal night, she would stop at the grocery store on the way home from work, picking up the same rotation of items — chicken, vegetables, pasta, snacks for Zeke. She didn't even have to think about it anymore. The shopping list practically wrote itself.

By the time she got home, Quinn would already be working on dinner. Tonight, he was firing up the grill, his focus on the heat and the sizzle of the meat rather than her. Zeke would be running in circles, giggling, finding some imaginary game to keep himself entertained. The smell of charcoal and food cooking would fill the air as Kayla unpacked the groceries, her mind wandering as she went through the motions.

They would eat together, conversation light and easy — Zeke rambling about his day at school, Quinn making a joke about something at work, Kayla nodding along, smiling, responding at the right moments. There was love at the table, warmth even.

She had come to see over time though that something was missing. Or maybe something had settled. There was no excitement, no urgency, no spontaneity. It was the same routine they had followed for years, and while it was comforting in its familiarity, it also felt like something was slipping away.

After dinner, the cleanup process would be methodical. Plates would immediately be placed in the dishwasher (Kayla hated full sinks), leftovers packed away, then Zeke's bath time. Kayla would read him a bedtime story and give him goodnight kisses. And then it would be just Kayla and Quinn again.

They would settle onto the couch, an unspoken agreement to watch whatever show they had been trying to get through. Quinn would drape an arm around her, fingers idly tracing patterns on her shoulder. Sometimes, she would lean into him, seeking comfort in his touch. Other times, she would sit just slightly apart from him, the space between them feeling heavier than it should.

Sure, they still made love, but it had become just another part of the routine. It was predictable, structured, almost… mechanical. There were no surprises, no exploration, no… fire. It was good but not the kind of passion she once craved. Not the kind of passion she remembered from their early days, when they couldn't keep their hands off each other, when every touch sent shivers down her spine.

When she used to feel truly desired.

She wanted to shake herself out of it, to find a way to reignite something, to feel that rush again, but how? They had built a beautiful life together — a stable, loving home, a wonderful son, a marriage that by all outward appearances seemed strong. But beneath it all, there was something quietly gnawing at her. A flicker of restlessness she couldn't ignore.

Lying in bed at night, staring at the ceiling, she would sometimes wonder if Quinn felt it too. Whether he missed the fire. Whether he missed the version of them that used to exist before the routine took over. She had tried to bring it back by suggesting weekend getaways, initiating intimacy in new ways, hinting at new, adventurous sexual things she wanted to try. But Quinn, ever practical, ever predictable, would respond with polite interest that never seemed to lead anywhere.

Maybe this was just what marriage became after years together. Maybe she was foolish to think that kind of passion could last forever. Maybe the quiet comfort of predictability was enough. Isn't this how all marriages are?

Kayla didn't know what the stirring desire meant yet, but she knew it was there.

And soon, she would have to acknowledge it.

3

It wasn't that Kayla was unhappy. She loved Quinn. She loved Zeke. Their life together was warm, steady, and secure. And yet, there were those nights when she would lie awake in bed, staring at the ceiling, feeling a restlessness she couldn't quite name.

Earlier in their relationship, their nights had been filled with urgency, with whispered teasing and stolen glances that sent shivers down her spine. Now, everything felt like part of a schedule. Quinn would kiss her goodnight, and once a week they'd make love for a few minutes — always in the same way, always leading to the same conclusion — and then he'd roll onto his side and drift off to sleep, leaving Kayla staring at the darkened room, feeling… unsatisfied.

She hated that she felt this way. She hated that she wanted more. More excitement. More adventure. More of that raw passion that used to make her knees weak.

For weeks, she ignored the feeling, convincing herself it was just a phase. She buried it beneath the responsibilities of work, motherhood, and keeping their household running smoothly. But no matter how much she tried to push it aside, it lingered, whispering to her in the quiet moments of her day.

There were little things that reminded her of what they had lost — the way Quinn used to look at her when she stepped out of the shower, the way he used to surprise her by pulling her into a deep, urgent kiss in the middle of making dinner, the way they used to laugh breathlessly against each other's skin, completely lost in the moment.

Now, everything was routine. He kissed her the same way every morning, touched her the same way in bed, held her the same way after.

Kayla could predict every move before it happened. Quinn would reach for her the same way, pulling her onto him with an almost absent-minded gesture. His hands would travel in the same patterns, as if following a well-worn path. He'd kiss her, but it was mechanical, more of a means to an end than something meant to make her shiver. She would respond, trying to inject some spark into it, trying to make it feel urgent again. But within minutes, it would all fall into place exactly as expected.

They would then move to missionary. Slow, steady thrusts. He would groan, she would close her eyes, and then, just as she started to feel something more than just going through the motions, it would be over. He would kiss her shoulder, murmur something sweet, and then roll onto his side, sighing with contentment as sleep pulled him under.

Kayla, meanwhile, would stare up at the ceiling, pulse still racing but unfulfilled. Sometimes, she would reach between her own legs after he fell asleep, finishing what he started, needing to grasp onto something that felt like real pleasure. But most nights, she simply lay there, feeling a growing sense of emptiness.

She had tried to change things. A few months ago, she had surprised Quinn with new lingerie — something delicate and lacey, a deep crimson shade that made her feel sexy and powerful. She had sauntered into their bedroom, waiting for him to notice.

And he had. He smiled, his eyes darkening with appreciation. But then he simply pulled her onto the bed, kissed her, and everything unfolded exactly the same way it always did. Same touches. Same rhythm. He never even paused to admire the way the lace fit against her skin. By the time it was over, she felt foolish for trying at all.

There were also those times she suggested trying something new. Something bolder. One night, she whispered in his ear that she wanted to try a different position, wanted him to be rougher, to take control the way he used to when they were younger. She had hoped for a flicker of excitement in his eyes, some sign that he missed that version of them too.

Instead, he chuckled softly, kissing her temple. "Babe, we don't need all that," he murmured. "We're good the way we are."

And that was it. The discussion was over before it even began.

She wanted spontaneity. She wanted to feel desired. She wanted something that would jolt them out of their comfortable, predictable rhythm.

She didn't want to cheat. She didn't want to leave. But something had to change.

Something had to wake them up.

4

Kayla had been looking forward to a night out with her friends for weeks. Between work, being a mother, and the slow-growing restlessness in her marriage, she needed this more than she realized. It had been too long since she'd gotten dressed up, let loose, and just been herself — outside of being Quinn's wife or Zeke's mom.

Tasha, her best friend since college, had chosen a trendy new wine bar downtown for their outing. The place had an upscale yet cozy vibe, with mood lighting, plush velvet chairs, and a lively crowd of young professionals unwinding after a long week. A jazz trio played in the background, adding to the ambiance.

Kayla arrived a little late. Getting Zeke settled with the babysitter had taken longer than expected. When she walked in, she spotted Tasha immediately, already holding a glass of red wine, her dark curls framing her face as she animatedly told a story to two of their other friends, Laura and Deja.

"There she is!" Tasha exclaimed, waving Kayla over. "Girl, I was starting to think you weren't gonna make it."

Kayla laughed as she slid into the seat next to her. "You know it takes a whole operation to get out of the house these days."

Tasha rolled her eyes. "Tell me about it. But you're here now, and we are getting you a drink."

A waiter arrived, and Kayla ordered a glass of white wine. As the night went on, the drinks flowed, and so did the laughter. They caught up on work, life, and the usual gossip. Kayla hadn't realized how much she had needed this until now — the easy camaraderie, the feeling of being seen outside of her roles at home.

Then, after a few drinks, Tasha leaned in, lowering her voice like she was about to share a deep secret. "Ok, ladies," she said, her eyes sparkling mischievously. "I have something to tell you, and it is going to blow your minds. Something that you need to keep only between us."

Kayla and the others leaned in. "Ooh... what?" Deja asked, intrigued.

Tasha took a sip of her wine before speaking, and flashed a sly smile. "Eric and I... we've been swinging."

Kayla blinked. "Wait, what?"

"Like, swapping partners?" Laura asked, eyes wide.

Tasha nodded, and with a deep grin, said, "Yep."

There was a pause before Deja let out a loud laugh. "Girl, you are lying."

"I am dead serious," Tasha said, smirking. "And let me tell you, it has changed everything in our marriage."

Kayla felt her stomach flip, though she wasn't sure why. "Ok, hold on. You're just... out here sleeping with other people?"

Tasha chuckled. "Not just me. Both of us. Together. It's not like cheating or anything. It's an experience. And honestly? It's the most alive we've felt in years."

Kayla exchanged glances with Laura and Deja, trying to gauge their reactions. Laura looked intrigued, while Deja looked skeptical, almost judgmental. Kayla, on the other hand, felt something different entirely — a mix of shock, curiosity, and... something else she couldn't name.

"How did it even start?" Kayla asked.

Tasha leaned in, clearly enjoying their reactions. "It started small. We were at this bar one night, kind of like this, and we met this couple. They were flirty, fun, and we just hit it off. We exchanged numbers, and after a few weeks of talking, we got together for drinks again and they brought it up — asked if we'd ever thought about being with other people together."

"And you just… said yes?" Deja asked incredulously.

Tasha shrugged. "At first, we were shocked and weren't sure. We awkwardly left that night, but then we talked about it — a lot. We decided to set ground rules, and then one night, we met them at a hotel, had drinks, got comfortable, and…" She let the sentence hang in the air, watching their reactions.

Kayla could feel her pulse quicken. She took a slow sip of her wine. "And…?"

Tasha smirked. "And it was the best sex of my life! Hands down."

Laura let out a low whistle. Deja shook her head in disbelief. Kayla, meanwhile, felt heat rise to her cheeks.

Tasha continued, "But it wasn't just about the sex. It was about the excitement, the newness. And the best part? Afterward, when Eric and I went home, we couldn't keep our hands off each other. It was like we had rediscovered something."

Kayla felt a strange flutter in her chest. That was exactly what she had been craving — something to shake them up, something to bring back that burning desire she missed. But swinging? That was something she never would have considered.

"So, wait," Deja said, resting her chin in her hand. "You guys do this regularly now?"

Tasha nodded. "Not every weekend or anything, but yeah, when we find the right couple."

"And you don't get jealous?" Kayla asked, genuinely curious.

Tasha shook her head. "At first, I thought I might. But honestly? It's different when you're both in it together. It's not like he's sneaking around or I'm feeling neglected. If anything, it has brought us closer. We communicate better, we're more open about what we want… and girl, our sex life? Next. Level."

Deja scoffed. "I don't think I could ever do that."

Laura shrugged. "I mean… I can see how it could work, if you have that level of trust."

Kayla didn't say anything right away. She wasn't sure what to think. The idea was wild, unconventional, but it also made her feel something she hadn't felt in a long time — curiosity. Excitement.

Tasha noticed her silence and nudged her. "What about you, Kay? What do you think?"

Kayla hesitated, swirling the wine in her glass. "I don't know," she admitted. "I mean, I love Quinn. We have a good marriage. But…"

"But…?" Tasha pressed.

Kayla sighed. "I guess I've also just been feeling like something's missing. Like we're stuck in this routine, and no matter what I try to do, I can't shake it."

Tasha nodded knowingly. "That's exactly how I felt before we started!"

Kayla chewed her lip, her mind racing. She had always thought she and Quinn would figure things out on their own, that maybe they just needed more date nights or some new way to spice things up. But this? This was an entirely different possibility, one that thrilled and terrified her in equal measure.

The conversation eventually shifted to other topics, but the thought lingered. Even as the night wound down, even as she laughed and clinked glasses with her friends, Kayla couldn't shake the idea that had taken root in her mind.

As she rode home in the back of an Uber, the city lights flashing past the window, she found herself wondering — what if?

And once that thought was there, she knew it wasn't going away.

5

For the next couple days, Kayla couldn't stop thinking about what Tasha had said. It had only been a casual conversation over wine, yet it clung to her thoughts like a melody she couldn't shake. The idea of swinging both thrilled and terrified her, leaving her caught in a whirlwind of emotions she struggled to process.

At first, she tried to dismiss it. Surely this wasn't something she could seriously consider. She and Quinn had a good marriage — stable, loving, and full of respect. They had built a life together, one filled with laughter and companionship, even though the passion had dulled over the years.

But that was the problem, wasn't it? The passion. The fire. The raw, urgent need that used to burn between them had settled into something warm but predictable. She missed the feeling of losing herself in the moment, of being overwhelmed by desire. She had tried to rekindle it in small ways — buying new lingerie, initiating more, subtly pushing Quinn toward new things — but he never responded in the way she craved.

Now, the thought of what Tasha had described haunted her. It wasn't just about the sex. It was about the excitement, the newness, the way she spoke about feeling alive again. Kayla wanted that feeling. She desperately *needed* that feeling.

She wasn't naïve, though. This was dangerous territory. It's not like this was a subject you could bring up casually over dinner. If Quinn reacted badly, would it change things between them forever? Would he think she was unsatisfied with him? Would he see it as a betrayal, an insult to their marriage?

The thought of hurting him made her stomach twist. The last thing she wanted was to create a rift between them. But then another question followed closely behind —

What if he was just as restless as she was? What if, deep down, he felt the same?

That question lingered, refusing to be ignored.

Kayla's body had betrayed her in the days that followed. She found herself more aroused, more eager to be close to Quinn, as if testing herself to see if she could push these thoughts away with sheer will. She initiated more often, hoping to light that spark that would reignite what they had lost. At first, Quinn seemed surprised by her sudden hunger, but he never questioned it. He went along with it, kissing her, touching her, responding in the way he always had.

Their intimacy had become almost routine. Quinn would press soft kisses against her neck, trail his hands over her body, and move through the motions like he was following a script. There was no spontaneity, no unpredictability. She loved him, but she longed for something that wasn't so... structured.

One night, she tried something different. She bought a lacy black set of lingerie, something bolder than she'd ever worn before. It left little to the imagination and accentuated every curve of her sexy caramel brown body. When Quinn walked into the bedroom, she was waiting for him, stretched across the bed, her wrists and ankles lightly tied to the bedframe.

His brows lifted in surprise, but instead of the smoldering hunger she had hoped for, he hesitated. "What's... this?"

"I thought we could try something new," she murmured, tilting her head invitingly. "Spice things up a little."

Quinn chuckled, rubbing the back of his neck. "You didn't have to do all this, babe. I love the way things are."

Something inside her deflated at his words. She forced a smile, trying to shake off the sting. "I thought it would be fun."

He climbed onto the bed, pressing a kiss to her forehead. "Of course. Let's have some fun."

But as he moved above her, touching her the same way he always did, she knew he wasn't really into it. He was doing it for her, but not because he desired it. And that realization left a hollow feeling in her chest.

She tried again later that week, pushing boundaries in small ways — whispering dirty things in his ear, taking control in bed, touching him in ways she never had before — but each time, Quinn followed her lead, but never matched her energy. It was as if he was indulging her.

Kayla felt like she was grasping at something just out of reach, and no matter what she did, she couldn't pull it close enough to hold onto.

Kayla found herself lying awake most nights, replaying the things Tasha had said over and over again. The idea of swinging refused to leave her mind.

It wasn't just the words themselves — it was the confidence in which she spoke them. The way she made it sound so simple, so natural, as if opening up her marriage to other people was as ordinary as trying a new restaurant. But could it really be that easy?

Imagining what it would be like to step outside of their marriage — not in a way that broke them, but in a way that strengthened them — sent a thrill down her spine. Could it bring them closer? Could it make them want each other the way they used to?

But there was the risk. The enormous… terrifying… risk.

How would she even begin to ask Quinn if he wanted to sleep with other people?

She practiced it in her head, trying to find a way to frame it that didn't sound insane. Maybe she could ease into it, joke about it at first. Or maybe she could test the waters by asking if he ever fantasized about being with someone else. Would that lead to an honest conversation, or would it scare him? Would it make him think she wanted to cheat?

Her hands felt clammy just thinking about it.

Fear was holding her back, so she buried it. She let the idea sit, lurking just beneath the surface, waiting for the right moment to be brought into the light.

That moment came sooner than she expected.

During a particularly tense therapy session, they had been discussing communication. The weight of their unspoken issues had been growing heavier with each visit. It was like they were walking through a dense fog, both of them aware of something lingering just beyond their reach but too afraid to confront it directly.

Their therapist, Dr. Emily Simmons, sat across from them, her notebook resting lightly in her lap. "Kayla, Quinn… I want you both to take a moment and really reflect on this question: What is something you need from your partner that you feel you're not getting?"

The silence stretched. Kayla could feel Quinn glance at her, waiting for her to speak first. Her heart pounded as she clenched her hands together in her lap.

The words sat on the edge of her tongue, ready to be swallowed back, to be locked away. But something inside her refused to hold them in any longer.

She took a breath and said it out loud.

"I need… more."

Quinn turned his head toward her, his expression shifting from neutral to confused. "More?"

Kayla swallowed hard. "More excitement. More passion. I feel like we've lost something, and I don't know how to get it back. I keep trying to get it back, but nothing has worked."

Dr. Simmons nodded encouragingly. "That's an important realization, Kayla. Can you give an example of what 'more' would look like for you?"

Kayla's hands clenched even tighter. She felt Quinn's eyes on her, waiting. She had spent weeks agonizing over whether to say it, but now the moment was here and she had to push through the fear.

She licked her lips, exhaled sharply, and forced herself to say it.

"I want to explore things. Try new things. I… I want to push boundaries."

Quinn's brows furrowed slightly, confusion flickering across his face. "Like what?"

Kayla hesitated. This was it. The moment that could change everything.

She closed her eyes for a second, steeling herself, then met his gaze. "Like... swinging."

The room went completely silent.

Quinn blinked. His expression was unreadable at first, and that terrified her. His mouth opened slightly, then closed. Finally, after what felt like an eternity, he let out a strained laugh.

"Wait... what?" His voice was low, almost as if he wasn't sure he had heard her correctly.

Kayla's stomach twisted, but she refused to back down. "I want to try swinging," she repeated, her voice firmer this time. "You know... exploring things. With other people."

Quinn sat back in his chair, running a hand through his hair. "Jesus, Kayla. Where is this coming from?"

Dr. Simmons leaned forward slightly, her voice calm. "Quinn, let's take a second before reacting. Kayla, can you explain what led you to this realization?"

Kayla took another deep breath, her pulse pounding in her ears. "I've been feeling stuck," she admitted. "Like we've been going through the motions for so long. I love you, Quinn. I really do. But I feel like we lost something along the way. And I don't know how to get it back."

Quinn's jaw tightened. "And you think sleeping with other people is the answer?"

She bit her lip. "It's not... not just about sex. It's about excitement. About trying new things together. About breaking out of this rut we're in."

Quinn shook his head, rubbing his hands over his face. "Kayla, I don't even know what to say right now."

Dr. Simmons interjected, her voice steady. "It's natural to feel shocked, Quinn. This isn't an easy topic to bring up. But Kayla, I do want to ask — have you given thought to what you're hoping this will accomplish?"

Kayla nodded. "I want to feel desired again. I want to see *us* again, not just as parents or roommates who share a bed, but as lovers. I want to bring something new into our relationship, not to replace what we have but to enhance it."

Quinn exhaled slowly, staring at the floor. His mind was clearly spinning.

Dr. Simmons turned to him. "Quinn, how are you feeling about this?"

He let out a dry laugh. "Honestly? I don't know. I mean… I *get* what she's saying. I feel the rut too. But this? Swinging? That's a huge leap."

Kayla swallowed the lump in her throat. "I know it is. And I'm not saying we have to do anything. I just… I want us to talk about it."

Another stretch of silence. Quinn looked at her, really looked at her, and Kayla felt exposed. Vulnerable, like she had just torn open her chest and laid everything inside out in front of him.

Finally, he sighed. "I don't know, Kayla. I need time to process this."

Dr. Simmons gave them both a reassuring nod. "That's completely understandable. What's important is that you've opened a dialog. I encourage you both to take time to reflect on this conversation and how it makes you feel — both individually and as a couple."

Kayla felt the weight of the moment settle around them. She had done it. She had said the thing that had been clawing at her for weeks. And now, there was no turning back.

Whether that was a good thing or not remained to be seen.

6

The days that followed their therapy session weren't hostile but they were definitely tense. Quinn was quietly processing, and Kayla tried to give him the space to do so. She knew this was a lot to take in. She had spent weeks wrestling with the idea before even saying it out loud. Expecting Quinn to adjust in mere days was unfair, but the waiting still gnawed at her.

They tiptoed around each other, neither willing to be the first to bring it up. Their conversations remained light — work, Zeke, dinner plans — but the unspoken weight of their last session hung over them. Then, on a Sunday afternoon, as they sat on their back patio sipping coffee, Quinn finally exhaled and spoke.

"I've been thinking about what you said."

Kayla set her cup down carefully. "And?"

He rubbed his eyes and then ran his hand down his face. "I still don't know if I get it. Or if I want it. But I'm willing to try if it's something you need."

Relief flooded through her, though she tried not to show it too much. "Really?"

Quinn nodded, though his face was still troubled. "Yeah. But there has to be rules. And if at any point I feel like this isn't working, I need you to respect that and we need to stop."

Kayla reached for his hand, squeezing it. "Of course. This only works if we both want it."

He studied her for a moment before sighing. "How did you even start thinking about this, anyway?"

She hesitated. She promised Tasha that it would stay between them, but Quinn was looking at her expectantly. "A friend. Someone I trust."

His brow furrowed slightly, but he nodded. "Then maybe you should talk to her. Figure out how people even start something like this and rules we should have in place."

That night, Kayla texted Tasha: *Need to talk. Got time this week?*

Tasha responded almost immediately: *For you? Always. Come by for wine tomorrow night.*

The next evening, Kayla arrived at Tasha's place, a modern townhouse filled with warm light and the scent of vanilla candles. Tasha, ever the perfect host, handed her a glass of wine before leading her to the couch.

"Ok," Tasha said, tucking her legs under her. "What's up?"

Kayla took a deep breath. "So... Quinn and I have been talking about swinging."

Tasha's eyes widened, then a slow grin spread across her face. "Oh. My. God. I knew it! You've been thinking about it ever since we talked, haven't you?"

Kayla laughed softly. "Maybe."

Tasha clinked their glasses together. "Girl, welcome to the club. So, tell me everything. Where's his head at?"

"He's... open. Very hesitant, but open. He says he'll try it, but only if we have clear boundaries and can stop at any time."

Tasha nodded approvingly. "Good. That's exactly the right approach. You both have to feel safe if you adopt the lifestyle."

Kayla swirled her wine, hesitating before speaking again. "How do we even start? Like, where do we even find people? How do we make sure it's... right?"

Tasha smirked. "Oh, that's the fun part. There are apps, websites, exclusive clubs — it's a whole world out there. But since you're just starting, I'd go the app route. It gives you time to talk to people, set expectations, and find the right fit."

Kayla nodded. "Which apps do you recommend?"

Tasha grabbed her phone and pulled up a list. "Here are the ones I use. Some are invite-only, but I can get you in. Others are more open but still high-quality."

Kayla glanced at the screen, taking mental notes. "And once we're on there?"

Tasha leaned back. "Just create a profile, but be honest about what you're looking for. Don't feel like you have to rush into anything. And most importantly — set your ground rules now."

Kayla raised an eyebrow. "What kind of rules?"

Tasha ticked them off on her fingers. "Only play together or separately? Full swap or just soft play? How often? Who gets final say on partners? Are there any hard stops? And —" she pointed at Kayla's wine glass, "—be honest about jealousy. It's normal at first. You just have to be able to talk through it."

Kayla exhaled. "That's... a lot."

Tasha grinned. "Yeah, but it's worth it. The first time is nerve-wracking, but once you find the right person, it's exhilarating. Trust me."

Kayla's mind was spinning, but excitement coiled in her stomach. This was happening.

The next night, after Zeke had gone to bed, Kayla and Quinn sat together in the dim light of their living room, laptops open as they scrolled through different apps and forums.

Quinn let out a low whistle. "There's... a lot of people doing this. A lot more than I thought."

Kayla chuckled. "Yeah, apparently we're late to the party."

He shifted uncomfortably, his brows furrowing as he continued to scroll. Kayla noticed his hesitation, the way his jaw tightened ever so slightly. She reached out and rested a hand on his knee.

"Babe, we don't have to do this if you don't want to," she said gently.

Quinn exhaled and leaned back into the couch. "It's not that I don't want to, it's just... I don't know. This is all really new. I don't know where to start."

Kayla nodded, understanding his trepidation. She had done more research than he had, read forums, listened to stories, even talked to Tasha about it. She wanted to help him ease into it rather than pushing him into the deep end.

"Ok, so let's make this simple. What would make you feel the most comfortable for our first time?" she asked.

He hesitated, chewing on the inside of his cheek before answering. "I guess... I don't know if I'm ready to see you with another guy yet. That might be too much for me."

Kayla had expected that. She had already thought about this and had a plan in mind. "What if our first time was just with another woman?" she offered. "No other guys. Just us and her. Would that feel less intimidating?"

Quinn blinked, clearly relieved. "Yeah. Yeah, absolutely."

Kayla smiled, glad she had found a way to ease his mind. "Ok, then that's what we'll do."

They continued browsing, and after some discussion, they settled on one of the invite-only apps that catered to couples looking for a shared experience.

Once Kayla got the invite from Tasha and their profile was approved, their inbox was immediately flooded with invitations — some polite, some crass, others enticing in ways Kayla hadn't expected.

Quinn scrolled through the messages, shaking his head. "Some of these people have zero chill."

Kayla laughed. "Welcome to online dating."

Then, amid the flood of messages, one stood out.

Her name was Lacey and her profile was striking — a stunning woman with dark, wavy hair and piercing green eyes, her pictures both elegant and sultry. In one, she lounged on a bed in white lace lingerie; in another, she smirked at the camera over the rim of a cocktail glass.

Their first messages were playful yet direct:

Lacey: "So, first time dipping your toes into the water?"

Kayla: "You could say that. We're looking for someone we both connect with."

Lacey: "Smart choice. Chemistry is everything. I'd love to meet and see if we click."

The rush was intoxicating. As they set up a date, Kayla felt her heart race.

There was no turning back now.

7

They chose an upscale but dimly lit restaurant, the kind of place where the candles flickered and the waiters spoke in hushed tones. The atmosphere was thick with anticipation, the air perfumed with the scent of expensive wine and sizzling steak. Nervous energy crackled between them as they arrived early, deciding to have a drink at the bar before Lacey showed up.

Kayla sipped her cocktail, her fingers drumming lightly against the glass. "Are you nervous?" she asked, glancing at Quinn.

He chuckled, taking a slow sip of his whiskey. "A little. Feels like a first date."

Kayla smirked. "That's because it kind of is."

The minutes passed, the drinks dulling their nerves just enough, and then she walked in.

Lacey.

She moved like she owned the room. Her long, dark waves cascaded over her shoulders in loose, careless curls, and her emerald-green eyes sparkled with something just shy of mischief. She wore a sleek black dress that hugged her curves in all the right places, the hemline riding up just enough to tease but not reveal. A delicate gold chain rested at her collarbone, drawing attention to the elegant dip of her neck. Her lips, painted a deep shade of red, curled into a knowing smile as she scanned the room.

When her gaze locked onto Kayla's, a slow, deliberate smile spread across her lips. Kayla felt her breath hitch slightly. There was something about the way Lacey looked at her — like she was peeling back layers with just her eyes, like she already knew the answer to a question Kayla hadn't even asked yet.

Quinn stood as she neared the table, his mind racing with how to greet her. Should he shake her hand? Hug her? Give her a nod and subtle wave? Before he could decide though, Lacey leaned in smoothly, pressing a soft kiss to Kayla's cheek before turning to him with an expectant expression. He hesitated just a fraction too long, awkwardly extending his hand before thinking better of it and leaning in for a hug. The result was a clumsy half-handshake, half-embrace that made Kayla stifle a giggle.

Lacey's lips twitched with amusement as she pulled back, smoothing a hand over her dress. "Nice to meet you, Quinn," she said, her voice rich and velvety.

"You too," he replied, rubbing the back of his neck as they all sat down.

Lacey crossed her legs gracefully, one slender calf sliding over the other in a way that was both casual and entirely deliberate. She rested her elbow on the table, her fingers brushing over the rim of her water glass as she watched them with curiosity. "So, how are we feeling? Excited? Nervous?"

"A little of both," Kayla admitted with a small smile.

"Good." Lacey took a sip of her drink, her eyes twinkling. "That's the fun part."

Once the menus were in their hands, the conversation started slow but picked up with the first round of drinks. Lacey had a natural charm, effortlessly weaving between playful teasing and deeper, more thoughtful discussion. She talked about her experiences in the lifestyle, answering their hesitant questions without judgment.

"So, what made you two take this step?" Lacey asked, stirring her cocktail lazily.

Kayla glanced at Quinn, then smiled. "We love each other. A lot. But we realized we were missing something — excitement, maybe. I'm hoping it helps us find connection in a new way."

Lacey nodded, her gaze warm and understanding. "That's the best reason for couples to do this. To grow together, not apart."

She again ran her fingertip along the rim of her glass, her eyes dancing between them. "You know, most couples I meet, there's usually one partner who takes the lead. One who's a little more curious than the other."

Quinn cleared his throat, shooting Kayla a look. "Yeah, that would be her."

Kayla rolled her eyes playfully. "Don't let him fool you. He's just as intrigued."

Lacey smirked. "I like intrigued."

There was something about the way she said it, the way her voice dipped slightly, that sent a shiver down Kayla's spine.

"So, tell me," Lacey continued, twirling her straw between her fingers, "have you two ever played with someone else before or is this your first time?"

Kayla hesitated, glancing at Quinn. "First time."

Lacey's smile widened. "I love newbies."

Quinn exhaled, laughing nervously. "Is that a good thing?"

Lacey winked. "That depends. Are you good students?"

Kayla felt her cheeks warm. Quinn shifted in his seat.

Lacey leaned in slightly, lowering her voice. "I could teach you both a lot. If you're willing."

Kayla swallowed. She hadn't expected Lacey to be so forward, but she liked it. She liked the way Lacey's gaze lingered, the way she seemed completely at ease in this situation while she and Quinn fumbled through their nerves.

As the night wore on, the initial tension melted away and was replaced by an undeniable chemistry. Kayla felt it in the way Lacey's eyes lingered on her, in the way Quinn leaned in just a little closer when she spoke. There was something electric between them, something Kayla hadn't felt in a long time.

When dinner ended and the check was paid, Lacey reached for her purse and smiled. "So, what do you think?" she asked, her gaze flicking between them. "Do we click?"

Kayla and Quinn exchanged a look. The answer was already clear.

Lacey grinned, reaching into her bag. She pulled out a small card and slid it across the table toward Kayla. "I have a suite at the Mirabelle downtown. Why don't you two come by for a nightcap?"

Kayla's heart hammered in her chest. She hadn't expected to take the next step tonight. She thought this was just a 'getting to know you' date. She looked at Quinn, searching his face for hesitation, but all she saw was the same curiosity, the same thrill.

"We'd love to," Kayla said, reaching for the card.

Lacey's smile deepened. "Good." She leaned in, her lips grazing Kayla's ear as she whispered, "I have a feeling this is going to be fun."

8

The car ride to the Mirabelle was quiet, but the air between them buzzed with an unspoken intensity. Kayla stole glances at Quinn, noticing the way his fingers tapped rhythmically against the steering wheel, his jaw set in contemplation.

"You're thinking about her," she murmured, a small smile tugging at the corner of her lips.

Quinn let out a short, guilty laugh, shaking his head. "I think we both are."

Kayla exhaled, pressing her palms against her thighs. Her body hummed with anticipation, her skin already tingling at the thought of what was about to happen. She had imagined this moment so many times, playing out different scenarios in her head, but now that it was real, she felt the weight of it settling in her chest.

When they pulled into the Mirabelle's circular driveway, Quinn handed his keys to the valet with slightly shaky hands, which Kayla noticed. She wasn't sure if it was nerves, excitement, or both. Probably both.

They stepped through the glass doors into the hotel's sleek, dimly lit lobby. The marble floors gleamed under the chandeliers, and the scent of fresh-cut lilies lingered in the air. Kayla's heels clicked against the polished surface as they made their way toward the elevators, her pulse pounding with every step.

Quinn pressed the button for the twelfth floor, exhaling slowly as the elevator doors slid shut. He turned to Kayla. "Are we really doing this?"

She bit her lip, nodding. "We are."

The elevator climbed in silence, the tension in the enclosed space thick and heady. Kayla felt Quinn's hand brush against hers, and without thinking, she laced her fingers through his, grounding herself in the familiarity of his touch. He squeezed back.

The doors opened with a soft chime, revealing a long, quiet hallway bathed in warm golden light. Room 1208. Kayla repeated the number in her head as they walked past doors, each step heavier than the last.

They stopped in front of the door, hesitating for the briefest moment. Quinn shifted beside her, rolling his shoulders as if trying to shake off his nerves.

"Last chance to back out," he murmured.

Kayla looked at him, her heart pounding, her body already thrumming with anticipation. "Do you want to?"

Quinn inhaled deeply, then exhaled, shaking his head. "No."

Kayla lifted her hand and knocked.

The door opened almost instantly, as if Lacey had been waiting on the other side. She was barefoot now, her sleek black dress replaced with a silky, wine-colored slip that clung to her curves like liquid. Her dark hair tumbled over her shoulder in soft waves, and her lips curled into a knowing smile.

"Right on time," she purred, stepping aside and motioning for them to enter.

The suite was breathtaking. Floor-to-ceiling windows offered a sweeping view of the city skyline, the lights twinkling like a sea of stars. A bottle of champagne sat chilling in a silver bucket on the bar, and soft, sultry music played from hidden speakers, setting the mood.

Kayla felt her breath hitch as Lacey closed the door behind them, the faint click echoing in the room.

"Make yourselves comfortable," Lacey said, padding across the plush carpet toward the bar. "I was just about to pour myself a drink. Would you like one?"

"Whiskey," Quinn said immediately, his voice a touch rougher than usual.

Kayla hesitated. "Champagne, please."

Lacey poured their drinks with an easy grace, handing Quinn his glass first before turning to Kayla. When Kayla reached for it, Lacey's fingers grazed hers — deliberate, lingering just a moment too long. A thrill shot through Kayla at the contact.

Lacey sank onto the couch, her posture relaxed and confident, as if she belonged there. She took a slow sip of her drink, eyes flicking between them. "So, tell me. What are you two feeling right now?"

Kayla let out a nervous laugh. "A little overwhelmed."

Lacey smiled. "That's understandable."

Quinn exhaled, running a hand through his hair. "It's just... this is new for us."

"Of course it is," Lacey said, her voice soothing. "That's what makes it exciting. The unknown, the anticipation. It's all part of the thrill."

She set her glass down and leaned forward, resting her chin in her hand. "And what about you, Kayla? How do you feel?"

Kayla swallowed. "Excited, but nervous."

Lacey's lips curved. "That's my favorite combination."

The room felt smaller somehow, more intimate. Kayla glanced at Quinn, who met her gaze with a silent question. Are we really doing this?

Kayla inhaled, steadying herself, then turned back to Lacey. "So... what happens now?"

Lacey's smile deepened as she stood, crossing the room with slow, measured steps. She stopped in front of Kayla, reaching down to take her hand, pulling her gently to her feet.

"Now," Lacey murmured, her fingers brushing Kayla's cheek, "we see where the night takes us."

Kayla's breath hitched as Lacey leaned in, her lips hovering just above hers, the warmth of her breath sending shivers down her spine. It was a moment suspended in time, charged and heavy with possibility.

And then, finally, Lacey kissed her.

The kiss was soft at first, a gentle exploration, but it then became deeper, more insistent. Kayla melted into it, her fingers tangling in

Lacey's hair, her body pressing closer without thinking. The taste of champagne lingered on Lacey's lips, and Kayla sighed against her mouth.

Quinn stood frozen for a moment, watching as his wife kissed another woman for the first time. There was something undeniably hypnotic about the sight, the way Kayla responded so naturally, as if she had done this a thousand times before.

Then, just as smoothly, Lacey turned to Quinn. He barely had time to react before she leaned in and kissed him with the same deliberate slowness. Her lips were soft, her perfume intoxicating, and for a second, all he could do was let himself fall into it.

Kayla let out a soft laugh, shaking her head. "That sure helped us get out of our heads."

Quinn exhaled. "Yeah… I wasn't expecting that."

Lacey smirked. "Good. Surprises keep things interesting."

She nodded toward the plush chair near the window, telling Quinn, "Why don't you sit down for a bit? Watch. Get comfortable."

Quinn hesitated for only a second before nodding and taking a seat. His heart was racing, but curiosity — and excitement — kept him there.

Lacey walked up to Kayla, her movements slow and deliberate. Without breaking eye contact, she leaned in and kissed her again. This time, it was even deeper, more purposeful. Her hands traced over Kayla's sides, teasing along the edges of her curves but never fully touching.

Quinn swallowed hard, watching as Lacey's fingertips skimmed just close enough to Kayla's chest and hips to make them both shiver. She was playing with both of them, and it was working.

Kayla let out a soft sigh against Lacey's lips, and Quinn felt the heat between them growing thicker. His nerves had been replaced by something else entirely — pure anticipation.

Lacey finally pulled back slightly, glancing over her shoulder at Quinn. "Still nervous?" she asked playfully.

He let out a slow breath and smirked. "Nope. Not anymore."

9

Lacey stepped back, her fingers moving to the straps of her slip. The room was quiet except for the sound of breathing — theirs, hers, the shared anticipation hanging in the air like a charged wire. With slow and deliberate movements, she slid one strap off her shoulder, then the other, her emerald eyes never breaking contact with Kayla's. The flickering city lights beyond the window cast shadows over her skin, accentuating every delicate movement.

Kayla's heart pounded so loudly she was sure Quinn could hear it.

Lacey hesitated right above her nipples for just a moment, teasing the suspense, a playful smirk curving her lips as she noted Kayla's shallow breath and the way Quinn's fingers clenched into the armrest of his chair. Then, with fluid grace, she allowed the silky fabric to glide down her frame, revealing smooth, golden skin beneath. The slip pooled at her feet, and she stood tall, poised, her body adorned in the evening glow.

Quinn sucked in a breath beside Kayla. She barely noticed — her focus was entirely on Lacey. On the way her body curved, on the effortless confidence she carried in every movement.

Lacey took a slow step forward, closing the distance between herself and Kayla. She reached out, the tips of her fingers tracing a delicate line down Kayla's arm, sending a shiver through her body. Kayla had never been touched like this before, at least not by another woman. There was something different about it — it was softer and more intentional, yet just as electric. She exhaled sharply, her lips parting slightly.

"You're shaking," Lacey whispered, her voice warm and knowing. "Are you nervous?"

Kayla swallowed hard, forcing herself to meet Lacey's eyes. "A little."

Lacey smiled.

Her fingers dipped lower, brushing along Kayla's wrist before moving to the zipper of her dress. With agonizing slowness, she pulled it down, her touch featherlight, teasing, all the while looking Kayla in the eyes. Kayla felt Quinn shift beside her, his presence grounding her even as she teetered on the edge of something completely unfamiliar.

As the fabric loosened, sliding over her shoulders, Lacey leaned in, her lips barely grazing Kayla's ear. "Just breathe," she murmured, her breath sending a rush of warmth down Kayla's spine.

Kayla's dress fell to the floor, leaving her in nothing but delicate lace. The cool air of the hotel room kissed her bare skin, making her hyper-aware of every sensation — the way Lacey's fingers traced absent patterns along her collarbone, the way Quinn's eyes roamed over her with an intensity she hadn't seen in years.

Lacey's gaze flickered to Quinn, amusement dancing in her emerald eyes. He had started to rise from his seat, his body urging him forward, his jaw tight with restraint.

"Not yet," Lacey purred, lifting a single finger. The command was playful, but firm.

Quinn exhaled sharply and leaned back, his knuckles white against the armrest. Kayla could feel the tension radiating from him, an energy she hadn't felt in their marriage in such a long time. It sent a pulse of exhilaration through her veins.

Lacey returned her focus to Kayla, her hands skimming along the bare skin of her waist. Every touch was slow and deliberate, as though she were mapping Kayla, committing every inch and reaction to memory. Kayla had never felt so... seen. So thoroughly studied. It was intoxicating.

Her lips hovered near Kayla's neck, brushing so close yet never quite meeting skin. Kayla's breath caught in her throat. She had spent years being worshiped by Quinn, being adored, but this was something else. This was someone entirely new, an experience entirely unknown, and it made her feel alive in a way she hadn't realized she was missing.

Lacey finally closed the gap, pressing a soft, open-mouthed kiss just below Kayla's jaw. Kayla gasped at the warmth of it, the tenderness. Her eyes fluttered shut, a mixture of nerves and exhilaration flooding through her. She could feel Quinn watching, feel the way his presence heightened everything, but she was lost in this new sensation.

"You taste sweet," Lacey murmured, her lips lingering against Kayla's skin.

Kayla shivered.

Lacey's hand moved lower, following the gentle curves of her body, exploring her without hurry. It was unlike anything Kayla had ever known — so deliberate, so slow, yet filled with so much tension she felt like she might burst.

Across the room, Quinn let out a low, uneven breath. He was still holding back, still watching, but his eyes were dark with something Kayla recognized instantly — desire, pure and unfiltered.

Lacey pulled back slightly, tilting Kayla's chin with the tips of her fingers. "Do you want me to stop?" she asked, her voice hushed but steady.

Kayla's answer came before she could second-guess it.

"No," she whispered. "Don't stop."

Lacey's smile was slow and knowing. "Good girl."

And then she kissed her.

It was softer than Kayla expected. But beneath that softness, there was something undeniably deliberate, something laced with intent. Kayla melted into it, her body responding before her mind could catch up. Lacey's lips parted slightly, her hands still skimming over Kayla's sides, pulling her in closer, deepening the connection between them.

Kayla let out the smallest of sighs, tilting her head as she surrendered to the moment. The world outside of this room faded away, leaving only the warmth of Lacey's mouth against hers, the heat of Quinn's stare, the undeniable shift in the air between all of them.

When they finally pulled apart, Kayla opened her eyes slowly, her head spinning.

Lacey grinned, brushing her thumb across Kayla's lower lip. "That," she whispered, "was fun."

Quinn, still watching, still holding back, let out another slow breath.

10

With gentle guidance, Lacey laid Kayla back onto the bed, her fingers ghosting over her arms before settling on her waist. The weight of Lacey's body pressing down against her was both foreign and electrifying, sending an unfamiliar heat through her core. Every nerve in Kayla's body seemed to hum with anticipation, a sensation so new yet so intoxicating she barely had time to process it.

Lacey's breath was warm against Kayla's skin, a tantalizing tease that left goosebumps trailing in its wake. She placed the lightest of kisses along Kayla's collarbone, moving at a languid pace as though she had all the time in the world. The patience in Lacey's touch was unlike anything Kayla had ever known. It wasn't hurried or mechanical — it was deliberate. It was teasing. It was like Lacey was unwrapping her slowly, savoring the process.

Kayla arched slightly, her breath hitching as Lacey's lips hovered over the swell of her chest. The anticipation was maddening, her body responding before her mind had the chance to catch up. A slow exhale passed from Lacey's lips as she kissed her way downward, her hands exploring, learning, memorizing.

Kayla barely recognized herself in this moment. She had never thought she would be here, beneath another woman, reveling in the way her touch sent shivers of electricity through her veins. There was something entirely different about this — something softer, more sensual, yet just as intense. It felt like an unraveling, a breaking apart of everything she thought she knew about herself.

Sensing Kayla's lingering nervousness, Lacey reached for her hand and guided it to her chest, encouraging her to explore. Kayla hesitated for only a moment before surrendering, her fingers brushing over Lacey's soft skin, feeling the soft rise and fall of her breathing. That small act shattered any final thread of hesitation.

Lacey smiled against her skin. "That's it," she whispered. "Just feel."

A newfound boldness surged through Kayla. She leaned forward, her lips grazing Lacey's collarbone, and this time, it was Lacey who let out a breathy sigh. The sound sent a thrill through Kayla's body, igniting something deep inside her — something powerful. She had been touched, desired, and explored, but this was different. This time, she was the one in control, the one discovering.

Quinn, still seated in the chair a few feet away, felt an almost unbearable pull toward them. His fingers curled around the arms of the chair, his breathing heavy as he watched. Every inch of him wanted to move, to touch, to join. The intensity of the moment was intoxicating, but frustration stirred within him — watching, waiting, unsure when he would be allowed to cross the invisible barrier keeping him in place.

Lacey knew this. She felt his gaze burning against her skin, and it only added to her amusement. She had seen men look at her like this before, but the fact that it was Quinn — Kayla's husband, her partner — added a layer of tension that made her pulse quicken.

Kayla's lips moved lower, kissing over the smooth curve of Lacey's stomach, her breath uneven with both excitement and nerves. The sensation of warm, soft skin beneath her lips was completely different from anything she had ever experienced before, and she found herself drawn to it. The sound of Lacey's quiet moan sent a thrill of satisfaction through her, spurring her forward.

Lacey arched slightly, trailing her fingers through Kayla's hair before guiding her head downward. Kayla hesitated only briefly before yielding, giving in to the moment fully. It wasn't just about physical pleasure — it was about discovery, about embracing the unknown, about surrendering to something that both terrified and exhilarated her.

She eased down between her thighs like she was slipping into warm water, her breath ghosting across soft, parted skin. The scent met her first — earthy and heady, like rain on hot pavement mixed with something innately human. Her mouth watered, her hands gripping Lacey's thighs, thumbs brushing gently as she leaned in and tasted her.

The first stroke of her tongue was soft, exploratory — a silent question. The answer came in the form of a breathless moan and the slow roll of hips beneath her hands. She smiled and went deeper, savoring the way the flavor spread. It was sweet and salty, wild and intimate, like nectar pulled from sacred fruit.

She sucked lightly, then again, letting the juices flood her mouth, her lips wet and chin slick. Her tongue moved with unhurried reverence, tracing every fold and every pulse, until Lacey began to tremble. That's when she felt it — fingers threading through her hair, slow at first, then tugging tight.

The grip tightened as her mouth worked with more pressure and hunger, feeding off each gasp, each tightening muscle. Lacey's hand fisted in the top of her hair now, holding her there, not to control but to beg for more — for deeper, for harder, for that unbearable edge.

And she gave it. Her tongue moved with precision, her mouth relentless, the taste of her like sunlight and sin. The hand in her hair pulled tighter, more urgently, grounding her in the intensity of the moment. She moaned into her, the vibration sending another shudder through Lacey's body.

Everything was slick now — skin, breath, want. Lacey cried out, hips pressing up, thighs trembling around Kayla's ears. But she didn't stop. Not yet. She was lost in it, intoxicated by the taste of Lacey, needing to drink every last drop of her pleasure.

Quinn exhaled sharply, his pulse hammering in his ears. The waiting was driving him wild. He shifted in his seat, wondering if this was all he was meant to do — watch and nothing more. He was used to being the one in control, used to guiding the rhythm of intimacy, but here, he was at the mercy of Lacey's teasing.

Just as his restraint began to fray, Lacey turned her head slightly and met his gaze. A teasing smirk played at her lips, her expression one of pure mischief.

"Not yet," she whispered, her voice like silk.

Quinn groaned, running his hands along his upper thighs as he forced himself to stay seated. Lacey was enjoying this too much — knowing he was on the edge, knowing she controlled the pace.

Kayla barely registered any of this. There was no world beyond the grip in her hair, the taste in her mouth, and Lacey unraveling beneath her. She had always wondered what it would feel like to be with another woman, but she had never expected this — this overwhelming wave of desire, this hunger to learn, to take, to give.

Lacey shifted, rolling Kayla beneath her once more. Her lips brushed against Kayla's ear, her breath hot and heavy.

"You're incredible," she murmured, and the words sent a rush of pride through Kayla's chest.

Then Lacey turned again, her gaze finding Quinn's. Slowly, deliberately, she ran her hands along Kayla's thighs, parting them, teasing. Quinn let out a sharp breath, his restraint hanging by a thread.

And then, finally, Lacey met his eyes once more.

"Now," she said.

Quinn didn't need to be told twice.

11

Quinn didn't hesitate. The moment Lacey granted him permission, he stood quickly, his pulse pounding, closing the space between them. Every part of his body hummed with anticipation, a desire so fierce it bordered on impatience. But just as he leaned in toward Lacey, eager to finally join in, she placed a single finger against his lips, stopping him with a slow, teasing smile.

"Not yet," she murmured, her voice carrying that same intoxicating authority.

His breath hitched, the restraint driving him mad, but he obeyed. Lacey's gaze flicked downward, an unspoken order in her eyes. A silent demand. He understood instantly.

With measured movements, Quinn reached for the hem of his shirt, pulling it over his head. The cool air of the room kissed his tanned skin, his body already burning with pent-up energy. He unbuckled his belt, his fingers clumsier than usual, fumbling slightly in his eagerness. He could feel both Kayla's and Lacey's eyes on him, watching, waiting. It was strange, standing there under their combined scrutiny, vulnerable and exposed, but somehow, that only fueled the fire coursing through his veins.

When he finally stepped out of the last of his clothing, he returned to the bed, standing before them, completely bare.

Lacey didn't rush. She let her eyes roam over him, her expression unreadable at first. Then, slowly, her lips curved into something approving. "Ok," she whispered, her voice barely above a breath. "Now."

Relief flooded through him as he finally moved, finally let himself sink into the moment. He leaned down, capturing Lacey's lips in a slow, deep kiss, his earlier urgency replaced with something else — something darker, richer. He wanted to take his time. Wanted to listen to her body, to learn how she responded, to savor the moment that had been so long in the making.

Lacey melted into him, her body molding against his as her fingers traced down the ridges of his stomach, igniting sparks in their wake. Her mouth was soft, teasing, her tongue barely brushing against his before retreating, making him chase her. He groaned against her lips, his hands tightening around her waist, pulling her closer.

Kayla, still entangled in Lacey's embrace, looked up and watched them. The sight of her husband, standing naked before another woman, his hands gripping her waist, his mouth consuming hers — it should have felt strange. Maybe even wrong. But instead, a slow burn ignited deep in her core.

She hadn't expected this. Hadn't expected to feel this way. But instead of jealousy, she felt something else. Something deeper.

Desire.

Kayla's fingers curled into the sheets as she studied them, watching as Quinn's hands explored, as Lacey responded with quiet sighs of pleasure. Her body reacted before her mind could catch up, a wave of heat rolling through her. She swallowed, heart hammering against her ribs.

She wanted more.

Lacey must have sensed it, because she suddenly pulled away from Quinn, her lips glossy, her breathing slightly uneven. She turned her attention back to Kayla, her fingers grazing her cheek, her gaze unreadable yet knowing.

"Now you two," she murmured, her voice smooth, commanding yet inviting. "Kiss each other."

Kayla's breath caught in her throat.

She turned toward Quinn, her pulse quickening as her eyes met his. For a moment, they simply stared at each other. Kayla saw something in his expression that sent a shiver down her spine — pure, unfiltered longing. It was a look she hadn't seen in years. A look she had sorely missed.

The moment stretched between them, heavy with anticipation.

Then, as if pulled by an invisible force, their lips met.

It was different than usual. Deeper. More urgent. There was no routine, no practiced movements. This was raw, untamed. Quinn's hands found Kayla's waist, pulling her against him, and she melted into him, her fingers threading through his hair.

A soft sigh escaped her lips, swallowed by the kiss.

She had almost forgotten how this felt. How it felt to want him like this.

Quinn's grip tightened on her hips, as though grounding himself in the moment. It wasn't just the kiss — it was the weight of everything leading up to it. The build-up. The hesitation. The release. The rediscovery.

Lacey watched them with a satisfied smile, her presence serving as a catalyst rather than a distraction. She shifted closer, every movement deliberate, until she was at the edge of the bed. Her fingers grazed over Quinn's lower back, feather-light at first, then firmer, coaxing his awareness away from Kayla's mouth just long enough for her to position herself.

Quinn was so consumed by Kayla's kiss that he barely registered Lacey kneeling beside him, until he felt her hand wrap around him. His entire body jolted at the sudden contact. She stroked him once, twice, slow and steady, before leaning forward.

Her lips closed over the head of his cock, warm and impossibly soft, and Quinn let out a sharp gasp. His hand instinctively gripped Kayla's hip as his knees threatened to buckle. Then, with a slow, hungry pull, Lacey slid him deeper into her mouth, her tongue pressing firmly against the underside as she took more of him in.

"Fuck…" Quinn's voice cracked, guttural and raw, as a groan tore out of him. His eyes fluttered shut, the sensation overwhelming. The tight heat of her mouth, the wet glide of her tongue, the suction pulling him deeper with each bob. It was almost too much.

Lacey found her rhythm quickly. Her lips glided down the length of him in long, deliberate strokes, her throat relaxing as she drew him in further each time. Quinn's thighs trembled, his abs tightening as she pushed nearly to the base, her nose brushing his skin before she pulled back with a wet, obscene sound. His breathing grew ragged, every exhale punctuated by another broken groan.

Kayla, still pressed against his chest, felt the shift immediately. She pulled back, her lips swollen, her breath quickened, and tilted her gaze downward. The sight made her stomach drop and her pulse skyrocket—Lacey's lips stretched around her husband's cock, her head bobbing in a steady rhythm, her hand twisting at the base while saliva glistened over him in the dim light.

Kayla had expected jealousy, some primal anger rising at seeing another woman with him. But all she felt was a deep, molten heat between her thighs, so fierce it startled her. Watching Quinn unravel under Lacey's mouth was intoxicating — his head thrown back, his body shuddering, the desperate noises tearing out of him.

She reached up, cupping his cheek to bring his eyes back to her. His pupils were blown wide, his lips parted as he panted for air.

"You ok?" she whispered, though the question carried more desire than concern.

Quinn met her gaze, his voice low and ruined with lust. "Yeah," he groaned, his hips twitching against Lacey's mouth. "More than ok."

Kayla kissed him again, hard and hungry, as Lacey continued below — Quinn's body trapped deliciously between them both, drowning in sensation.

The night had shifted into something uncharted, something thrilling, something that neither of them had known they needed.

But here, in this moment, with Lacey's quiet guidance, they weren't just indulging in an experience.

They were unraveling years of routine.

They were peeling back layers of themselves they hadn't realized were buried.

They were reconnecting.

And neither of them wanted it to end.

12

Kayla knelt beside Lacey, her lips trailing over the smooth warmth of her skin in slow, lingering kisses. There was something intoxicating about the way Lacey responded — her breath hitching, her fingers threading through Kayla's hair in a silent command, her body yielding, inviting. Kayla could feel the slight tremor beneath her fingertips, the way Lacey's pulse quickened under her lips. The sensation was unlike anything she had ever experienced before — softer, yet just as consuming. A different kind of hunger.

Lacey sighed, the sound rich and throaty, as she guided Kayla's movements with a delicate but firm touch. Kayla followed instinctively, learning Lacey's body through the subtle ways she reacted. A whisper of a sigh here, a sharp intake of breath there. Each response only urged Kayla forward, her own body stirring with an intensity that was new, thrilling, and utterly unexpected.

Quinn, still caught in the blissful haze of the moment, felt his pulse roar in his ears. The sight of Kayla, her lips exploring Lacey's skin, the way her body pressed so intimately against another woman's, sent a wildfire through his veins. His breathing turned shallow, his chest rising and falling in uneven waves as he tried to steady himself. The anticipation was unbearable, every part of him thrumming with need, yet he remained frozen in place, savoring every second of what was unfolding in front of him.

Then, just as suddenly, Lacey pulled back from Quinn, her emerald eyes flickering with mischief. She turned toward Kayla, her lips curling into a knowing smile as she reached out, brushing a strand of hair behind Kayla's ear.

"Now it's your turn," she murmured, her voice laced with something dark and sweet, like honey laced with spice.

Kayla hesitated only for a moment, the weight of the moment pressing against her. Then, without a word, she turned her attention to Quinn. Their eyes locked, and in that instant, something shifted. The smoldering tension between them, the years of routine and predictability — it all burned away, leaving behind nothing but raw, unfiltered desire.

Quinn's gaze darkened as he watched her, his jaw tightening. Kayla had seen that look before — years ago, when their passion had been wild and unpredictable, before marriage and life settled into routine. That unguarded hunger, that unspoken need, that had been missing for so long.

Now, it was back.

Without breaking eye contact, Kayla leaned toward him, her touch featherlight as she ran her fingers down his chest. She took her time, reveling in the way his muscles tensed beneath her fingertips, the way his breath grew uneven with each second. She wanted him to feel this, to feel her, the way she was feeling everything at once.

Then, slowly, deliberately, she moved lower.

Quinn inhaled sharply, his hands bracing against the edge of the bed as Kayla's lips brushed against his skin. The warmth of her breath sent shivers coursing through him, every nerve in his body firing at once. And then, with a slow, deliberate motion, she took him into her mouth.

Quinn's entire body tensed, his head tilting back slightly as a deep groan rumbled in his chest. His hands clenched at his sides as he fought the overwhelming urge to move, to take control, to let go completely. But he didn't. Not yet. He wanted to savor this, to let it wash over him like a slow-building storm.

Kayla alternated between deep, languid movements and slow, teasing flicks of her tongue, each motion sending Quinn spiraling further into bliss. She could feel the way his thighs tightened beneath her hands, the way his breath grew more ragged with each passing second, the way his dick pulsated with excitement. There was something powerful about this — about knowing she was the one unraveling him, about seeing him lose himself so completely.

And then, just as she was getting lost in the rhythm, she felt something else.

A whisper of fingertips tracing along the curve of her back. A touch so light it was barely there, yet it sent a shockwave through her body.

Lacey.

Kayla shuddered as Lacey's hands moved lower, ghosting over the swell of her hips before sliding further down. Her touch was patient and deliberate, drawing lazy circles against Kayla's skin, teasing her with the promise of something more. It was a slow, agonizing build — one that made Kayla's breath come faster, her body aching for more.

Quinn, lost in his own pleasure, barely registered the shift at first. But then he opened his eyes, just enough to see the way Lacey positioned herself behind Kayla. The way her hands roamed, the way her lips brushed against Kayla's shoulder, her breath hot against her skin.

He had never seen Kayla like this before, and it excited him.

13

The three of them moved toward the bed in an almost dreamlike haze, the weight of anticipation making every movement feel heavier, charged. Lacey climbed onto the mattress first, settling in the center. She propped herself up on her elbows, her emerald eyes flicking between Kayla and Quinn with a knowing smirk, as if she could sense the storm of emotions brewing in both of them.

Kayla followed next, her breath unsteady, her pulse hammering beneath her skin. She wasn't sure if it was nerves, excitement, or something in between, but every inch of her was alive, aware of the newness of what was happening. She glanced at Quinn, searching for reassurance, and found it in the way he looked at her — not just with hunger, but with something deeper. Understanding. Trust.

They both knew this was uncharted territory, but there was no turning back now.

Kayla and Quinn positioned themselves on either side of Lacey, their bodies sinking into the mattress as hands found skin, mouths found lips. The kissing started slow, deliberate. Kayla traced her fingers along Lacey's jaw before capturing her lips in a deep, lingering kiss, reveling in the softness, the contrast. Lacey's lips molded to hers effortlessly, teasing, testing, until Kayla let herself give in, let herself stop thinking and simply feel.

Quinn, unable to hold back, pressed his mouth to Lacey's neck, his teeth grazing the sensitive skin just below her ear. Lacey let out a slow sigh, tilting her head back to give him more access. His hands roamed along her sides, feeling every curve, every shift of her body beneath him.

Kayla, emboldened by the sound, let her lips wander lower, tracing along the elegant slope of Lacey's collarbone, her skin impossibly smooth. Her fingers followed, mapping out every inch of her body as if memorizing her shape. It was intoxicating, feeling the way Lacey responded to her touch, the small gasps she let slip.

Lacey's hands roamed just as freely, her fingertips dancing between Kayla and Quinn, teasing, guiding. There was a sense of unhurried exploration, of savoring each moment as if time had slowed to a crawl.

Then, without warning, Lacey shifted, sitting up slightly and catching Kayla's gaze. She ran a hand down her own body, a slow, sensual motion before she leaned in and whispered against Kayla's lips, "Lie back for me."

Kayla hesitated for a fraction of a second, her pulse spiking. The request sent a thrill through her, but with it came an entirely new level of vulnerability. She had never had another woman's lips, another woman's touch, in this way, on a part of her body that only men have kissed. But as she looked into Lacey's eyes — full of patience, full of certainty — something in her melted.

She obeyed.

Kayla settled onto her back, the cool sheets beneath her a stark contrast to the heat radiating from her body. Lacey positioned herself between Kayla's legs, gently spreading them apart. Kayla's breath caught in her throat. She had no idea what to expect. Would it feel different? More intense? Less?

And then Lacey's lips met her.

A sharp gasp escaped Kayla before she could stop it. Her fingers gripped the sheets as a new kind of pleasure rippled through her, unfamiliar and overwhelming. Lacey was slow at first, methodical, as if savoring the moment as much as Kayla was unraveling from it. Her touch was different — softer than Quinn's but no less intense. The way she moved, the way she adjusted to Kayla's body, was precise, intentional.

It was like she knew exactly how to draw pleasure out of her.

Kayla's head fell back against the pillows, her chest rising and falling rapidly. Every nerve in her body was alight, her senses overloaded in the best possible way. Her hands instinctively reached down, threading through Lacey's hair, tugging gently as her hips shifted against her.

She barely noticed Quinn moving until she felt his hand on her stomach, his thumb drawing slow circles against her skin. She opened her eyes, finding him watching her — watching the way her body responded, the way her lips parted with every sharp inhale. His gaze was dark, filled with something she hadn't seen in years.

Desire. Pure, unrestrained desire.

Lacey, sensing Quinn's attention, turned her head just enough to meet his gaze. A slow, teasing grin spread across her lips before she lifted her hand and motioned for him to come closer.

Quinn hesitated, looking at Kayla, silently asking for her permission.

Kayla, breathless and flushed, gave him a slow, knowing smirk. "Get in there."

That was all he needed.

Quinn shifted forward, his body aligning behind Lacey's. He reached for her, his hands running along the smooth curves of her waist before gripping her hips. His breath came in ragged bursts as he pressed against her, feeling her warmth, her readiness.

And then, he pushed forward.

A deep, guttural sound escaped him as he sank into her, the sensation unlike anything he had ever known. Lacey exhaled sharply, her body arching, but she didn't stop. She kept her attention on Kayla, her movements never faltering, her rhythm never breaking.

Kayla, caught between the sensations of Lacey's touch and the sight of Quinn moving behind her, felt her body tighten, her mind slipping into something primal. It was electric, the way it all blended together — Quinn's deep, slow thrusts, Lacey's skilled mouth pleasing her in ways that felt new, the sounds of their collective pleasure filling the room.

Quinn kept his eyes locked on Kayla the entire time, watching her, reading her, feeling her. And when she finally gasped his name, her fingers digging into Lacey's shoulders, he knew.

This was something they could never come back from.
And he didn't want to.

14

Sunlight streamed through the sheer curtains, casting a warm glow over the tangle of limbs and sheets on the bed. Kayla slowly blinked awake, her body still humming with the remnants of the night before. She felt warmth on either side of her — Quinn's arm draped over her waist, Lacey's hair tickling her shoulder.

Lacey stirred first, stretching luxuriously before rolling onto her side. She met Kayla's gaze and smiled, a knowing glimmer in her eyes. "Morning," she murmured, her voice husky with sleep.

Kayla exhaled a quiet laugh. "Morning."

Quinn grumbled something incoherent into the pillow before shifting, rubbing his face. When he opened his eyes, his gaze moved between the two women before he sighed deeply. "That actually happened," he said, his voice still laced with disbelief.

Lacey smirked as she sat up, slipping gracefully out of bed. "It did," she confirmed, stretching before gathering her clothes from the floor. She dressed leisurely, buttoning her dress while Kayla and Quinn remained curled under the sheets, watching her.

As she reached the door, she turned back, her gaze settling on Kayla. "Call me sometime," she said with a wink. Then, with a final glance between them, she slipped out, leaving behind the lingering scent of her perfume.

For a moment, there was only silence between Kayla and Quinn.

Then, they both let out deep, simultaneous breaths, falling back against the pillows.

Quinn ran a hand through his hair, staring up at the ceiling. "Well," he said finally, "that was… a lot."

Kayla turned onto her side, propping herself up on one elbow to look at him. "Good 'a lot' or bad 'a lot'?"

He turned his head toward her, searching her face before breaking into a slow grin. "Good. Definitely good."

Kayla mirrored his smile. "Yeah," she admitted, voice soft. "I didn't expect to feel… so free."

They lay there for a few moments, letting the weight of the experience settle.

Finally, Quinn reached over, lacing his fingers with hers. "So… what now?"

Kayla thought for a moment before squeezing his hand. "Now? We figure out where this takes us."

And for the first time in a long time, she had no doubt that wherever that was, they'd be going there together.

For the next few days, Kayla and Quinn attempted to slip back into their normal routines. Work, school drop-offs, grocery shopping — it was all the same, yet somehow, everything felt different.

They hadn't spoken much about their night with Lacey. Not because they were avoiding it, but because neither of them quite knew what to say. The unspoken weight of it lingered between them like an electric current—thrilling, uncertain, and undeniably present.

At dinner, they laughed at Zeke's stories about his soccer practice, and at night, they curled up in bed as they always had. But something had shifted. Quinn noticed it in the way Kayla glanced at him when she thought he wasn't looking, the way her fingers lingered a little longer when she touched him. Kayla, in turn, noticed the way Quinn seemed more present, more engaged. There was a quiet understanding between them now, an unspoken acknowledgment that they had ventured into unknown territory together — and enjoyed it.

Still, neither of them initiated a conversation about what came next.

15

A week passed and Kayla started feeling the urge again. One evening, after putting Zeke to bed, she curled up on the couch with her phone, scrolling through profiles. The rush of anticipation bubbled in her stomach as she browsed, each new possibility reigniting the excitement she had felt that night with Lacey.

She found a few profiles intriguing — a single Black male with a confident, smoldering gaze, and a married couple who radiated warmth and energy. She studied their bios, considering what each experience might be like, then took a deep breath and turned to Quinn.

"I found a few interesting profiles," she said casually, hoping to gauge his reaction.

Quinn's brow lifted slightly. "Already?"

Kayla shrugged. "I just... I don't know, I liked how it made me feel."

Quinn hesitated before shifting closer, glancing at the screen. He took in the images, his expression neutral until his gaze lingered on the profile of the single male.

"A guy?" he asked, voice clipped.

Kayla sighed, anticipating his resistance. "We agreed to explore together. That doesn't mean just women, Quinn."

His jaw tightened. "I just don't know if I can handle that."

Kayla softened her tone. "You didn't think you could handle

watching me with Lacey, either, but you ended up enjoying it."

Quinn rubbed the back of his neck. "That was different."

"Is it?" Kayla pressed. "I'm not saying we have to do anything right now. But I at least want to consider our options."

After a long silence, Quinn exhaled and nodded slowly. "Fine. What about the couple?"

Kayla smiled, sensing his compromise. "I actually think they seem like a great fit."

Quinn still felt a twinge of unease, but he could see how excited Kayla was, and part of him wanted to push past his own insecurities for the sake of their shared experience.

"Ok," he said. "Let's meet them."

16

The stylish downtown lounge was buzzing with energy when Kayla and Quinn arrived. The warm amber glow of dimmed chandeliers cast a golden hue over the sleek, modern decor. The low hum of jazz intertwined with the occasional bursts of laughter from nearby tables, creating an atmosphere that felt both intimate and alive.

Kayla spotted Mia and Jason first. They were seated in a plush, curved booth near the back of the lounge, the kind of secluded spot that promised good conversation and even better chemistry. Mia was striking — shoulder-length caramel waves, deep brown eyes that glimmered with mischief, and an easy, confident smile. She exuded an easy charm, the kind of woman who could light up any room just by being in it. Jason, by contrast, had a quiet, self-assured presence. He was broad-shouldered, dressed in a crisp button-down with the sleeves casually rolled up to his elbows, exuding an air of relaxed confidence.

As Kayla and Quinn approached the booth, Mia's face lit up. "You made it!" she said warmly, sliding over to make room. "I was just about to text you and make sure you hadn't chickened out."

Kayla laughed, slipping into the seat beside her. "Not a chance."

Quinn and Jason exchanged firm handshakes as they took their seats. "Good to finally meet you," Jason said, his voice deep and steady.

"You too," Quinn replied, settling in. He noticed how effortlessly Jason carried himself — relaxed, easygoing, the kind of guy who could command a room without even trying. It put Quinn at ease... but also made him hyper-aware of the contrast between them.

A waiter appeared, taking their drink orders. Kayla opted for a glass of Malbec, Mia ordered a mojito, while the men went for old fashions with rye.

"So," Mia said, crossing one leg over the other and turning to Kayla. "Tell me, how's this whole adventure been going for you two so far?"

Kayla felt the warmth of the wine spread through her as she exchanged a quick glance with Quinn. "Honestly? A mix of excitement and nerves," she admitted. "But I think that's part of what makes it so thrilling."

Mia's lips curled into a knowing smile. "Exactly. The best things in life come with a little bit of fear."

Jason chuckled, sipping his drink. "That, and a lot of communication." He turned to Quinn. "That's been the biggest thing for us. Being open about how we're feeling, checking in constantly."

Quinn nodded, digesting the words. He liked Jason. There was something reassuring about him — no arrogance, no weird possessiveness, just someone who seemed genuinely confident in his relationship.

"Have you two been in the lifestyle long?" Kayla asked, leaning in slightly.

"About two years," Mia answered. "We took our time at first, dipped our toes in slowly. The first couple we met? Complete disaster." She rolled her eyes playfully. "Zero chemistry, too many expectations. We swore we'd never do that again."

"But then," Jason added, smirking, "we met another couple who changed our minds."

Mia nodded. "They were fun, easygoing. No pressure. That's when we realized this could actually be a really positive thing for us."

Quinn swirled the amber liquid in his glass. "And has it been?"

Jason met his gaze directly. "Without a doubt."

Mia glanced at Kayla, tilting her head. "And you? What's been your favorite part so far?"

Kayla hesitated, considering her words. "I think it's just... discovering new things about myself. About us. Pushing boundaries in a way that actually feels freeing instead of scary."

Mia's smile widened. "That's what I love to hear."

Quinn was quiet, absorbing the conversation. He realized he wasn't just paying attention to what was being said — he was watching. Watching how Mia's hand rested on Kayla's knee, the subtle way Jason's arm draped across the booth, his fingers idly tracing circles against Mia's lower back. It was all so natural for them, and yet, for Quinn, it still felt like uncharted territory.

He wasn't uncomfortable, but there was a weight pressing against his chest — the question that had been gnawing at him since they'd started this journey.

Could he really do this? Could he watch another man with Kayla and be ok with it?

The conversation flowed seamlessly from there — work, travel, favorite places to go out in the city. Mia and Kayla slipped into an easy rhythm, their laughter infectious, exchanging knowing glances throughout the night.

At one point, Kayla caught Quinn's eye, as if silently asking if he was ok. He gave her a small nod, exhaling as he took another sip of his drink.

Mia leaned in closer to Kayla, their knees pressing together. "So, tell me... do you think you and I would have fun?" Her voice was playful, teasing, but with a quiet intensity underneath.

Kayla felt a warm shiver dance along her spine. "I think we would."

Mia bit her lower lip, tilting her head slightly. "I was hoping you'd say that."

Jason grinned, turning to Quinn. "And you?"

Quinn cleared his throat, meeting Jason's gaze. "I think... I think I'm figuring it out."

Jason's expression softened, as if understanding exactly what Quinn meant. "That's ok, man. It's a process."

By the time they finished their drinks and stepped outside, the air between the four of them had shifted — charged with possibility. The city lights flickered around them, the distant hum of traffic filling the space between words.

Mia turned to Kayla with a teasing smile. "We should do this soon," she said, her tone laced with suggestion.

Kayla's pulse quickened. "I'd like that."

Jason clapped a hand on Quinn's shoulder. "We'll be in touch."

Quinn nodded, smiling, though his stomach was still twisted in knots. The night with Lacey had been great, but the reality of what they were planning still loomed over him. He was out of his depth, still struggling to navigate the push and pull of this new world.

As they walked to their car, Kayla slipped her hand into Quinn's. "Be honest with me. How are you feeling?"

Quinn took a moment before answering. "Excited… but extremely nervous."

Kayla squeezed his hand. "That's ok. We'll go at our own pace."

He exhaled, glancing at her. "Are you sure about this?"

She smiled, tilting her head up toward him. "I am. Are you?"

He wasn't sure.

17

The week leading up to their date with Jason and Mia was filled with quiet anticipation — at least, for Kayla. She spent it texting back and forth with Mia, coordinating schedules and setting up logistics. It felt almost surreal, planning something so intimate in such a casual, practical way. It was almost as if they were arranging a double date with friends, not something that had the potential to shift the very foundation of their marriage. But beneath the excitement, there was a steadiness to it, a confidence that reassured her this was the right next step.

The messages between her and Mia were flirtatious but light.

Mia: Can't wait for Friday! What are you wearing? (For dinner, I mean. Or… otherwise *wink*)

Kayla: Haha, good question. Something cute but easy to take off, I guess?

Mia: Oooh, now you're speaking my language. I'll make sure Jason doesn't wear too many layers ;)

Kayla giggled as she read the texts, feeling the thrill build inside her. She liked the way Mia flirted — playful, but not overly aggressive. It felt easy. Right.

Yet, as much as she enjoyed the lead-up, Kayla could sense Quinn's hesitancy growing. She noticed the way he avoided bringing up the plans unless she mentioned them first. He would then nod along, responding when necessary, but his tone lacked the same enthusiasm he had before they met Lacey.

"Do you think we should book a hotel room?" Kayla asked one evening as they lay in bed, her phone resting on her stomach as she waited for Mia's reply.

Quinn hesitated. "A hotel?" he asked, his voice carefully neutral.

She studied him for a moment, the way his jaw was set a little too tightly. "Are you ok?"

He forced a smile. "Yeah, just... a lot to think about."

She reached out, lightly grabbing his forearm. "Talk to me, babe. What's on your mind?"

He sighed. "I guess... I just don't know what it's going to feel like. Watching you with another guy."

Kayla softened, shifting closer. "That's fair."

"It's not jealousy," Quinn added quickly, though he wasn't sure if that was entirely true. "It's just... different. I liked seeing you with Lacey. It turned me on. But this? This is uncharted territory."

She nodded, understanding. "It's different for me too," she admitted. "Don't you think it was the same for me watching you with Lacey? I don't want you to do anything you're not ready for, though."

Quinn hesitated. He wanted to be ready. He wanted to give Kayla this experience. But the idea of seeing another man touching her, being inside her... it sent an uncomfortable heat through his chest. It wasn't anger or possessiveness. It was something more primal, something that made his stomach twist. Would it change how he saw her? Would it change how she saw him?

"I think I just need to see it to understand it," he finally said. "I won't know how I feel until we're in the moment."

Kayla nodded. "That makes sense. And remember, if at any point you want to stop, we stop. No questions. No pressure."

Quinn swallowed. "Ok."

The next few days were filled with a strange mix of tension and normalcy. They went through their usual routines — work, parenting, meals, and evenings spent on the couch watching their favorite shows. But there was an unspoken charge in the air, an undercurrent of anticipation that neither of them fully addressed.

Kayla, for her part, was excited. She had never felt so desired, so free to explore this side of herself. It wasn't just about the sex — it was about stepping into something new, about unlocking a part of her she had kept hidden for so long. She knew this was a big leap, but it felt right.

Quinn, on the other hand, found himself more distracted than usual. He would be reviewing a deposition at work and suddenly his mind would wander to images he wasn't sure he was ready to see. He imagined Jason touching Kayla, kissing her, pressing against her in ways that only he had for years.

And the strangest part? His reaction wasn't as simple as jealousy.

He thought about Lacey. About how seeing Kayla with her had ignited something in him. Would this be the same? Or would it be different?

One night, as they lay in bed, Quinn finally asked the question that had been weighing on him all week.

"Are you... excited? About him?"

Kayla turned her head to face him, her expression thoughtful. "I'm excited about the experience, and it's not only about him. I think he seems great but I do also like Mia a lot."

Quinn exhaled, staring at the ceiling. "I don't know if I'm ready for this."

Kayla reached for his hand, squeezing it. "Then we wait. We don't have to do this."

He hesitated before shaking his head. "No. I don't want to stop you from having this. I just need to wrap my head around it."

She studied him for a long moment before pressing a soft kiss to his shoulder. "We'll be ok," she whispered. "Trust me."

Quinn exhaled and nodded. He wanted to believe her. He really did.

18

Kayla slipped into a floral-patterned summer dress, the soft fabric hugging her in all the right places. The dress was light and flowing, cinched at the waist in a way that accentuated her curves. The pale yellow fabric, decorated with delicate blue and green flowers, made her skin glow with warmth. The neckline dipped just low enough to hint at the soft swell of her chest, while the hemline skimmed the middle of her thighs, teasing glimpses of her long, toned legs. As she moved, the fabric shifted around her like a whisper, brushing sensually against her skin.

She stepped in front of the mirror, adjusting the thin straps over her shoulders, tucking a stray curl behind her ear. She wasn't wearing anything extravagant — just a subtle shimmer on her cheekbones, a touch of mascara to darken her lashes, and a burgundy tint on her lips. But it was enough. She didn't need much. She already looked breathtaking.

Quinn sat at the edge of the bed, watching her. Something in his chest tightened, a sensation he hadn't felt in a long time — desire, yes, but also admiration, reverence. She looked so effortlessly beautiful, standing there in the soft light of their bedroom, the excitement in her expression making her even more radiant. He had always known Kayla was gorgeous, but lately, he was seeing her differently. Or maybe he was just seeing her again.

The realization hit him hard. When had he stopped looking at her like this? When had he let himself take her for granted, let himself stop feeling this heat in his chest every time she got dressed up?

His eyes traveled down the curve of her waist, the gentle slope of her hips, her toned thighs peeking out from beneath the hem of the dress. The way she moved, the way her bare shoulders gleamed under the glow of the vanity light, the way she looked at herself in the mirror with a hint of satisfaction — it was intoxicating. And the worst part? He wasn't sure if she was dressing up for him or for Jason.

That thought gnawed at the back of his mind as she turned to face him. She gave him a small smile, one that was both nervous and excited. "What do you think?" she asked, smoothing down the fabric of her dress.

Quinn swallowed, his throat suddenly dry. "You look..." He hesitated, searching for the right words. "You look incredible."

Her smile deepened. "Thank you."

She walked over to the closet, reaching for her nude heels—the strappy ones that made her legs look impossibly long — and Quinn's pulse spiked. He had always loved those shoes on her, the way they made her carry herself with a little extra confidence, the way they made her hips sway just a little more when she walked. And now, as she bent slightly to buckle them, he felt a sharp pang of something primal, something possessive.

His gaze flickered to his own reflection in the mirror across the room. He had put effort into his appearance tonight, too. A crisp button-down in a dark shade of navy, the sleeves rolled up just enough to hint at the muscles in his forearms. Fitted black slacks that sat comfortably on his frame, paired with polished shoes. He had even run a hand through his hair with some product, making sure he looked sharp. But looking at himself now, he wondered — was he dressing up for Kayla? Or was he doing it because he felt like he had something to prove?

"Are you ready?" she asked, grabbing her small clutch from the dresser.

Quinn nodded, standing up and adjusting his cuffs. "Yeah," he said, but he wasn't sure if he was answering her or himself.

As they made their way to the door, Quinn found himself watching Kayla with new eyes. The curve of her back as she walked, the way she checked her phone, probably reading a message from Mia. The way she bit her lip absently, lost in thought.

For the first time in a long time, he wasn't just looking at her. He was *seeing* her. Really seeing her. And the realization that he could lose her — either to this lifestyle or to someone else — sent a shiver down his spine.

As he opened the door for her and followed her out into the night, one thought echoed in his mind:

He wanted her. Not just tonight. Not just because of this new adventure they were on. He wanted her like he used to. And he wasn't sure if he could stand the thought of someone else wanting her just as much.

19

Kayla and Quinn weren't the first ones to arrive this time. Standing outside the hotel room, Quinn exhaled deeply as Kayla knocked on the door, anticipation swirling in her chest. She squeezed his hand reassuringly, but the tension in his grip told her everything — he was still fighting his nerves.

The door swung open to reveal Mia, who was absolutely stunning in a deep red, lace-trimmed dress that really accentuated her chest. The silky fabric draped over her rich, warm brown skin like it had been made just for her. Her dark curls cascaded over her shoulders, framing her striking features — full lips painted a sultry shade of red, deep brown eyes that shimmered with mischief. A teasing smile curled at the corners of her mouth, her confidence radiating in waves.

"Glad you made it," Mia said, her voice rich like honey, pulling Kayla in for a warm hug before stepping back to let them inside. Her embrace lingered just a second longer than necessary, her hands grazing Kayla's bare shoulders as she pulled away. A thrill shot through Kayla's spine.

Quinn followed, shaking Jason's hand as they exchanged knowing glances. Jason was dressed in a fitted black button-down, his relaxed posture exuding confidence, his sharp jawline accentuated by the low lighting of the room. Kayla thought he looked good — really good.

"Good to see you both," Jason said smoothly, clapping Quinn on the shoulder. "Hope you're ready for a good night."

Quinn let out a breathy chuckle. "Yeah… I think so."

Mia poured them drinks, handing Kayla a glass of wine before settling onto the plush loveseat with her own. "So, how was your week?" she asked, crossing one toned leg over the other, the slit of her dress exposing more of her smooth thigh.

"Busy," Kayla admitted, taking a sip of her drink. "Work, my son's school stuff, life. This is a much needed escape."

Jason leaned against the bar, swirling the amber liquid in his glass. "I hear that. We've been looking forward to this all week." His gaze flickered toward Kayla, his meaning clear.

Quinn let out a short breath, his fingers tightening around his glass. He had spent the last few days trying to quiet his overthinking mind, but here, in this dimly lit space, with Mia's sultry presence beside him and Jason's easy confidence across from him, the tension inside him was shifting. It wasn't quite gone, but it was morphing into something else.

Kayla noticed the way Mia's fingers traced the rim of her glass absentmindedly, the way her eyes kept drifting toward Quinn. The anticipation in the room thickened, unspoken words hanging between them like a drawn bowstring waiting to snap.

Mia set her drink down and leaned toward Quinn, brushing her fingertips along his forearm. "So, you never told me," she murmured, tilting her head slightly. "What did you think the first time you saw me?"

Quinn hesitated, caught off guard by her directness. He glanced at Kayla, as if asking for permission, before turning back to Mia. "I thought you were gorgeous," he admitted, his voice slightly lower than usual. "And… slightly intimidating."

Mia laughed, a rich, throaty sound. "Intimidating? That's a new one."

Jason grinned, leaning in. "Oh, she gets that a lot. But trust me, she likes it."

Mia shrugged, looking at Quinn playfully. "I mean, a little intimidation isn't always a bad thing. Makes things more fun."

Kayla smirked, feeling the heat in the room rise. "Oh, trust me, Quinn likes a little challenge."

Mia's eyes sparkled. "Perfect."

The conversation flowed effortlessly, the flirtation growing with each passing moment. At one point, Jason leaned in toward Kayla, brushing a strand of hair behind her ear. "You look incredible tonight," he murmured, his voice just above a whisper.

A shiver ran down Kayla's spine. "Thank you," she said softly, feeling the weight of his gaze on her.

After another round of drinks, the shift happened naturally. Mia made the first move. She stepped closer to Quinn, running her fingers lightly along his arm before pressing a slow kiss against his neck. He tensed at first, but she reached up, tilting his chin so their eyes met. Without hesitation, she kissed him fully. This time, he let himself sink into it, his hands resting lightly on her waist.

Kayla felt Jason's eyes on her. When she turned to face him, he was already close. They smiled at each other, wordlessly acknowledging what was about to happen. Jason's hands found her hips, pulling her in as their lips met. His kiss was slow and firm, his fingers tracing along the small of her back as he deepened it.

The two couples moved in sync, lost in their own worlds, until a slight misstep caused them to bump into each other. They broke apart, breathless, exchanging glances. Kayla turned to Quinn instinctively, bracing for hesitation, for jealousy.

But instead, he looked exhilarated. His gaze locked onto hers, and she could see it — the excitement, the raw hunger, the acceptance.

Jason smirked, stepping back slightly. "So… are we ready to move this somewhere more comfortable?"

Mia, still pressed against Quinn, trailed a finger down his chest and nodded. "I think we are."

Kayla swallowed hard, looking at Quinn one last time, silently asking him if he was truly ok. He reached for her hand, squeezing it gently before nodding.

And just like that, the night continued into the unknown.

20

Quinn had always thought he understood himself. He had spent years believing he knew where his boundaries lay, what he could handle, what he could not. But as he stood there, his lips still tingling from Mia's kiss, he realized that nothing could have prepared him for this moment.

Kayla and Jason had moved beyond the initial, playful stage of flirtation. Their kisses deepened, hands exploring, fabric shifting. Quinn watched as Jason slid the straps of Kayla's dress down her shoulders, exposing the smooth, nude expanse of her skin. Kayla's face was flushed, her eyes half-closed, lost in the moment. She looked breathtaking in a way that was different from what he was used to seeing — the Kayla who sat across from him at the dinner table, who curled up beside him at night. Here, she was glowing, electric, uninhibited.

Quinn's stomach tightened. He had been bracing for it, expecting it to hit like a gut punch, but the jealousy and possessiveness never materialized. Instead, something else settled in his chest — an unfamiliar, disorienting mix of apprehension and undeniable excitement. He felt like both an observer and a participant at the same time, trapped between the past version of himself and whatever this new experience was awakening inside him.

Mia's hands trailed down his chest, grounding him. "You ok?" she whispered, her voice soft, coaxing.

Quinn exhaled, nodding. "Yeah," he murmured, though he wasn't entirely sure it was true.

Mia studied him for a moment before a small smile curved her lips. "You will be," she said, and then, with slow, deliberate movements, she reached for the buttons on her dress.

His breath caught as she undid them one by one, revealing warm, smooth dark skin beneath the deep red lace of her lingerie. She stepped out of the dress, letting it fall at her feet, standing before him in nothing but that delicate fabric. The dim light of the room cast gentle shadows across her toned figure, highlighting the curves of her waist, the fullness of her hips. She was confident, utterly at ease in her own skin, and it stirred something in Quinn that he hadn't felt in a long time — a rush of admiration, of raw, physical attraction that had nothing to do with routine or familiarity.

Quinn swallowed hard, suddenly hyper-aware of the way her dark curls framed her face, the way her eyes held his as she reached for the buttons on his shirt. "Your turn," she murmured, slipping it off his shoulders.

The sensation of her fingers against his skin sent a shiver down his spine. He let her take control, let her undo the buckle of his belt, her knuckles brushing against his stomach. When she finally pushed his pants down, her eyes flicked up to meet his, and something unspoken passed between them. Approval. Anticipation.

Meanwhile, Jason was mapping Kayla's body with his hands, his fingers tracing the delicate curve of her spine. He studied her like she was something to be savored, his eyes darkening as her dress pooled at her feet.

"You're beautiful," he murmured, his voice thick with appreciation.

Kayla's skin burned under his gaze. It had been years since she'd felt this kind of attention, the thrill of a man seeing her in a new way. Jason's fingers skimmed over her waist, his touch light, exploratory, before his lips followed, pressing slow, open-mouthed kisses along the column of her neck. She let her head tip back, surrendering to the sensation.

She had been worried that this moment would feel strange — that allowing another man to touch her would feel wrong. But it didn't. It was exhilarating.

And then it happened. Kayla knelt before Jason, her fingers gliding down his torso as she settled between his legs, and took Jason in her mouth. Jason exhaled sharply, threading his fingers through her hair as she moved against him with newfound confidence. Quinn's stomach twisted as he watched, every nerve in his body on edge.

This was it, the moment he had been dreading, the true test of how far he could go.

His first instinct was to look away, to shield himself from the reality of what was happening, but he forced himself to stay present. He had agreed to this. He had wanted to prove — to Kayla, to himself — that he could handle it.

And then something unexpected happened.

Kayla glanced up at him.

Not Jason. Not Mia. Him.

Her expression was soft, questioning, as if silently asking if he was still with her in this, if he was ok. And somehow, that simple gesture grounded him in a way nothing else could.

Quinn released the breath he hadn't realized he was holding. His pulse slowed. He felt Mia's fingers gently tracing over his shoulder, her presence reassuring rather than intrusive.

Kayla wasn't lost in the moment. She was still his wife, still the woman he had built his life with. And even here, in this uncharted territory, she was thinking of him.

Quinn swallowed hard and nodded toward Kayla, a silent signal between them.

She smiled — just for him.

And just like that, something inside him shifted.

Mia's lips brushed against his jawline, her hands warm against his chest. He let his tension dissolve, let himself be carried into the moment. Maybe, just maybe, he didn't have to fight it anymore.

Maybe he could let go.

Quinn turned toward Mia, his hands slipping around her waist, pulling her closer. She tilted her chin up, her breath warm against his skin, her lips hovering just over his. He closed the distance, kissing her deeply, finally allowing himself to enjoy the moment for what it was.

As the night unraveled, the four of them moved between curiosity and passion, exploring this new dynamic together. There were moments of uncertainty, glances exchanged to check boundaries, whispered reassurances that they were all ok. But there was also pleasure, exhilaration, the realization that maybe — just maybe — this could be something more than either of them had imagined.

Kayla, breathless and flushed, looked over at Quinn again, and this time, there was something else in her gaze.

21

The room pulsed with a heady mix of excitement and tension, each moment stretching, heightening. The soft glow of the dimmed lamps cast shadows that flickered along the walls, the air thick with anticipation. They moved as pairs — Quinn and Mia drifting toward the bed, Kayla and Jason toward the sleek wooden table near the window. The shift felt natural, unspoken, as if an invisible current was guiding them forward.

Kayla's breath came in soft, uneven waves as Jason's hands slid along her sides, his touch warm, measured. He turned her around and placed his hand on the middle her back, guiding her to bend over the table. He moved with a quiet confidence, exploring, learning her body. Her fingers gripped the edge of the table for stability, her body humming with expectation, Jason's presence behind her both grounding and exhilarating.

Across the room, Quinn leaned back into the pillows, his hands instinctively finding Mia's waist as she straddled him. The sensation of her body against his sent a sharp thrill through him. She moved with deliberate ease, her fingertips tracing the rough stubble along his jawline before tilting his chin up to meet her gaze. Her deep brown eyes held something playful, teasing, as if daring him to let go completely.

"Relax," Mia whispered, brushing her lips just below his ear, her breath warm against his skin.

Quinn exhaled slowly, his fingers tightening slightly against her hips. It was strange, this feeling — not just the physical thrill, but the mental shift occurring within him. He had expected hesitation, even discomfort, but instead, he felt a slow unraveling of his fears. The barriers he thought he'd built between jealousy and acceptance had already begun to dissolve.

Kayla stole a glance across the room, locking eyes with Quinn. The moment stretched between them, charged and intimate in its own way. He wasn't lost in this. Neither of them were. They were still connected, even here, even now. The realization settled something deep inside her.

Jason's lips trailed along the back of her neck, his touch a stark contrast to Quinn's. It was more deliberate, more exploratory. He moved as though savoring every reaction, every shift in her breath. Her mind buzzed, caught in the strange and exhilarating dichotomy of newness and familiarity. She had never felt this way before — completely present, yet utterly untethered.

Mia, meanwhile, had begun to guide Quinn in a slow, deliberate rhythm, her hands mapping the contours of his body with a practiced touch. She leaned in closer, brushing her lips over his chest, her movements unhurried, savoring the moment. Mia lifted his hand, pressing it against her side, urging him to explore.

He met her gaze, something unspoken passing between them, and for the first time that night, he let himself surrender completely.

Kayla could feel Jason's breath against her ear as he traced his hands lower, pressing against the small of her back, drawing her into the moment. She shivered, absorbing the sensation, the unfamiliarity, the quiet confidence in his touch. Her body responded in ways she hadn't anticipated, her pulse a steady drumbeat in her ears.

But still, her mind flickered back to Quinn. She turned her head slightly, stealing another glance at him.

He was watching her. And not with jealousy. Not with hesitation. With something else entirely.

Acceptance.

For a moment, their eyes held, the connection between them still strong, still unbroken despite the circumstances. And with that, any lingering doubt dissipated. This wasn't about separation — it was about trust, about experiencing something side by side, redefining the limits of what they thought they knew about love, about intimacy.

Kayla let out a slow exhale, turning her attention back to Jason. She leaned into the moment, allowing herself to feel everything, to let go in a way she hadn't in years.

22

Later that week, Quinn and Kayla found themselves back in their therapist's office, sitting side-by-side on the leather couch, their hands loosely intertwined. The last time they were here, their voices had carried hesitation, uncertainty. But today, something was different. They looked lighter... freer.

Dr. Simmons studied them for a moment before leaning forward. "You both seem... different," she observed. "How have things been since we last spoke?"

Kayla and Quinn exchanged a glance before Kayla spoke first. "Honestly? Really good," she admitted. "We've had two experiences now, and it's been... exciting. Eye-opening."

Dr. Simmons nodded, her expression warm but measured. "Tell me more about that. What emotions have surfaced for both of you?"

Quinn exhaled, rubbing his palms against his jeans before answering. "At first, I was terrified," he confessed. "The thought of Kayla with another man — it felt like something I shouldn't be ok with. But when it actually happened... it was different than I expected. I wasn't losing her. If anything, I felt closer to her."

Kayla squeezed his hand. "I feel the same way. It's made me appreciate what we have more, not less."

Dr. Simmons studied them carefully. "That's a powerful realization. But I want to make sure you're both being honest with yourselves. Are there any lingering doubts? Any moments that made either of you uncomfortable?"

Quinn hesitated, then nodded. "I won't lie — there were moments where I had to push through some strong emotions. Watching Kayla with Jason... there was an initial shock. It's like my brain was fighting itself — one part telling me I should be jealous, but another part realizing it wasn't a threat."

Kayla smirked, turning to Quinn. "You weren't too bothered when Mia had her hands all over you, though."

Quinn chuckled, rubbing the back of his neck. "Ok, fair point." He turned back to Dr. Simmons. "That was another thing. I didn't expect to enjoy it as much as I did. The guilt was there at first, but then I saw Kayla watching me, and she wasn't hurt or upset — but excited. That changed everything."

Dr. Simmons nodded. "Tell me more about that moment. What was going through your mind?"

Quinn took a deep breath. "I guess I was waiting for permission to enjoy it. When I saw Kayla smiling, I knew she wasn't regretting this. That's when I let go."

Kayla turned toward him with a teasing grin. "Let go? That's an understatement. You and Mia were lost in your own world for a while."

Quinn smirked. "And you weren't?"

Kayla bit her lip, tilting her head. "Oh, I was. Jason knew exactly what he was doing."

Dr. Simmons interjected, her voice calm but curious. "How did it feel seeing each other with someone else? Was there ever a moment of fear?"

Kayla exhaled. "I thought there would be, but when I looked at Quinn with Mia, I didn't feel jealousy. I felt... turned on. And it wasn't just about the act itself — it was seeing him through fresh eyes. Watching someone else appreciate him, seeing how he responded to her touch... it reminded me of why I fell for him in the first place."

Quinn turned to her, a small smile tugging at his lips. "I felt the same way about you. Watching you with Jason — it wasn't just that you were enjoying yourself. It was the way you carried yourself. You were confident and free. And when you looked at me in the middle of it, I knew we were still connected."

Dr. Simmons tapped her pen against her notepad thoughtfully. "That's important — maintaining connection even while exploring something new. It sounds like you both felt reassured rather than threatened."

Quinn nodded. "Exactly. Even when we weren't touching, even when we were with other people, I felt her presence."

Dr. Simmons leaned back, her expression pleased. "That's a strong foundation. But I do want to ask — what happens now? Do you see this as something you'll continue, or do you feel like you've gotten what you needed from it?"

Kayla and Quinn exchanged another glance. Kayla was the first to answer. "I think we're still figuring that out. We both feel good about where we are, but we're not rushing to define it."

Quinn agreed. "We're taking it one step at a time."

Dr. Simmons smiled. "That's a healthy approach. As long as you continue to communicate and check in with each other, you'll be able to navigate this in a way that works for you both."

As they left the office that day, Quinn felt something settle in his chest. He and Kayla were walking an unconventional path, but it was theirs. And for the first time, he wasn't afraid.

23

Later that night, Kayla found herself sitting across from her coworker and close friend, Erika, in the dim glow of a chic downtown lounge. The music was low, the clinking of glasses and murmured conversations creating an intimate atmosphere around them.

Erika leaned forward, studying Kayla over the rim of her wine glass. "Ok, spill," she said, her tone light but her eyes sharp. "Something's been going on with you. I can feel it."

Kayla hesitated, glancing around as if to make sure no one was eavesdropping. This wasn't exactly the kind of conversation she wanted to have within earshot of strangers.

Erika smirked. "It's a man, isn't it?"

Kayla took a slow sip of her drink before setting it down. "Sort of," she admitted. "But also… not exactly."

Erika frowned. "Not exactly?"

Kayla exhaled. "Quinn and I… we've been exploring. Swinging, actually."

Erika's expression froze for a fraction of a second before she carefully set her glass down. "Wait—like, actually? You're telling me you and Quinn… with other people?"

Kayla nodded, feeling warmth creep up her neck. "Yeah."

Erika blinked, shaking her head as if trying to process the revelation. "Wow. I did not see that coming."

Kayla gave a nervous laugh. "I know. It surprised me, too."

Erika was silent for a long moment, sipping her wine. Then, in a quieter voice, she asked, "Did you enjoy it?"

Kayla nodded, her cheeks flushing. "Yeah, way more than I expected. Also… I was with a woman."

Erika leaned in, lowering her voice. "And? How was it?"

Kayla hesitated before answering. "It was… different. Exciting. The way she kissed me – so soft, but confident. And when things got more intense, I wasn't expecting how much I'd like it."

Erika's lips parted slightly. "Did you… want to stop at any point?"

Kayla shook her head. "No. I was nervous at first, but once I let myself go, it felt… freeing. She knew exactly what she was doing, and I just let myself be in the moment."

Erika leaned in, her curiosity piqued. "What was the best part? The excitement? The newness? Or just knowing you could do something so… different?"

Kayla thought for a moment, swirling her drink. "Honestly? It was knowing that Quinn and I could handle it together. That we could step outside of what we thought was normal and still feel connected."

Erika smirked, sipping her drink. "So, do you think you'd do it again?"

Kayla bit her lip, smiling. "Yeah. I think I would."

Erika shook her head in amused disbelief. "Damn, girl. I never would've guessed. So, what's next?"

Kayla grinned. "I guess we'll see."

They clinked glasses, and for the first time, Kayla felt the thrill of saying it all out loud — of owning her choices, without shame.

24

Erika sat at her desk, staring at her computer screen, but the numbers and emails in front of her blurred together. She sighed and leaned back in her chair, closing her eyes and rubbing her temples. She had barely gotten any work done all morning. Her mind was elsewhere — specifically, on Kayla.

Their conversation at the bar the night before had been playing on repeat in her head. Another woman. Kayla had kissed a woman, had been intimate with her. The thought made Erika's heart pound in a way she wasn't ready to confront.

She had always known she was different. It wasn't until her early twenties, after a drunken night with a college friend, that she admitted it to herself — she liked women. That night had been unexpected, but it had changed everything. The soft press of lips against hers, the way her body reacted — it was like a switch had flipped. After that, she stopped pretending. She pretty much only dated women, even had a serious relationship or two. There had been a couple of dates with men, mostly out of curiosity, but nothing ever clicked.

And then… there was Kayla.

The first time she saw her, it was like being hit by a bolt of lightning. Erika had always been drawn to confident, charismatic women, but Kayla was something else entirely. She had this effortless beauty, a warmth that drew people in. There was something so magnetic about her — the way she laughed, the way she carried herself with that easy grace, the way her eyes sparkled when she talked about something she loved. She wasn't just beautiful; she was radiant.

Erika had crushed on her silently, pushing those feelings down because Kayla was married, straight, and they were friends. It just wasn't something she could act on. But that didn't mean she didn't notice things like the way Kayla tucked a stray piece of hair behind her ear when she was deep in thought, the way she bit her lip when she was trying to concentrate, and the way she stretched in her chair, arms reaching high above her head, her toned stomach peeking out just enough to make Erika's breath hitch.

And then there were the stolen glances.

Erika wasn't proud of it, but she had spent years sneaking looks at Kayla throughout the workday. When Kayla would walk into a meeting, Erika's eyes would instinctively track her, taking in the way she moved, the way she smiled, the way her blouse clung just right to her. It was ridiculous, really — she felt like some lovesick teenager crushing on the unattainable girl. But she couldn't help it.

She had long since accepted that Kayla would never see her that way, so she buried the feelings and focused on being a good friend instead. But now? Now everything was different.

Kayla had been with another woman. And she had liked it.

Erika drummed her fingers against the desk, biting her lip. Should she say something? Should she admit that she had thought about Kayla that way for years? Would it ruin their friendship?

For so long, she had convinced herself that her feelings didn't matter, that they were just a byproduct of admiration, of a deep friendship that she had mistaken for something more. But if that were true, why did her heart speed up every time Kayla brushed against her in passing? Why did she sometimes catch herself fantasizing about what it would be like to kiss her, to feel her body respond to her touch?

And now, with the knowledge that Kayla was open to exploring with women... the door that Erika had always thought was firmly shut had been cracked open just the tiniest bit.

But did that mean she should step through it?

She exhaled and shook her head. No. Not a good idea.

Kayla was still figuring things out, still navigating her feelings. The last thing Erika wanted to do was push her into something she wasn't ready for. No, this was something she would have to keep to herself — for now, at least.

Instead, she opened her email and forced herself to focus. But deep down, she knew this wasn't the last time she'd wonder about what could be.

25

The next two weeks passed in a blur of normalcy. Kayla and Quinn fell back into their routines — work, parenting, daily errands... The intensity of their recent experiences lingered in the background, but they didn't talk much about what came next. They both needed time to process, breathe, and reassess how they felt about it all.

But one night, as Quinn sat on the couch scrolling through their swingers app, something caught his attention. A new couple had appeared in the feed, and they stood out immediately.

His eyes zeroed in on the woman first. She was absolutely breathtaking. Stunning deep brown skin, her curves accentuated perfectly by the way she posed in her profile pictures. Her body was toned, yet soft in all the right places, the kind of shape that instantly commanded attention. One picture showed her in a green silk dress, its plunging neckline teasing just enough to make Quinn shift uncomfortably on the couch. Another had her standing on a beach in a bikini, her black, wavy hair cascading over one shoulder, her full lips slightly parted in a sultry smirk. Her confidence practically leapt off the screen.

Quinn swallowed hard, his grip tightening on his phone. He felt a low warmth building in his stomach, and when he shifted, he realized his pants were already swelling with excitement. His eyes flicked to her husband. Tall, broad-shouldered, strong jawline — a guy who exuded an easy sort of dominance. He was attractive, objectively so, and Quinn knew immediately that Kayla would find him appealing.

But his focus drifted immediately back to the woman.

His fingers traced over the screen as he scanned every detail of her pictures, his breath hitching slightly as he imagined her in front of him rather than behind a screen. The way she looked directly into the camera — like she knew exactly the effect she had on men. On him. It wasn't just about her beauty; it was the way she carried herself, the way she seemed to own her sexuality unapologetically.

Quinn licked his lips, forcing himself to glance at the couple's bio. Experienced. Friendly. Open to meeting new couples. He exhaled slowly, his heart drumming a little faster.

"Hey, check this out," he said, trying to keep his voice even as he turned the phone toward Kayla.

Kayla, curled up on the other end of the couch, looked up from her own screen, lazily shifting to face him. She took the phone, her eyebrows raising as she scrolled through the couple's pictures.

"You seem eager," she teased, smirking as she flipped through the photos.

Quinn shrugged, trying to play it cool. "They just seem like a good match."

Kayla continued scrolling, lingering on the woman's bikini shot before shifting to a photo of her and her husband together at a bar, laughing, looking comfortable and self-assured.

"She's gorgeous," Kayla admitted, then turned her gaze to Quinn, her eyes gleaming with amusement. "You really like her, don't you?"

Quinn hesitated, his jaw tightening slightly before he let out a soft chuckle. "Sure, she's attractive."

Kayla grinned knowingly. "Right."

Her gaze flickered down briefly — Quinn was still trying to subtly adjust himself, but the evidence of his excitement was hard to ignore. Her smirk widened.

Without another word, she opened the chat feature and typed out a message, introducing them and asking if the couple would be interested in getting to know them.

Quinn watched, his stomach fluttering with anticipation. As the message sent, he let out a slow exhale, already wondering what it would be like if they said yes.

26

The chat with the new couple started off cautiously. Kayla had sent the first message, keeping it light and friendly, introducing herself and Quinn. The response was warm but measured, the other couple clearly testing the waters before revealing too much.

For the next day, the four of them exchanged messages, slowly peeling back layers of conversation. As they grew more comfortable, their personalities shined through. The woman, Simone, was witty and engaging, her messages filled with teasing humor and flirtatious undertones. Her husband, David, was more reserved but carried an air of confidence that made Kayla certain he would be just as charming in person.

Quinn found himself becoming even more drawn to Simone as the texts progressed. She was stunning in her pictures, but even more captivating through her words. There was an easy charisma about her, a sultry playfulness that made his pulse quicken. It had been a long time since he felt such a magnetic pull toward another woman, and he kept catching himself rereading her messages, feeling an almost guilty thrill in the anticipation of meeting her.

Simone: "So tell me, Quinn, are you the confident, take-charge type, or do you like a woman who tells you exactly what she wants?"

Quinn: "Depends on the situation. But something tells me you're very good at giving directions."

Simone: "I like a man who listens. Especially when I tell him where to put his hands."

Quinn swallowed hard, rereading the message twice. His body tightened, and he shifted in his seat, hoping Kayla didn't notice his growing excitement again. But as he glanced at his wife, he saw the slight smirk on her lips.

Kayla: "Careful, Simone. Quinn might start taking notes."

Simone: "Good. I hope he does."

Quinn exhaled, setting his phone down for a second before picking it back up, his fingers twitching with the need to keep the conversation going. This was the kind of banter he hadn't realized he'd been craving — playful, electric, filled with unspoken promises.

Meanwhile, Kayla and David had their own exchange going, though it was less overtly teasing and more quietly intriguing. David had a way of making Kayla feel seen, even through text, asking thoughtful questions about their dynamic and what she hoped to get out of the experience.

David: "Kayla, are you more excited or nervous about this?"

Kayla: "Both, if I'm being honest. But mostly excited. Quinn and I have never felt this kind of chemistry with another couple before."

David: "That's what Simone and I were saying. Sometimes you just know."

The conversation naturally shifted toward setting plans. Initially, they considered a casual first meeting, like a dinner or drinks, but as the conversation deepened, both couples felt a unique chemistry forming. By the end of the second day of chatting, they agreed to skip the introductory meeting and combine it into one.

Simone: "We're feeling pretty good about this. What if we meet at the hotel bar first? Have a drink, loosen up, and then head up to the room?"

Kayla: "I like that. Great idea."

David: "Should we exchange numbers? Just to make the logistics easier?"

Previously, they had kept all communication within the app, maintaining a layer of separation between their real lives and their explorations. This time felt different, though.

Kayla and Quinn exchanged a glance. It was another step toward breaking down boundaries, toward making this feel more real. But something about this couple made them feel at ease.

Kayla: "Yeah, sure, let's do it."

Moments later, Quinn received Simone's number, his heart pounding slightly as he saved it into his phone. This was happening.

That night, while Kayla was in the shower, Quinn found himself lying in bed, staring at Simone's name on his screen. He debated texting her directly — just a simple message, maybe something playful — but he hesitated. Would that cross a line? Would Kayla mind?

His thumb hovered over the keyboard before he finally typed: "Looking forward to finally seeing you in person."

A minute later, his phone buzzed.

Simone: "Looking forward to much more than that."

Quinn swallowed, the weight of anticipation pressing against his chest. His body responded instantly, warmth spreading through him as he imagined what was to come.

As Kayla and Quinn settled into bed that night, Quinn lay awake, staring at the ceiling, his mind buzzing with excitement.

This was the most he had been attracted to another woman since he first met Kayla. And now, all he had to do was wait for the night to arrive.

27

The night had finally arrived. Quinn and Kayla had planned to get to the hotel bar thirty minutes early to settle in, but when they walked inside, they immediately spotted Simone and David already seated at a high-top table, sipping on their drinks.

Simone looked even more breathtaking in person. She wore a fitted emerald green dress that hugged her curves perfectly, her dark curls falling effortlessly over her shoulders. David, dressed sharply in a tailored button-down and slacks, exuded quiet confidence.

The greetings were warm but restrained — quick hugs, friendly smiles — nothing that would draw attention from the other bar patrons. To any outsider, they were just two couples catching up over drinks.

Seated together, the conversation flowed naturally. They joked about first-meeting jitters, their experiences on the app, and how tricky it could be to balance this lifestyle with regular life. The chemistry between them was undeniable. Had this been any other situation, Quinn could have easily seen the four of them becoming close friends.

After a couple of rounds and an hour of conversation filled with laughter and easy banter, Simone leaned in, lowering her voice. "So... should we take this upstairs?"

Quinn felt his pulse spike. Kayla and David exchanged glances before Kayla nodded. "Yeah, let's go."

The four of them stood, walking toward the elevator. The air between them was charged with anticipation. As they stepped inside, they found themselves joined by a few other hotel guests.

Quinn was about to press the button for their floor when he felt a firm yet subtle squeeze on his backside. His breath hitched, and he turned slightly, catching Simone's sly grin. Kayla and David weren't even aware of what she was doing. It was a private, secret moment between the two of them, and the realization sent a ripple of excitement through him.

He had been looking forward to this all week, but now it felt real in a way it hadn't before. The prospect of what was about to happen left him both nervous and electrified.

As the elevator continued its ascent, he stole a glance at Kayla. She was smiling, engaged in quiet conversation with David, her body language relaxed. If she had any second thoughts, she wasn't showing them.

Simone's fingers lightly trailed off him just as the elevator chimed. The doors opened.

And just like that, it was time.

<h1 style="text-align:center">28</h1>

The moment they entered the hotel room, an almost electric energy crackled between them. The air felt different — exciting, charged, unspoken anticipation lingering in the space between them.

They fell into more conversation, laughter puncturing the air. The chemistry was undeniable. The four of them genuinely liked each other, their personalities meshing in a way that felt seamless. The conversation was lively, full of teasing and flirtation that had become second nature to them over the past few days of messaging.

Simone sipped her drink, her dark eyes flickering with amusement. "So," she said, resting her elbow on the back of the couch, her body angled toward Quinn. "What were you thinking when you first saw our profile?"

Quinn chuckled. "Honestly? I thought you were way too gorgeous to be real."

Kayla smirked, nudging him. "He wasn't the only one staring at your pictures. Trust me."

Simone tilted her head, her full lips curving into a playful smile. "Oh?"

Kayla shrugged, swirling the wine in her glass. "Let's just say Quinn wasn't the only one impressed."

David laughed, his deep voice smooth and relaxed. "Well, I'd say we're all impressed with each other. That's why we're here, right?" His hand casually landed on Kayla's knee, his fingers brushing lightly over the hem of her dress.

Quinn found himself stealing glances at Simone throughout the conversation. Her presence was magnetic, her every movement deliberate. When she tucked her hair behind her ear, when she laughed and placed her hand lightly on his arm, even the way she leaned in when she spoke, it was intoxicating.

Then, she excused herself to the bathroom. Quinn's eyes instinctively followed her, his gaze trailing the smooth curve of her back, the way her emerald dress clung to her hips, emphasizing her toned, shapely figure. The sway of her perfect ass had his pulse quickening, an undeniable tightness forming in his pants. He quickly averted his gaze, but Kayla caught it. She smirked knowingly, taking a slow sip of her wine before whispering, "You are not subtle."

Quinn chuckled, shaking his head. "She's just... breathtaking."

Kayla glanced toward the closed bathroom door, her expression thoughtful. "Yeah, she really is."

A few minutes later, the door to the bathroom clicked open.

Simone stepped out, and the air in the room seemed to pause. Her emerald dress was gone, replaced by a black lace lingerie set that clung to her like shadow and light. Its sheer panels accentuated every perfect curve, delicate straps tracing her curves like whispers, framing her sculpted figure with breathtaking precision.

His eyes drank her in. The subtle contrast of the lace against her deep brown skin was stunning. His eyes followed the arc of her collarbone, the swell of her breasts framed by the intricate lace, the smooth plane of her abdomen narrowing to a tight waist and flaring hips. Her toned, long legs moved with fluid grace, every step infused with effortless sensuality. She didn't just wear the lingerie — she commanded it.

He wasn't the only one affected. Kayla's lips parted slightly, her eyes widening as she took in the sight of Simone standing before them, her body glowing under the soft hotel lighting. She had expected to spend most of her night focused on David, but now, seeing Simone like this, an unfamiliar craving stirred within her. It was different from what she'd felt before. It was stronger, more visceral.

Simone smiled, clearly enjoying their reactions. She stepped forward, walking toward Quinn first. He was still sitting, his grip tightening around his glass as she approached. She placed a single finger under his chin, tilting his face up toward her.

"I take it you approve?" she murmured, her voice like silk.

Quinn swallowed hard, his voice slightly hoarse. "Very much."

She smirked and ran a slow, teasing hand down his chest before turning to Kayla. Her gaze softening just slightly as she reached out and tucked a loose strand of Kayla's hair behind her ear.

"And what about you?" Simone's voice dropped to a near whisper, her breath warm against Kayla's cheek. "You like what you see?"

Kayla let out a slow breath, nodding. "Yeah," she admitted, voice barely above a whisper. "I really do."

Simone's smile deepened, a spark of satisfaction flashing in her dark eyes. She turned back toward David, who had been watching the entire exchange with an amused grin. "Well," she teased, tilting her head, "I figured we could stop pretending like we're just here to talk."

David chuckled, finishing the last sip of his drink before setting the glass down on the table. "I think that's fair."

Quinn's heart hammered in his chest, his entire body buzzing with anticipation as Simone reached for his hand, gently guiding him to stand. Her touch sent an electric current through him, and when she leaned in, pressing a soft, lingering kiss against his jawline, he exhaled sharply, every ounce of tension flooding from his body.

Kayla licked her lips, eyes flickering between Simone and David. A slow smile formed as she leaned forward. "I like the way you think."

29

As Quinn and Kayla remained frozen in place, still processing Simone's boldness and beauty, she took a step forward, her gaze locked on Kayla's. Without hesitation, she reached out and cupped Kayla's face, pulling her in for a deep, slow kiss.

Quinn felt something stir in his chest — jealousy? Intrigue? He wasn't sure. All he knew was that watching his wife locked in an embrace with a woman he so desperately desired sent his mind into a tailspin. His breathing hitched as Simone deepened the kiss, her hands sliding into Kayla's hair, her fingers tugging ever so slightly.

Kayla melted into it, letting out the softest sigh. Her hands found Simone's waist, her fingers grazing against the warm skin beneath the sheer lace of her lingerie. For a moment, Quinn could see nothing but them — the way their bodies pressed together, the way Kayla's hesitation gave way to something primal.

He had always found Kayla breathtaking, but seeing her like this — untamed, eager, lost in the moment — was something entirely different. His pulse pounded, and his grip on his glass tightened. The room around them seemed to blur, as if the only thing that existed was the two of them, tangled together in a moment he never could have imagined.

Then, Simone pulled back, her lips curving into a knowing smile. "That was fun," she teased, her voice husky. She traced a single finger along Kayla's jawline before turning to David, who had been watching with an amused smirk. Taking Kayla's hand, she placed it in his. "I think you two should get acquainted."

Kayla hesitated for only a moment, her gaze flickering toward Quinn. He saw the unspoken question in her eyes — Are you ok? — and though his heart was pounding, he managed a slow nod.

David stepped forward, his hands warm as he slid them over Kayla's waist, pulling her close. He murmured something to her, something Quinn couldn't hear, and Kayla laughed — a breathy, almost nervous sound that sent an odd thrill through Quinn's chest. Then, David tilted her chin up and kissed her.

Simone then stepped closer to Quinn, stopping just a few inches away. Holding his gaze, she reached behind her back and unhooked her bra, letting the lingerie slide down her arms and fall to the floor.

Quinn sucked in a sharp breath.

She was absolutely stunning. More than that, it was as if every idealized vision of a woman he'd ever had was standing before him in flesh and blood. The smooth, deep brown of her skin was luminous under the soft glow of the hotel lighting. Her curves were elegant, the toned lines of her body telling a story of strength and grace.

For a long moment, he couldn't move. Couldn't think. He felt like a teenager again, seeing something forbidden and intoxicating for the first time.

Simone's lips twitched as if she could read his thoughts. She took his hand, guiding it to her waist before moving it lower, pressing it against the curve of her backside. The heat of her skin, the firmness beneath his palm, sent a jolt through him.

Her confidence was staggering, effortless. She didn't wait for permission. She knew exactly what she wanted, and Quinn found himself utterly captivated by her presence.

Then, just as deliberately, she reached between his legs, her fingers grazing him through his slacks. His breath caught, his body reacting instantly.

"Do you like what you see?" she murmured, her voice like silk.

Quinn exhaled shakily. He couldn't even form words.

Simone grinned, her fingers pressing just a little harder. "No worries, you don't have to answer," she whispered. "I can tell you do."

She leaned in, her lips brushing just below his ear, her breath hot against his skin. "Let me help you relax, Quinn," she purred, her hands moving to unbutton his shirt.

He let Simone slide his shirt from his shoulders, her fingers grazing over his chest as she traced the lines of his muscles. He let himself forget about the tension in his body, the warring emotions in his mind. Instead, he focused on the warmth of her skin, the way she smelled — something rich and heady, like jasmine and spice.

Across the room, Kayla and David were lost in their own moment. David had peeled the straps of her dress down her shoulders, exposing the delicate lace of her lingerie. Kayla shivered beneath his touch, arching slightly as his lips traced along the curve of her neck.

Quinn swallowed hard, his pulse erratic as he watched his wife give herself over to someone else. And yet... there was something beautiful about it. It didn't feel like betrayal. It was something new.

Simone's fingers curled under his chin, pulling his attention back to her. "Don't look away," she whispered, her lips ghosting over his jaw. "Let yourself see her. Let her see you."

Quinn did as she said. His gaze met Kayla's just as David's hands slid down her back, pulling her even closer. Her lips parted slightly, her breath uneven, but when her eyes locked onto Quinn's, something unspoken passed between them.

This wasn't about loss. It wasn't about jealousy.

It was about trust. About discovery.

Simone smiled knowingly, pressing herself against him as she tilted her head toward Kayla. "You see that?" she whispered. "She's still yours, Quinn. Don't worry."

30

The energy in the room shifted in an unspoken agreement. Quinn, Kayla, Simone, and David moved toward the bed together, a tangle of limbs, laughter, and whispered encouragement. Unlike their last experience, where they had drifted into separate spaces of the room, this time they remained together, a connected mass of bodies exploring, testing, and surrendering to the unknown.

Simone and Kayla found themselves alternating between the men and each other. Every touch, every lingering look between them held something more profound than simple curiosity. When Kayla kissed Simone again, there was no hesitance, only hunger.

Quinn tried to focus on the moment, on the experience, but there was a gnawing awareness forming in the back of his mind. Kayla wasn't just experimenting anymore; she was savoring, losing herself in Simone in a way that felt different. More than once, Quinn caught himself feeling a flicker of something he couldn't name. Was it jealousy? Was it competition? He wanted Simone — badly — but so did Kayla.

David, ever the composed observer, smirked slightly as he leaned toward Quinn. "Looks like our ladies have their own plans tonight."

Quinn chuckled, though it didn't quite reach his eyes. "Yeah, seems that way."

Simone, completely attuned to the power she held, flicked her gaze between them. "Don't worry," she murmured. "I have enough to go around."

Her words sent a new rush of exhilaration through Quinn, but beneath that thrill, something else brewed. A realization that what they had started wasn't just about trading partners — it was about exploring deeper, more personal desires. And for the first time, Quinn wasn't sure if he was ready for where this path might lead.

As Kayla turned her attention back to David, she was struck by the sheer presence of him. He was strong but smooth, exuding confidence with every movement. His hands, large and firm, rested on her waist before sliding up her sides in a way that sent a shiver racing down her spine. His fingers trailed over her chest, teasing but intentional, and she found herself leaning into his touch instinctively.

"You're beautiful," he murmured, his voice deep and resonant. The way he said it was different from how Quinn spoke to her — David's words carried a quiet reverence, a patient appreciation.

Kayla's breath hitched as he moved closer, brushing his lips over the sensitive spot just beneath her ear. Her hands roamed over his chest, feeling the taut muscles beneath her fingertips. The contrast between them — his strength and her softness — made every moment feel heightened, every touch electric.

David lifted her effortlessly and, with Kayla's legs wrapped around his, guided her onto the bed, his body hovering just above hers. His weight, his heat, the sensation of his breath against her skin, it overwhelmed her in the best possible way. She was keenly aware of every movement, every shift, her senses tuned to the way his hands explored her body with deliberate precision.

Quinn watched from the side, captivated. Kayla wasn't just responding. She was thriving, lost in the sheer pleasure of the moment.

David shifted, his lips tracing a path down Kayla's stomach and kept going until he rested his face between her legs. Her back arched violently in response, a soft gasp escaping her lips. He moved slowly, savoring every reaction, every taste, his hands gripping her thighs as if memorizing the shape of her. Every flicker of pleasure sent waves of heat coursing through her, a slow build of anticipation that had her clutching at the sheets beneath her.

Meanwhile, Simone turned her attention back to Quinn. She could see the conflict warring inside him, the struggle between curiosity and control. So she did what she did best. She took away the choice.

Sliding up beside him, she captured his lips in a slow, searing kiss. Quinn groaned into her mouth, his restraint unraveling as he finally let himself fall into the moment. Simone's hands mapped his body, her nails digging into his back as she deepened the kiss.

Quinn felt his inhibitions dissolving, his desire for Simone taking hold. He reached for her, pulling her closer, his fingers tracing the curve of her hip. She let out a soft moan, arching against him, their bodies pressing together in a way that sent sparks dancing along his skin.

Simone leaned into him, whispering something teasing in his ear before shifting to straddle his lap. Her body moved with an effortless rhythm, their connection deepening as Quinn surrendered fully to the moment. His hands explored her curves and chest, tracing the lines of her body as they melted into each other, completely lost in sensation.

Across the bed, Kayla let her head fall back against the pillows, her breathing ragged. David moved with a slow, deliberate rhythm, his touch coaxing her deeper into sensation. She felt unburdened, freed from expectation, allowed to simply exist in this moment of pure indulgence.

Quinn, still tangled with Simone, turned his head slightly, catching a glimpse of Kayla lost in pleasure.

This was their journey. And for now, he was content to let it unfold.

31

The morning after, Kayla and Quinn entered their house in silence. The weight of the previous night settled between them like an unspoken truth neither of them was ready to confront. They had shared so much, continuing to cross boundaries that once felt immovable, yet now, standing in the familiar warmth of their home, it felt oddly distant, like the night had happened in another world entirely.

Quinn set his keys on the kitchen counter while Kayla slipped off her coat, neither making eye contact. Their movements were routine, methodical, but the air between them remained thick with something unspoken.

"I'm going to take a shower," Kayla finally said, her voice even but distant.

Quinn nodded. "Yeah. Me too."

She disappeared down the hallway, and Quinn exhaled deeply, running a hand through his hair. He had expected this — the awkwardness, the uncertainty — but now that it was here, it gnawed at him in a way he hadn't anticipated. He wasn't sure what the right thing to say was. He wasn't even sure what he was feeling.

The rest of the day passed in a haze of small talk and avoidance. They fell back into their routine, but there was an undercurrent beneath every interaction. They had done this before, returning to normal after an experience, but something about this time felt different. As much as they tried to act like everything was the same, they both knew it wasn't.

That evening, they prepared for Kayla's office party. She stepped out of their bedroom in a sleek, red dress that hugged her figure perfectly, its deep neckline accentuated by the soft waves of her dark hair. Quinn, dressed in a tailored navy suit with a crisp white shirt, couldn't help but admire her.

"You look amazing," he said, his voice sincere.

Kayla met his eyes, a flicker of warmth passing between them. "You don't look too bad yourself."

For a moment, it felt like them again. But just as quickly, the moment passed.

They arrived at the venue, a beautifully decorated event hall lined with twinkling lights and decorations. Soft jazz music played in the background as Kayla introduced Quinn to a few of her colleagues. They engaged in polite conversation, laughing in all the right places, sipping on cocktails as the night unfolded.

Kayla played the part effortlessly. She knew how to work a room, flashing the right smiles, making the appropriate comments, nodding along at the jokes and stories she had already heard a dozen times before. To an outsider, she appeared the picture of a woman having a great time. She threw her head back in laughter at the CFO's anecdote about a failed merger, clinked glasses with a junior associate who had just secured his first big client, and leaned into Quinn when their boss made a toast to long-lasting partnerships and hard work.

But it was all a performance.

Inside, she felt detached, her mind elsewhere. Every smile, every charming exchange was carefully placed, but none of it felt real. She could still feel Simone's hands on her, the ghost of her lips against her skin. The electricity of that night had lingered far longer than it should have, trailing behind her like a shadow. She didn't want to be here. She wanted to be somewhere else, with someone else.

She could sense Quinn watching her, studying her a little too closely. He saw through the performance, knew her well enough to recognize that something about her wasn't quite right. But he didn't say anything. He just kept sipping his drink, nodding at conversations he wasn't really listening to.

Then Kayla spotted Erika and grabbed Quinn's arm. "I'll be back in a bit, ok?"

Quinn nodded, watching as she made a beeline for her friend.

Kayla pulled Erika into a quieter room just off the main hall, her pulse quickening. "I have to tell you something."

Erika arched an eyebrow, intrigued. "Oh? Did you guys have another playdate?"

Kayla's lips parted slightly before she nodded. "Yes, but it was… different this time."

Erika crossed her arms, leaning in slightly. "Different how?"

Kayla hesitated, then exhaled. "With the wife – her name was Simone – I really enjoyed it more than I expected. More than I should have."

Erika smirked. "I knew it!"

Kayla's brows furrowed. "Knew what?"

"That you'd like being with a woman. Tell me about her. What did she look like?"

Kayla's stomach twisted at the memory. "She was… incredible. Confident. Drop-dead gorgeous – highly toned but still very curvy. She knew exactly what she was doing, too. I couldn't stop thinking about her even when I was with her husband David."

Erika's eyes darkened slightly, curiosity burning behind them. "So, are you saying you're into women now? Or just Simone?"

Kayla bit her lip, struggling with the question. "I don't know. Maybe… both?"

Erika exhaled, shaking her head in amusement. "Damn. I wish I could have been a fly on that wall."

Kayla chuckled, but the sound was tinged with uncertainty. "It felt… natural. And I think Quinn noticed. He's been acting funny ever since."

Erika tilted her head. "Noticed what?"

"That I was more into her than I was into David. That I wanted her more than Quinn, more than anything else."

Erika nodded knowingly. "And how do you think that makes him feel?"

Kayla sighed. "I don't know yet."

Erika reached out, touching Kayla's arm lightly. "Be careful, Kay. Feelings like that can get messy."

Kayla nodded, her mind racing. "I know."

They returned to the party, slipping back into the festive atmosphere, but the weight of the conversation lingered. Kayla had unlocked something new inside of herself, and she wasn't sure if she could push it back into the box.

Neither was Quinn.

Later, still at the party, Quinn received a text from Simone: "Had a great time last night. I'd love to do that again sometime."

He stared at the message for a long moment before locking his phone, forcing a smile as one of Kayla's coworkers passed by and clinked their champagne glass against his.

32

A few weeks had passed, and neither Kayla nor Quinn brought up their experience with Simone and David. It took them both a while to process the experience.

They slipped back into their usual rhythm — work, parenting, family dinners — but there was something different in the air. It wasn't tension, exactly, but an unspoken awareness of what had happened. They had taken another step into this world together, and yet, neither seemed to know how to address it. The silence on the subject stretched longer than Kayla had expected.

For Kayla, it wasn't just the experience itself that lingered — it was Simone. It was the way she had touched her, the way she felt beneath her fingertips, the way her body had responded. She had considered herself completely straight before, never giving too much thought to the idea of being with a woman. But now, she wasn't so sure. She had now had sexual experiences with three women and enjoyed it more than she had with the guys. Had she always harbored this attraction, buried under the expectations of a conventional life? Or was it something new, something unlocked by the freedom of those encounters?

She found herself thinking about it more than she wanted to admit. Was it just Simone? Or was it something deeper?

And then, as the days passed and their routine settled again, the restless itch returned.

One night, after Zeke had gone to bed and they were curled up on the couch watching a show neither of them were paying attention to, Quinn casually broached the subject.

"So," he started, taking a sip of his drink. "Are we going to do this again?"

Kayla turned her head toward him, slightly caught off guard. "Do what again?"

Quinn smirked. "Come on, Kay. You know what I mean."

She studied his expression. He wasn't pushing, but he was curious. Maybe even a little eager.

"I don't know," she admitted. "Are you ready for that?"

Quinn exhaled through his nose. "I think so. It's weird, but I liked how it made us feel after." He glanced at her. "I mean... if you want to."

Kayla felt a warmth in her chest. The fact that he was coming to her about it, rather than waiting for her to bring it up, meant a lot.

She bit her lip. "I do. But can I pick this time?"

Quinn raised an eyebrow. "Pick?"

She nodded. "The last two times, we kind of went with the first couple we really connected with. I want to be the one to make the choice this time."

Quinn seemed puzzled but shrugged. "Ok. Sure. Just let me know what you find."

The next evening, after Quinn had fallen asleep, Kayla curled up with her laptop on the bed next to him and began scrolling through profiles. This time, she wasn't looking for another couple.

She wasn't even sure if she was looking for another woman.

Then she saw it.

A profile of a single man.

He was handsome in a rugged way — dark skin, short-cropped hair, piercing light green eyes. His profile picture was simple but confident, his body toned and muscular, his smile easy and inviting. There was something different about him, something intriguing.

She had never been with two men at the same time. The idea alone sent a thrill through her. She wasn't sure if it was the taboo nature of it, or if it was the fact that, for once, she would be the center of attention in a way she never had been before.

She also figured that this would be a good opportunity to explore what her sexual preferences truly were. Does she still like being with men, as well as women? Or was she a lesbian, finding contentment in men but not excitement.

She clicked on his profile and began typing.

Kayla: *Hi there. I really liked your profile. You seem interesting.*

It didn't take long for him to respond.

Man: *Well, that's a hell of a compliment. Interesting how?*

Kayla smirked to herself.

Kayla: *You seem confident. Like you know exactly what you want.*

Man: *I do. And I have a feeling you do, too.*

She felt warmth spread through her body. He was flirtatious, but not aggressive. Confident, but not cocky.

Kayla: *Maybe. I guess we'll find out ;)*

Man: *I like a woman who takes control. So tell me... what exactly are you looking for?*

She hesitated for only a second before replying.

Kayla: *An experience. Something new. Something… exciting.*

Man: *You're speaking my language.*

They exchanged messages late into the night, the conversation growing more suggestive, the chemistry undeniable. By the time she finally closed her laptop, she had already set a date to meet him.

Now, she just had to tell Quinn.

Two nights later, over dinner, she decided to bring it up.

"Hey," she said, swirling her fork in her pasta. "I, uh, found someone."

Quinn glanced up. "Already? Damn, you don't waste time."

She smiled. "Well, I wanted to find the right person."

Quinn leaned back in his chair, flashing her a grin. "So, who is it?"

Kayla hesitated. "Well, it's… a man."

Quinn's fork clattered against his plate. "Wait, what?"

Kayla kept her voice calm. "A single man. Just him. Not a couple."

Quinn's expression shifted from confusion to something more unsettled. "So, now you want to do this without me?"

She reached across the table, grabbing his hand. "No. Not at all. You would still be there. But I thought… why not switch things up?"

Quinn's jaw tensed. "Why?"

Kayla took a deep breath. "Because our first time was with just Lacey, a single woman. And I went along with that because it was what you were comfortable with. But if this is truly about exploration, it's only fair that I get to explore what I want, too."

Quinn rubbed the back of his neck. "I don't know, Kay. That feels different."

She raised an eyebrow. "Does it? You got to have two women. Why is it different for me to have two men?"

Quinn sighed, clearly struggling. "It just… I don't know. The idea of watching you with another guy like that — it feels different than watching you with another woman or another couple. Even when you were with the other guys, it somehow made it feel better that their wives were also there."

Kayla nodded, understanding but holding her ground. "I get that. But if we're doing this, we can't have different standards for what we each get to explore."

Quinn was quiet for a long moment before finally exhaling. "You already set up the date, didn't you?"

Kayla chewed her lip and gave him a sheepish look. "Yes."

Quinn shook his head but let out a small chuckle. "Jesus, woman."

She reached for his hand again. "I promise, if it gets to be too much, we stop. Just like you asked for in the beginning."

Quinn exhaled through his nose. He was still hesitant, but he nodded. "Ok."

Kayla smiled, squeezing his hand. "Deal."

As they finished dinner, she could see that he was still processing. But she also knew one thing — he hadn't said no. And that meant they were moving forward.

33

The tension between Kayla and Quinn lingered in the days following their conversation. Even though he had agreed, Kayla could sense his unease, the way he seemed quieter than usual, lost in thought. She knew this was a big step — one that he hadn't been entirely prepared for.

So, in an effort to reset and reconnect, she suggested a weekend trip.

"Just us," she told him one evening as they lay in bed. "No distractions. No big conversations. Just a break from everything for a couple nights."

Quinn agreed, albeit cautiously, and two days later, they found themselves pulling up to a luxury resort nestled in the countryside, a couple of hours outside the city. The grand entrance, lined with palm trees and soft golden lighting, felt like a world away from their everyday routine.

After checking in, they made their way to their room — a spacious suite with a private balcony overlooking a glistening pool. The moment they stepped inside, Kayla exhaled deeply, already feeling the weight on her chest lift.

"This was a good idea," she said, tossing her bag onto the bed.

Quinn nodded. "Yeah, it was."

Kayla pulled out her phone and quickly booked a spa appointment for the next morning. "I set up a treatment for myself tomorrow morning," she said, glancing up at him. "Gonna pamper myself a little."

Quinn smirked. "Good. You deserve it."

She walked over and wrapped her arms around his waist, resting her head against his chest. "Let's enjoy this weekend. No pressure, no stress. Just you and me."

He kissed the top of her head. "Agreed."

That afternoon, they explored the resort, starting with the pool. The water was cool and inviting, and they spent a blissful hour floating under the sun and enjoying cocktails from the nearby bar. Quinn seemed to relax more with each passing drink, his usual sharp edges softening. Kayla reveled in the moment, in the way he laughed with her, in the way he seemed present in a way he hadn't been in weeks.

Later, they moved to the hot tub, sinking into the bubbling warmth as the evening breeze set in. Quinn draped an arm over Kayla's shoulder, pulling her close as they talked about everything and nothing — old memories, funny stories, the things they had been too busy to bring up in their day-to-day lives.

For the first time in a while, they felt at ease with each other.

The next morning, Kayla woke early for her spa appointment, leaving Quinn to sleep in. The spa was tucked away on the quieter side of the resort, a tranquil space filled with soft music and the scent of lavender.

She was first treated to a luxurious massage, the therapist's hands working out the tension in her back and shoulders. Next came a facial, followed by a waxing session that left her skin smooth and refreshed. By the time she was done, she felt like an entirely new person.

Before heading back to the room, she decided to spend a few extra minutes in the sauna.

As she settled onto one of the wooden benches, the heat enveloping her, another woman entered. She was tall, with sun-kissed skin and light brown hair tied into a loose bun. She looked to be in her mid thirties, carrying herself with a confidence that was both effortless and inviting.

"Mind if I join you?" the woman asked, her voice warm.

"Not at all," Kayla said, sitting up slightly.

The woman sat down with a relaxed sigh. "I'm Jessica."

"Kayla."

Jessica gave her a friendly smile. "Here for the weekend?"

Kayla nodded. "Yeah, just a little getaway with my husband. You?"

Jessica stretched her legs out in front of her. "Same. Just needed some time away from work, kids… all of it."

They quickly fell into easy conversation, sharing bits and pieces of their lives. Jessica had two kids, a demanding but fulfilling career, and a husband who she adored. Kayla told her about Quinn, Zeke, and a career that wasn't quite as fulfilling as Jessica's.

They continued talking for a while, bonding over shared experiences, before Jessica suddenly grinned. "Hey, we should do dinner together tonight. You and your husband, me and mine."

Kayla smiled. "That sounds great."

They exchanged room phone numbers and planned to meet at the resort's main restaurant that evening.

Dinner with Jessica and her husband, Mark turned out to be an unexpected highlight of the trip. The four of them hit it off instantly, sharing stories, drinks, and laughter. Mark was charming, a bit reserved compared to Jessica's outgoing nature, but warm and engaging. Quinn seemed to enjoy himself too, loosening up as the night went on.

They lingered at the restaurant longer than they had expected, ordering dessert and another round of drinks, their conversation flowing effortlessly. When they finally got to the elevator, they discovered they were staying on the same floor.

As they walked down the hallway together, chatting the whole way, they reached Jessica and Mark's room first. The couple turned, smiling warmly. "We'll have to do this again before we all leave," Jessica said.

"Definitely," Kayla agreed, giving Jessica a warm hug.

Jessica and Mark disappeared into their room, and as their door shut, something caught Kayla's eye. A small door hanger, hooked onto the handle.

A pineapple.

An upside-down pineapple.

Her breath hitched slightly. Tasha had told her about this. This was a well-known symbol in the swinging community.

She glanced at Quinn, who had also noticed the door hanger but didn't realize what it was. Their eyes met, and Kayla felt a slow, knowing smile spread across her lips.

"Well," she murmured. "That's interesting."

Quinn, still not knowing what was going on, said, "What is?"

Kayla told him about the upside-down pineapple, and how it was a symbol indicating that they were fellow swingers and open to swinging, swapping partners, or having a third person join.

Quinn chuckled under his breath. "Very interesting."

As they continued walking down the hall toward their room, Kayla's mind was already spinning. This weekend was supposed to be a break, a reset. But maybe — just maybe — it was about to become something more.

34

The next morning, Kayla and Quinn walked into the resort's breakfast lounge, both feeling refreshed from their weekend away. They found a small, sunlit table near the windows and settled in, ordering coffee and fresh fruit while waiting for their omelets to arrive.

Halfway through their meal, Kayla glanced up just as Jessica and Mark entered the room. Jessica caught her eye, grinning as she whispered something to Mark. He chuckled, nodding in agreement. The two couples exchanged polite waves before Jessica and Mark moved toward the buffet station.

Kayla took another bite of her food before setting down her fork. Without much thought, she lifted her hand and waved them over. "Why don't you two join us?" she called with an easy smile.

Quinn's eyebrows raised slightly in surprise, but he quickly masked it with a sip of his coffee. He had assumed they'd keep their interactions casual — friendly, but contained. This, however, was something different.

Jessica and Mark exchanged a brief glance before walking back to the table with their plates. "If you're sure we're not intruding," Mark said as he pulled out a chair.

"Not at all," Kayla said cheerfully. "We were just talking about how beautiful this place is."

For the next hour, the four of them talked easily, laughing over their travel stories and sharing details about their lives outside the resort. The chemistry between the couples was undeniable, though subtle. There were lingering glances, shared smiles, and a growing familiarity that made their interactions feel... charged.

At one point, Jessica excused herself to the bathroom, and Kayla stood up to join her. "We'll be right back," she said, throwing Quinn a quick glance before following Jessica down the hallway.

In the restroom, Jessica leaned against the marble sink, adjusting her hair in the mirror. "Your husband's adorable, you know," she said with a smirk.

Kayla chuckled as she checked her lipstick. "Yours isn't bad himself."

Jessica grinned. "Mark is great, but there's something about Quinn... strong, quiet, but you can tell there's depth there." She met Kayla's eyes in the mirror. "He's very attractive."

Kayla felt her stomach flutter slightly. "Thank you. You think so?"

Jessica turned, facing her fully. "I know so."

There was something in her tone — playful but not entirely innocent. Kayla felt warmth creep up her neck but kept her composure, giving a coy smile. "Well, I'm sure Quinn would appreciate the compliment."

Jessica winked. "I hope so."

They shared a moment of knowing silence before heading back to the table.

Before parting ways, they made plans to meet at the resort's bar for happy hour later that evening. The easy camaraderie between them had only grown, and Kayla was more than a little curious about where it might lead.

Later that evening, the four of them met at the resort's bar, securing a round table near the windows overlooking the pool. The place was lively, with a soft buzz of chatter mixed with the smooth sounds of a Motown cover band warming up for their set.

Jessica took a seat between Mark and Quinn, while Kayla sat on the opposite side. They ordered cocktails, a few small plates to share, and fell back into their rhythm of easy conversation.

As the drinks flowed, so did the playful banter. At some point,

Quinn and Jessica drifted into their own side conversation, their voices lowered just enough to create a sense of exclusivity. Seeing this, Kayla turned toward Mark, engaging him in a similar way.

"So," she said, swirling her glass. "How long have you and Jessica been married?"

"Eleven years," Mark said, smiling fondly. "Feels like a lifetime and a blink at the same time."

Kayla nodded. "I know exactly what you mean."

Mark took a sip of his drink before tilting his head. "And you and Quinn? How long?"

"Eight years," she said. "But it feels like we've been together forever."

Mark chuckled. "I get that."

They continued talking, sharing details about their lives, their kids, and their shared love of travel. It was natural and easy, but there was an undercurrent of something else — a quiet intrigue that neither acknowledged directly but both felt.

Toward the end of happy hour, the band began their set, and a small dance floor opened up near the stage. Jessica perked up immediately. "We should dance," she said, grabbing Kayla's hand and pulling her to her feet before she could protest.

Kayla laughed as they made their way to the floor, the two of them easily falling into the rhythm of the music. Mark and Quinn stayed behind for a few moments, watching them with amused expressions before deciding to join them.

The four of them danced together, their bodies moving in sync with the sultry notes of the saxophone. The energy was electric, the playful tension from their conversations bleeding into their movements. Kayla felt alive, completely present in the moment, her body buzzing with the warmth of the drinks and the intoxicating energy of the night.

Then, she noticed something.

Jessica kept bumping into Quinn. Subtle at first — a light touch, a brush of her hip — but it soon became clear that it was intentional. The way she moved, the way she glanced at him beneath her lashes, it was unmistakable. And he didn't seem to mind.

35

The music pulsed through the dimly lit lounge, the rhythm setting the tone for what had become an intoxicating evening. The drinks had flowed freely, the laughter had come easily, and the dancing had shifted from playful to something more suggestive.

Kayla wasn't sure when the change happened, but she could feel it in the air—an almost electric charge crackling between the four of them. They alternated between dancing as a group and in pairs, their bodies moving together with effortless chemistry. At times, the husbands switched partners, Mark spinning Kayla around while Jessica pulled Quinn closer, whispering something in his ear that made him smirk. The line between friendship and flirtation blurring with every passing moment.

The couples weren't just dancing anymore. They were teasing.

When Jessica danced with Quinn, her touches lingered longer, her body pressing subtly against his. Kayla noticed the way Jessica would tilt her head slightly, allowing Quinn's hand to graze her neck, the way their eyes locked as they moved in sync.

Similarly, Kayla felt the firm grip of Mark's hands at her waist, guiding her movements in time with the music. His fingers traced small circles on the small of her back, and though it was barely noticeable, the sensation sent a shiver down her spine. When she glanced up at him, he grinned as if he knew exactly what he was doing.

Then came the moment that solidified everything.

A sultry jazz number filled the room, the saxophone crooning low and sensual, and the four of them instinctively came together. Jessica and Kayla found themselves facing each other, mere inches apart, both of them swaying to the rhythm. Behind them, their husbands moved in close, Mark's hands on Kayla's hips, Quinn mirroring the motion with Jessica.

The heat between them was undeniable.

Jessica's lips parted slightly as she met Kayla's gaze, her eyes flickering with something both knowing and mischievous. Kayla's breath hitched, the tension tightening between them like an invisible thread. Behind her, she could feel Mark's warmth radiating against her back, his hands never moving inappropriately but still making his presence known.

Across from her, Quinn caught Kayla's eyes, his expression unreadable but intense. She could see it in his face — he knew exactly what was happening.

She raised an eyebrow, silently asking him: *Are you ok with this?*

Quinn hesitated for only a second before giving a small, almost imperceptible nod.

In that single, unspoken exchange, they had made a decision.

This wasn't just a friendly vacation connection anymore.

This was a date.

The night stretched on in a haze of movement, whispered words, and lingering touches. When they finally decided to call it a night, the four of them walked back to their rooms, the tension still humming between them like a charged wire.

As they approached Jessica and Mark's suite, Jessica reached into her clutch and pulled out the key card, sliding it into the door. She pushed it open but then turned back, her gaze lingering on Kayla and Quinn.

With a sly grin, she leaned against the door frame. "Well," she murmured, voice laced with invitation, "are you coming in?"

36

The night had been a blur of passion, a whirlwind of tangled limbs and whispered moans, of fevered kisses and uncharted sensations. It had lasted for what felt like hours — exploring, indulging, giving in to desires none of them had known they harbored so deeply. When exhaustion finally overtook them, they collapsed into the large bed, bodies intertwined, breathless and satisfied.

Kayla had never experienced anything like it.

Now, in the soft glow of morning, she stirred beneath the sheets, her body still warm from the night before. She felt Jessica beside her, their legs tangled together, the weight of her arm draped lazily across Kayla's stomach. Behind her, she could sense Quinn, the steady rise and fall of his chest, while Mark lay on the other side of Jessica, his arm slung over her waist.

The air was thick with the scent of sleep and last night's indulgences. It was quiet, except for the soft sounds of breathing, the occasional shifting of limbs.

As Kayla tried to gently untangle herself from the sheets, Jessica stirred beside her, her lips curving into a slow smile as her eyes fluttered open.

"Good morning, gorgeous," she murmured, her voice husky with sleep.

Kayla felt a spark ignite deep within her. Before she could respond,

Jessica leaned in, pressing a soft kiss against her lips. It was a slow, lingering kiss, warm and unhurried.

Kayla sighed into the kiss, allowing herself to sink into it. The way Jessica's lips moved against hers sent shivers down her spine, her body already waking up in ways that were still new to her. Jessica's fingers trailed along Kayla's side, tracing soft, lazy patterns, her touch featherlight but charged with promise.

What had started as a gentle good morning quickly deepened, their lips parting, their kisses growing more fervent. Kayla found herself getting lost in it, her body pressing instinctively closer to Jessica's as hands roamed, as fingers mapped familiar territory with renewed curiosity. Almost in unison, their hands slowly roamed down each other's bodies, stopping once they felt the warmth they were searching for.

A quiet moan escaped from one of them, though neither knew who. What mattered was that they were here, entangled once again, as if the night had never truly ended.

The shifting of the sheets caused movement on the other side of the bed. A sleepy groan sounded behind Kayla, and when she finally broke away from Jessica, she turned to see Quinn and Mark stirring, their eyes heavy with sleep but widening slightly as they took in the scene before them.

"Well," Quinn murmured, his voice thick with grogginess and something else entirely, "that's one way to wake up."

Jessica giggled, running her fingers through Kayla's hair before turning to face the men. "Couldn't help ourselves."

Mark chuckled from beside her, rubbing a hand over his face as he sat up slightly. "Don't let us stop you."

Kayla felt warmth creep up her neck, but it wasn't embarrassment. It was something far more exhilarating. Last night had been wild, but this morning? This was something different. Something intimate.

Jessica reached out, her fingers grazing Quinn's arm as she whispered, "Care to join?"

Kayla's breath hitched. The game had begun again.

And none of them wanted to stop.

37

The drive home from the resort was quiet but comfortable. Kayla and Quinn were both lost in their thoughts, replaying the past two days, the memories still fresh in their minds. There was something surreal about stepping back into their normal lives after everything they had experienced.

They picked up Zeke from Mark's parents' house, where he had spent the weekend. The moment he saw them, he ran into Kayla's arms, excitedly recounting his time with his grandparents. It was a grounding moment—reminding her of the life they had built, the responsibilities they carried, and the reality they were returning to.

Back at home, Kayla busied herself in the kitchen, making Zeke a late breakfast while Quinn unpacked their bags. The smell of pancakes and eggs filled the house, the normalcy of the moment both comforting and strangely disorienting.

The day passed in a blur of domestic tasks — grocery shopping, tidying up, playing with Zeke. By the time the evening rolled around, Kayla was exhausted but relieved. Their weekend away had been exhilarating, but she was grateful for the quiet comfort of their home.

Once Zeke was in bed, Kayla curled up on the couch beside Quinn, resting her head against his shoulder as they mindlessly watched a show. It wasn't long before Quinn reached for the remote, muting the television before turning to her.

"So," he said, his voice casual, but his expression anything but. "Are we going to talk about it?"

Kayla blinked, feigning innocence. "Talk about what?"

Quinn smirked. "You know exactly what."

She bit her lip, playing with the edge of the blanket draped over them. "Ok," she admitted. "Let's talk."

Quinn exhaled. "I mean… it was fun, right? Jessica and Mark."

Kayla nodded, a small smile playing on her lips. "Yeah. It was more than fun."

Quinn hesitated for a moment before continuing. "I didn't expect to enjoy it as much as I did."

Kayla tilted her head to look at him. "Me neither."

They sat in silence for a moment, both digesting their feelings. There was no awkwardness, no regret — just mutual understanding.

"I know that wasn't what we planned but I think it was exactly what we needed," Quinn admitted. "To let loose, to step outside ourselves for a little bit. It being spontaneous instead of manufactured really added an element."

Kayla nodded, feeling the same. "And it didn't feel… wrong."

"No," Quinn agreed. "It felt natural. Like it wasn't forced."

Kayla shifted so she could look him in the eye. "Would you want to do it again soon?"

Quinn thought about it for a second before giving a small shrug. "Yeah, but I also don't want to rush into something else just because we had a great time."

Kayla smiled, appreciating his honesty. "Agreed. No pressure, no expectations. Just… seeing where things go."

Quinn nodded, leaning back into the couch, pulling her closer. "Exactly."

Just as she was about to relax into Quinn's embrace, her phone buzzed on the coffee table. She reached for it absentmindedly, unlocking the screen.

A new message.

From him.

The single guy she had been talking to before the trip.

Her stomach flipped as she opened it.

Hey, beautiful. Hope you had a good weekend. Let's set up a time to meet.

Kayla felt Quinn shift beside her, his eyes flicking to her screen. He raised an eyebrow, reading the message.

"Well," he murmured, a slow smirk forming on his lips. "That's interesting timing."

Kayla swallowed, her pulse quickening. "Yeah. No kidding."

Quinn studied her expression for a moment before nodding toward the phone. "So… what are you thinking?"

Kayla met his gaze, a thrill running through her. "I think it's something we should talk about."

38

Kayla and Quinn sat in silence for a few moments, the soft glow of the television flickering against the walls. The weight of the message lingered between them, unspoken but impossible to ignore.

"So," Quinn finally said, his voice measured. "Are you still wanting to meet him?"

Kayla turned to face him, searching his expression. He was trying to act indifferent, but she could sense his reluctance. "I do," she admitted. "Do you?"

Quinn exhaled, running a hand over his face. "I don't know. Like I said, it's just… different."

Kayla raised an eyebrow. "But different how?"

Quinn hesitated before answering. "Because it's just one guy. With Jessica and Mark, it was even. You were with him, I was with her. This… this feels different."

Kayla leaned closer, placing her hand on his arm. "You mean like how it was different when we were with Lacey?"

Quinn's jaw tensed. "That's not the same."

Kayla gave him a glare. "Isn't it? You had two women to yourself that night. I didn't say no. And if we're going to keep doing this, it has to be fair."

Quinn was quiet for a long moment. He knew she had a point, and he hated that he couldn't argue against it. His reluctance wasn't entirely about fairness, though. It was something else, something he couldn't quite put into words.

Kayla studied him carefully. "Are you jealous?"

Quinn scoffed, but his hesitation betrayed him. "No."

Kayla smirked. "You sure?"

He sighed, shaking his head. "I just don't know how I'm going to feel about it in the moment."

Kayla softened, understanding his hesitation. "And that's ok. If at any point it's too much, we stop. Remember?"

Quinn met her gaze, and after a beat, he nodded. "Ok. Fine. We can meet him."

Kayla smiled, leaning in to kiss him softly. "Thank you."

Later that night, when Kayla was alone, she picked up her phone and typed out a response.

Hey you 😊 *Had a great weekend. Let's definitely set something up.*

His reply came quickly.

Glad to hear it. Can't wait to see you in person.

Kayla's stomach did a slow flip as she smiled down at the screen.

They exchanged messages for the next half hour, the conversation growing increasingly playful. Kayla found herself blushing at some of his comments, his confidence evident in every word.

Eventually, they settled on a time and place. This time, Kayla and Quinn agreed to skip the usual drinks at the bar. It would instead just the three of them, meeting in private. It felt more direct, more intimate. But it also added to the tension.

As the date neared, Kayla could barely contain her excitement. She had never been with two men at the same time, and the thought of it sent an unfamiliar thrill through her.

The night finally arrived, and Kayla stood in front of the mirror, adjusting her dress. It was something simple yet elegant — black, form-fitting, with a scooped neck that rested right along the top of her breasts – teasing just enough to keep things interesting.

Quinn watched her from across the room, his expression

unreadable. "Damn. You look good."

Kayla smirked playfully. "I know."

Quinn shook his head with a chuckle. "Cocky tonight, huh?"

Kayla turned to face him fully. "You nervous?"

Quinn hesitated. "A little."

Kayla walked over, running her fingers down his chest. "Just remember—we're in this together."

Quinn nodded, though he still looked uncertain.

They arrived at the hotel room first, the space feeling larger in the quiet stillness. Kayla checked her phone — he was on his way. Her pulse quickened with anticipation.

Twenty minutes later, a knock came at the door.

Quinn inhaled deeply before stepping forward to open it.

Standing in the doorway was a tall, tattooed, toned man with smooth dark skin. He was even better looking in person than in his profile picture. His fitted black button-up shirt accentuated his broad shoulders, and his tailored pants showed off his powerful build.

Kayla's breath caught in her throat. He was gorgeous.

His lips curved into a slow smile as his deep brown eyes locked onto hers. "Well, damn," he said, his voice deep, both rich and smooth. "You look even better than I imagined."

Kayla felt a flush creep up her neck. "Likewise."

The man introduced himself to Quinn, and said his name was Tate. Quinn shook his hand and then stepped aside, letting him in. "Come on in, man."

The energy in the room shifted as he stepped inside, closing the door behind him. There was very little small talk this time. There was no need for it.

He walked toward the bed and motioned for them to come closer. Kayla felt her pulse quicken as she took a step forward, Quinn following beside her.

Then, without hesitation, the man reached for the buttons of his shirt, slipping it off in one fluid motion. His sculpted chest and defined abs looked like something carved from stone.

Kayla swallowed hard.

Then, as he unfastened his belt and slid his pants down, she froze.
Her eyes widened as she gasped softly.
Because this man had the biggest dick she had ever seen.

39

For a long moment, Kayla and Quinn stood frozen, their eyes locked onto the man in front of them. The tension in the room thickened, a mix of awe, surprise, and something else neither of them could quite name.

A slow, knowing smile spread across the man's face. He had clearly seen this reaction before. "Didn't expect that, did you?" he teased, his voice deep and smooth.

Quinn, still staring, exhaled sharply. "Jesus," he muttered, unaware he had even spoken aloud.

Kayla finally broke her trance, her cheeks flushing as she let out a small laugh. "Yeah, you could say that."

The man took a step toward her, his presence commanding, confident. He reached for her hand, pulling it towards him. He guided her hand across his muscular abs, continuing to lower it until she had her hand wrapping around him. She could barely fit her hand around it. He then reached for her waist, his touch firm but gentle as he pulled her closer. Kayla let herself be drawn in, her heartbeat quickening as he leaned down and captured her lips in a slow, deep kiss. His hand trailed down her back, sending shivers through her body until it finally settled on her ass, gripping it possessively.

The kiss deepened, with Kayla melting into it, her fingers curling into his strong shoulders. For a brief moment, she forgot Quinn was even in the room until she felt a hand on her lower back. She turned slightly, finding Quinn standing behind her, his eyes filled with something between curiosity and arousal.

Kayla reached back, pulling Quinn behind her. His body pressed against hers, his lips finding the side of her neck as the other man continued kissing her. The sensation of being surrounded by both of them sent an unfamiliar but thrilling rush through her. She was the center of their attention, the focus of their desire, and she loved every second of it.

Tate's hands explored her body, tracing over the curves of her dress before tugging at the fabric. Quinn's hands weren't far behind, both men moving in unison as they undressed her. The three of them moved to the bed, their bodies tangling together, their touches exploratory and eager.

Kayla had never experienced anything like this. The feeling of two men completely focused on her, devoted to her pleasure, was overwhelming in the best possible way. They moved through different positions, her body adjusting to the new sensations, her pleasure heightened by the sheer novelty of the experience.

At one point, she attempted to take the man into her mouth, but his sheer size proved challenging. He chuckled, running a reassuring hand through her hair before gripping the back of her hand with his large hand. "Take your time," he murmured, his voice filled with amusement and desire.

Every inch of her was worshipped that night, every part of her touched and explored. She had never felt so desired, so completely consumed by pleasure. By the time they finally collapsed onto the bed, breathless and spent, she could barely move.

The man stretched, a satisfied grin on his face as he reached for his clothes. "That," he said, "was incredible."

Kayla, still catching her breath, laughed softly. "Yeah... it really was."

As he began getting dressed, Kayla, feeling playful and still high from the experience, smirked. "Can I take a picture?" she teased.

The man chuckled, clearly amused by the request. "Sure. Go ahead."

Quinn, however, stiffened slightly beside her as she asked the question, his jaw tightening. He said nothing, but Kayla noticed the way his expression shifted, the silent flicker of something possessive in his eyes.

She took the picture quickly, laughing at the sheer audacity of it before tossing her phone aside. The man finished dressing, flashing them both a charming smile. "Let me know if you ever want to do this again."

With that, he walked to the door, gave one final wink, and disappeared into the night.

Kayla let out a deep exhale, turning toward Quinn. "That was…"

Quinn nodded, still looking at the closed door. "Yeah."

She studied his face. "You ok?"

Quinn forced a small smile. "Yeah. Just… processing."

Kayla reached for his hand, squeezing it.

Replaying the last hour in her head, Kayla had come to one conclusion that night. She wasn't only into women. This also posed a question that she had to figure out – What does that say about Quinn?

40

The next morning, Erika's phone buzzed on her nightstand. Still groggy, she reached for it and squinted at the screen.

A text from Kayla.

Curious, she opened it. The moment her eyes adjusted to the image, she almost dropped the phone.

It was a picture of a naked man, his body toned and muscular, but that wasn't what shocked her — it was what was between his legs. It was the biggest penis she had ever seen, larger than anything she had imagined was even possible. It looked like something out of a horror movie.

Her heart pounded as she fumbled for the call button. Kayla picked up almost instantly, laughing hysterically on the other end.

"What the actual hell, Kayla?" Erika gasped. "Who—what—when—What the fuck is that?"

Kayla's laughter deepened. "I take it you're impressed?"

"Impressed?! That thing is a damn weapon! Where did you even find him?"

Kayla grinned. "Oh, just a little adventure last night."

"Tell me everything," Erika demanded. "Now."

For the next fifteen minutes, Kayla recounted every detail, sparing nothing. Erika listened, enraptured, occasionally gasping or groaning in disbelief.

"Kayla, you are living in a completely different universe than me," Erika finally said, shaking her head. "I need to hear more. Drinks tonight?"

"Absolutely," Kayla agreed.

That evening, they met at their favorite bar, slipping into a cozy corner booth with cocktails in hand. Erika leaned in eagerly. "Ok, I need details. And don't skimp on the good stuff."

Kayla smirked and launched into a deeper retelling, of both the night before and of her weekend with Jessica and Mark. Erika listened, wide-eyed, taking it all in.

When Kayla mentioned how much she enjoyed being with Jessica, Erika's expression flickered. She tried to brush it off, but Kayla noticed.

"What?" Kayla asked, tilting her head.

"Nothing," Erika said quickly, waving a hand. "Go on."

Kayla narrowed her eyes, knowing her friend's tells after so many years. "No, no, no. That was definitely a look. What is it?"

Erika shook her head. "It's nothing."

"Liar." Kayla smirked. "Spit it out."

Erika took a deep breath, looking down at her drink. She hesitated for a long moment, then finally, she reached across the table, placing her hand over Kayla's.

"Ok," Erika exhaled, her voice softer now. She took a very long, deep breath, and said, "I want to join you guys one of these times."

Kayla blinked, caught completely off guard. "Wait. What?"

Erika swallowed hard. "I've been thinking about it. And after hearing everything, I just... I want to experience it, too."

Kayla was stunned, but then a slow smile spread across her face. "Well, damn," she murmured, leaning in closer. "That just made things interesting."

41

The next day, while at work, Kayla couldn't shake the conversation with Erika from her mind. She had always considered Erika one of her closest friends. Sure, Erika was incredibly attractive, but she had never entertained the idea of being with her.

Now, she found herself wondering: what if?

Every time she saw Erika that morning, Kayla noticed she was acting strange — quiet, distant, not her usual confident self. It was clear she was avoiding Kayla, something that had never happened before. Kayla waited until lunchtime, then casually walked over to Erika's desk.

"Hey," she said, leaning against the edge. "Let's grab lunch."

Erika barely looked up. "I can't. I have a lot to do."

Kayla raised an eyebrow. "Are you sure? I wanted to talk about what we discussed last night."

That got Erika's attention. She hesitated, her fingers tightening around her pen before she sighed. "Fine. But just for a little while."

They left the office and headed to a small café a few blocks away. They took a seat in a corner booth, the energy between them different than usual. Erika seemed almost shy, something completely unlike her.

Kayla decided to break the ice. "I have to admit, last night caught me off guard," she said. "But I've been thinking about it."

Erika looked up, her eyes searching Kayla's. "And?"

Kayla exhaled. "I feel like I at least need to think about it, talk it out. Because, to be honest, I never thought of you that way before.

Erika gave a small, nervous chuckle. "Yeah, well, I never thought I'd actually work up the courage to say it."

Kayla stirred her drink. "I haven't mentioned it to Quinn yet. I was thinking about the first time he met you, though. He could barely talk. You make him nervous."

Erika laughed, some of her usual confidence returning. "I remember that. It was kind of adorable."

Kayla smiled. "But I need to know… why now? Why ask this now?"

Erika hesitated, taking a slow sip of her drink before answering. "Because I've always been attracted to you, Kayla." She swallowed hard. "I knew you were off-limits, and I respected that. But hearing about everything you've been doing… you enjoying your time with those women… it made me realize I had to say something. Otherwise, I'd regret it forever."

Kayla didn't respond right away. She hadn't expected such honesty. "And Quinn?" she asked. "You're ok with him being involved?"

Erika nodded. "I've been with guys before, but my preference has always been women. I don't mind if he's there. I know you're a package deal."

Kayla bit her lip, considering. "I'm intrigued," she admitted. "But I'm also worried. What if it changes our friendship? What if things are weird at work? And what if I think it's just a one-time thing, but one of us starts developing feelings?"

Erika reached across the table, taking Kayla's hand. "That's not going to happen," she said firmly. "I promise you, this is just something I want to experience. If it happens, it happens. If it doesn't, then nothing changes."

Kayla still wasn't sure. Her mind raced with possibilities, with potential consequences. She needed something to push her one way or the other.

Erika must have sensed that hesitation, because, after a long moment, she smirked. "I have an idea."

Kayla eyed her. "Oh?"

"Come to the bathroom with me."

Kayla blinked. "Excuse me?"

Erika stood, smiling, extending a hand. "Come on."

Curious and slightly amused, Kayla followed her. The moment the bathroom door shut behind them, Erika moved in, pinning Kayla aggressively against the wall. Before Kayla could even react, Erika captured her lips in a deep, slow kiss.

Kayla gasped softly, her hands instinctively gripping Erika's arms. The kiss wasn't just playful — it was deliberate, sensual. Erika's lips moved expertly against hers, her body pressing close, her fingers tracing along Kayla's waist. It was hot. It was intense.

And it changed everything.

When Erika finally pulled away, she grinned. "So… still unsure?"

Kayla was breathless, her heart pounding. She touched her lips, still feeling the heat of Erika's kiss.

42

On the drive home from work, Kayla's mind was a blur. She kept thinking about the kiss — about Erika's lips, the way she felt pressed against her, the way her body had instinctively responded. At random moments, she found herself absentmindedly touching her lips, reliving the moment in her head.

Erika had always been one of her closest friends, but now things felt different. It wasn't just the proposal that lingered — it was the possibilities it presented.

Would it be possible to sleep with Erika and still maintain their friendship? Could things go back to normal afterward? She wasn't sure, and that uncertainty made her nervous. But at the same time, she couldn't deny the rush she had felt when Erika kissed her. There was undeniable chemistry there. And if she were honest with herself, there always had been.

She wasn't even sure how Quinn would react. Kayla knew he found Erika attractive — hell, he had been flustered and tongue-tied around her the first time they met. But would he think it was strange to sleep with one of her best friends? Would that be crossing a weird line?

More than anything, Kayla was also afraid of saying no to Erika and damaging their friendship. If she declined, would Erika feel embarrassed? Would things between them shift regardless?

By the time she pulled into their driveway, Kayla had begun forming some ground rules — things that would make her feel more comfortable if they chose to go through with this.

One biggie: Quinn wouldn't be allowed to sleep with Erika. He could make out with her, touch her, but penetration was off-limits. The idea of watching them together in that way made her uneasy. Instead, when things escalated, she would be the one having sex with Quinn while also engaging with Erika.

Would Quinn think that was fair? Probably not. But Kayla wasn't willing to compromise on that.

That night, Kayla made Quinn's favorite dinner and put on some background music, setting the atmosphere to make him feel relaxed. He had always struggled with simply unwinding, and she wanted him to be in a good mood before broaching the subject.

After Zeke was put to bed, Kayla sat beside Quinn on the couch. She took a deep breath, then finally spoke. "I have something to tell you."

Quinn gave her a curious look. "Uh-oh."

Kayla exhaled. "I talked to Erika."

Quinn's brows furrowed. "About what?"

Kayla hesitated, then said, "About... us. About the lifestyle."

Quinn sat up straighter. "Wait—Erika knows?!?"

"She does now," Kayla admitted. "I trust her, Quinn. I know she won't say anything."

Quinn let that sink in, then gestured for her to continue.

Kayla took a deep breath, looking down before finally raising her eyes to meet his. "She asked if she could join us."

Quinn blinked. "Join us?"

Kayla nodded. "For one time. On a date."

Quinn was stunned silent, clearly processing. She could see the flicker of excitement in his eyes, but also hesitation. "And how do you feel about it?" he asked.

Kayla bit her lip. "I think... I need to think about it more. But I wanted to talk to you first."

Quinn rubbed his jaw, considering. "So, let me get this straight. One of your best friends wants to have a threesome with us?"

Kayla nodded. "Yep."

"And you're actually considering it?"

Kayla sighed. "I don't know. I mean, I kissed her and that kind of changed some things."

Quinn's eyes widened slightly. "You what?"

Kayla hesitated but then decided there was no point in holding it back. "She kissed me first, actually. In the bathroom. And... I liked it."

Quinn exhaled, running a hand through his hair. "Ok. So... where does that leave us?"

Kayla took a deep breath. "I would have some ground rules if we decided to do this."

Quinn smirked. "Of course you would..."

She rolled her eyes. "Hear me out. You can kiss her, touch her, even go down on each other. But no penetration."

Quinn frowned. "Wait, why not?"

Kayla folded her arms. "Because I don't want to see that. I don't know if I can handle it. I can handle everything else, but not that."

Quinn tilted his head. "Kayla, when we were with Tate, you told me it had to be fair. That I had to let you experience it if I expected you to let me experience things. But now, when it's my turn—"

"This is different," Kayla cut him off. "This is Erika. She's my best friend. I don't want to be unable to look at her — or you — the same way afterward."

Quinn sighed, running a hand down his face. "That's one hell of a limitation."

Kayla softened. "I get that. And I get that it's not completely fair. But it's the only way I'd feel ok about it."

Quinn stared at her for a long moment before sighing. "Ok. No penetration."

Kayla reached for his hand, squeezing it. "Thank you."

He gave a small chuckle. "But you realize you just guaranteed I'm going to spend half the night wondering what it would have been like, right?"

Kayla laughed. "I'll make it worth your while."

Quinn smirked. "You better."

With that settled, Kayla reached for her phone and sent Erika a message.

Kayla: *Come over for dinner tomorrow night. Stay late so we can talk.*

Erika's response was almost immediate.

Erika: *Looking forward to it.*

As Kayla set her phone down, she let out a deep breath. Tomorrow was going to be interesting.

Later that night, as Kayla drifted off to sleep, Quinn lay beside her, his thoughts still running. He wasn't entirely sure how he felt about the rules, but he had agreed.

Then, sometime around midnight, his phone buzzed on the nightstand. Groggily, he reached for it, blinking at the screen.

It was another message from Simone.

She included a picture this time — a sultry, teasing shot of her in a sheer black bra and panties, her body posed perfectly. The message beneath it made his heart pound.

Simone: *I was just thinking about you. I'd love to meet up again.* 😉

Quinn exhaled, staring at the screen for what seemed like ten minutes.

43

The next morning at work, Kayla noticed that Erika seemed to be in an unusually good mood. It wasn't just her energy. It was the way she moved, the way she carried herself. There was something different about her today, something almost electric.

Kayla's suspicions were confirmed when she saw what Erika was wearing. Typically, Erika dressed conservatively for work, favoring loose blouses and slacks that did little to show off her body. But today, she had chosen a fitted pencil skirt that hugged her hips perfectly, a silky blouse that draped over her curves in a way that left little to the imagination, and high heels that make her legs look even more toned than usual. The confidence in her posture, the way she smiled knowingly at Kayla — it was all intentional. She was trying to impress her before their dinner.

Kayla wasn't immune to it. The sight of Erika like this stirred something in her, something new and thrilling. The two women exchanged discreet glances throughout the morning, neither wanting to be too obvious.

At one point though, when they were both in the break room heating up their lunches, Erika walked past Kayla, her hand brushing lightly against Kayla's hip. The touch was subtle but unmistakably deliberate. Kayla felt a shiver run through her. Erika knew exactly what she was doing, and Kayla was more than willing to play along.

That evening, Kayla wanted to make everything perfect. She prepared a thoughtful dinner — tenderloin steak, baked sweet potatoes, and grilled asparagus. On the way home, she even stopped to pick up her favorite cheesecake for dessert.

By the time Erika knocked on the door at six o'clock, the house was filled with the warm scent of the meal. Kayla greeted her with a hug, feeling the closeness linger just a little longer than usual.

"Something smells amazing," Erika said as she stepped inside.

Quinn greeted her with a smile and a quick hug. "Hope you came hungry."

Erika grinned. "Always."

Before dinner, Zeke insisted on showing Erika all of his toys, tugging at her hand and pulling her into his room. Kayla watched them interact with a smile, finding it endearing. Erika had always been good with Zeke, and seeing them together gave her a strange, comforting feeling.

Dinner itself was surprisingly normal. They talked about work, the weather, and politics, with Zeke chiming in every so often with his own stories. It wasn't until Quinn had taken Zeke to bed that the atmosphere shifted.

Kayla and Erika stayed in the kitchen, cleaning up and plating the cheesecake. As they worked, Erika lowered her voice. "So... have you said anything to him yet?"

Kayla glanced at her. "Quinn?"

Erika nodded.

"I did, last night. He was surprised, to say the least."

"And?" Erika pressed, watching her closely.

"He's open to it," Kayla admitted, "but he wanted to talk things through first."

Erika exhaled, as if she had been holding her breath. "That's good."

Kayla smirked. "You seem nervous."

Erika let out a soft laugh. "I am. This is... a big deal."

Kayla nodded. "I know."

Once Zeke was asleep, they moved out to the patio with their drinks and dessert. The night air was crisp but pleasant, and the mood was lighter than Kayla had expected.

Erika was the first to break the tension. "Ok, so let's talk about the awkward elephant in the room."

Quinn chuckled. "Go for it."

Erika looked between them. "I know Kayla told you about my idea last night. How do you feel? Are we doing this?"

Kayla took a sip of her drink before answering. "I think we need to talk about it first — really talk about it. Because this isn't just some random encounter. This is our friendship. This is our work. I don't want to ruin what we have."

Erika nodded. "Neither do I. Trust me, I've thought about all of that."

Quinn leaned back in his chair. "So let's start there. What happens after?"

Erika smiled knowingly. "Nothing changes unless we want it to. I'm not looking for anything beyond what we agree on. I value what we have too much to risk that."

Kayla glanced at Quinn, who seemed to be absorbing everything. "And what about work?"

Erika shrugged. "Same answer. Nothing changes. We act like we always do. No one has to know."

Kayla let that sink in before finally turning to Quinn. "What are you thinking?"

Quinn had been quiet throughout most of the conversation, listening but not reacting much. Now, he exhaled slowly and gave a small smile. "I think… Sure. I'm ok with it."

A grin spread across Erika's face. Kayla felt her own relief settle in.

"Good," Kayla said. "But… I do have some ground rules."

Erika smirked. "That doesn't surprise me."

Kayla nodded. "First, Quinn can kiss you, touch you, even go down on you if you're into that. You can even go down on him, if you want. But no penetration."

Erika raised an eyebrow but didn't seem offended. "That's fair."

"Second, we do this one time. If we want to revisit it, we'll talk about it later, but there are no expectations beyond that."

Erika nodded. "Agreed."

Quinn smirked. "Anything else?"

Kayla shook her head. "I think that covers it."

Erika leaned back, sipping her drink. "Then I guess the only thing left is where and when."

"I was thinking next weekend," Kayla said. "Instead of a hotel, what if we did it at your place?"

Erika's eyes lit up. "I like that idea. I'll make cocktails and snacks. We can make a night of it."

Quinn chuckled. "Fancy."

Erika grinned. "What can I say? I like to host."

When the evening wound down, they walked Erika to the door. She turned first to Quinn, leaning in and pressing a lingering kiss to his lips. Given the dynamics of the situation, she figured it would be best to start with him, providing an ice-breaker before their big date.

Then, without hesitation, she pivoted and kissed Kayla. This time, there was no uncertainty, no testing the waters. It was full of promise, full of certainty.

When she pulled away, she had a sly grin on her face. "See you guys soon."

With that, she turned and walked out, leaving Kayla and Quinn standing in the doorway, both slightly stunned.

Kayla finally let out a breath. "Well... that just happened."

Quinn laughed, shaking his head. "Yeah. Yeah, it did."

As they shut the door behind them, Kayla felt her stomach flutter with anticipation. The decision had been made. Now, there was only one thing left to do — follow through.

44

A couple of days had passed since Quinn had received Simone's text, but he had yet to respond. He wasn't sure what to say. He thought about telling Kayla multiple times. After all, transparency was one of their core rules. But every time he considered it, he hesitated.

Part of it was guilt. Part of it was excitement.

The truth was, ever since Kayla had revealed her kiss with Erika, something in him had shifted. He trusted Kayla, but the thought still lingered. If they weren't already planning a threesome with Erika, would she have told him? It had made him question things in a way he hadn't before. And now, here he was, staring at Simone's text and wondering if this was his own little secret to keep.

He finally gave in and typed out a response.

Quinn: *Hey, sorry for the late reply. Been busy. You caught me off guard with that pic.*

Simone: *Good. That was the point.* 😏 *So... are you gonna let me catch you off guard in person?*

Quinn exhaled sharply, his body tensing. He knew he shouldn't be doing this, but the temptation was overwhelming. Simone was, without question, one of the most stunning women he had ever seen. She had a body that was nearly unreal, a face that made heads turn in every room she walked into.

And she wanted him. That alone sent a thrill through his veins.

Quinn: *I'd be lying if I said I wasn't tempted.*

Simone's response was immediate.

Simone: *Then stop lying.*

Quinn let out a low chuckle, shaking his head. He glanced toward the hallway, making sure Kayla was nowhere near before typing again.

Quinn: *I'd have to talk to Kayla first. See when she's available.*

Almost instantly, the three little dots appeared, signaling that Simone was responding. Then they disappeared. Then came back again. It was as if she were debating how to respond.

When the response finally came through, Quinn sat up straighter.

Simone: *I was actually thinking… maybe just us this time.*

His pulse jumped.

Quinn: *Just us?*

Simone: *Yeah. I mean, we've already done it before. I know you. You know me. Why complicate things?*

Quinn rubbed his hand over his jaw, his heart pounding. This was uncharted territory. Up until now, every experience they had was mutual — he and Kayla together, experiencing new things as a couple. This… this was something else.

Quinn: *Damn, Simone. That's unexpected.*

Simone: *Is it, though?*

Quinn swallowed hard. He wanted to say yes, but was it really? Simone had always been forward, always confident. She didn't play games. And right now, she was being crystal clear about what she wanted.

Quinn: *I'd still need to tell Kayla.*

Simone: *That's up to you. I already told my husband. He's cool with it. Your choice.*

Quinn's stomach tightened. He stared at his phone, the weight of the moment sinking in. If he told Kayla, she would say no. That much he knew.

But did he have to tell her? He had already been with Simone. This wasn't a new experience. It was just… a repeat.

That was the justification he kept repeating to himself.

After a long moment, he finally responded.

Quinn: *Yeah, I'd like that. Let's set something up soon.*

Simone's reply came quickly.

Simone: *I like the sound of that.*

Quinn sat there for a moment, staring at the screen. Then, before he could think twice, he deleted the entire conversation, but not before saving her photo in a hidden folder on his phone.

For the first time since they started swinging, he had kept something from Kayla.

And he wasn't sure how to feel about it.

45

In the days leading up to their planned night together, Kayla and Erika's work dynamic shifted. There was no denying that something had changed between them, even though neither had directly addressed it.

At first, the awkwardness was subtle — longer-than-usual pauses in conversations, sidelong glances that lingered for far too long. Kayla found herself catching Erika staring at her when she wasn't looking, only for Erika to quickly avert her eyes and pretend to be focused on her computer.

And then there was the flirting. It was playful, teasing, but also secretive, existing just beneath the surface where no one else could see.

One morning, as Kayla walked into the break room to grab her coffee, Erika was already there, leaning casually against the counter. "Good morning," Erika said with a smirk, her tone laced with something just shy of innocent.

Kayla poured her coffee, offering Erika a knowing glance. "Morning."

Erika's eyes flickered over her, taking in the fitted pencil skirt Kayla had chosen that day. "Looking nice," she said casually, but there was an edge to it.

Kayla smirked. "So do you."

They both lingered there for a beat too long, neither wanting to move first. It was Kayla who finally broke the moment, grabbing her coffee and turning to leave, but just as she passed Erika, she felt a delicate touch at the small of her back, the lightest graze of fingers. It was fleeting, but unmistakable.

She didn't stop walking, but she felt the heat rise in her cheeks.

Throughout the day, the subtle touches continued. When Erika passed behind her at her desk, her fingertips skimmed Kayla's shoulder. When they were working on a project together in the conference room, their knees brushed under the table, and neither moved away.

At lunch, Kayla was microwaving her meal when Erika joined her again. This time, when she passed Kayla, she deliberately brushed her curves along Kayla's side, her hand grazing over her waist and moving slightly down the side of her thigh. It was quick, subtle, and impossible for anyone else to notice, but it sent a jolt of electricity through Kayla.

She turned to Erika with a raised eyebrow. "Are you trying to get us caught?"

Erika grinned. "What, you don't like a little risk?"

Kayla laughed softly, shaking her head. "You're dangerous."

"And yet, you're smiling."

Kayla didn't deny it.

The anticipation between them was building, a slow, tantalizing burn that neither wanted to extinguish. Every exchanged glance, every stolen touch only made the wait feel longer.

By the time Friday arrived, Kayla knew two things for certain: she wanted Erika in a way she never had before, and whatever happened that weekend was going to change everything.

46

Since they started swinging, Kayla had noticed a distinct change in Quinn. He had become more adventurous, more spontaneous, and, to her delight, more eager in bed. The frequency of their intimacy had increased dramatically, and for the first time in a long time, their physical connection felt new again.

Sex with Quinn had always been good, just... predictable. He had his go-to positions — missionary, Kayla on top, and occasionally doggy style. That was it. Kayla had always been the one pushing for variety, for experimentation, but Quinn had never been particularly open to it. Now, things were shifting.

She wasn't sure if it was because he had been with other women, or if he simply saw her in a new light, but either way, she wasn't about to complain. What she did know was that his confidence had grown, and with it, so had his willingness to explore.

One particular night stood out in Kayla's mind. She had just finished her evening shower, steam still clinging to the bathroom mirror as she wrapped herself in a towel. As she reached for the lotion on the counter, she heard Quinn enter behind her.

Without saying a word, he pressed her against the counter and bent her forward, his hands firm on her hips. Her breath caught in her throat. This was new. Quinn had always been gentle, predictable — never one to take control so boldly.

He bent her forward, one hand sliding up her back as the other wrapped around her waist. Their eyes met in the mirror, and for the first time, she saw something raw and unfiltered in his gaze — something possessive. He leaned in, his lips grazing her ear.

"Stay just like that," he murmured.

The anticipation sent a shiver down her spine.

That moment had stayed with her. It was unlike anything they had done before, and she had craved more of it ever since.

So, a few nights later, just days before their planned night with Erika, she decided to push Quinn's newfound boldness a little further.

She prepared carefully. After taking another long shower, she shaved, moisturized, and slipped into their bedroom with a plan in mind. She reached into the nightstand, pulling out the soft fabric straps she had used once before — a failed attempt at bringing something new into their bedroom. That night, Quinn had hesitated, his discomfort clear. But now… now she had reason to believe things might be different.

Kayla climbed onto the bed, lying on her stomach as she secured her wrists and ankles to the posts. She was completely naked, her body stretched out and vulnerable in the soft glow of the bedside lamp.

She heard him approaching, the sound of his footsteps muffled by the carpet. When he entered, he was looking at his phone, distracted by an email.

"Hey, I was just—" His voice cut off mid-sentence.

Kayla turned her head slightly, catching his stunned expression as his eyes went wide. He stared at her, taking in the scene before him.

She smiled. "There's a blindfold on the nightstand," she said, her voice smooth. "Put it on me."

For a moment, he didn't move. She could see the conflict in his eyes — his hesitation warring with the obvious excitement that was already building in his stance.

Then, finally, he smiled.

It was a slow, almost boyish grin, filled with something she hadn't seen in a long time — genuine excitement.

Quinn stepped forward, picking up the blindfold. As he did, his gaze flickered to a bottle of lube, a question forming in his expression, but he said nothing. Instead, he slid the soft fabric over Kayla's eyes, tying it securely behind her head.

The moment she was in complete darkness, every sensation became more intense.

She felt his fingertips trace the curve of her spine, moving downward with deliberate slowness. When his hands reached her hips, he paused, his touch featherlight. Then, without warning, his palm smoothed over her freshly waxed skin. He exhaled sharply.

"Damn," he muttered under his breath, his fingers sliding lower.

She shivered. "Like that?"

He didn't answer, but the way his hands gripped her thighs spoke volumes. He spread them slightly, then ran his fingers teasingly over her, dipping down but never fully touching where she wanted him to. He was drawing it out, building anticipation in a way that was completely unlike him.

Kayla moaned, her body arching slightly.

Then, just as she was about to beg him to do more, she felt him shift behind her. The rustling of fabric told her he was undressing. She turned her head slightly, sensing his movements even without sight.

"Wait. Come here. Stand next to the bed," she whispered.

He hesitated for a second, then obeyed. She could feel his presence beside her, could sense his body heat. She tilted her head up slightly, opening her mouth in silent invitation.

He groaned softly. "Damn, Kayla."

Then he gave her exactly what she wanted.

As the night progressed, Quinn surprised her again. He moved in ways he never had before, trying things he once resisted. And then, as they shifted again, Kayla murmured a request against his skin.

"The lube," she whispered.

He stilled for a moment, his breath uneven. "What?"

"The lube," she repeated. "On the nightstand."

She could feel his hesitation. Then she felt the bed shift as he reached for it.

When he returned to her, he pressed a kiss to her shoulder, then moved lower. His hands traced her body as he prepared her, slow and careful.

He put some lube in her, but then she whispered, "Not there." It took Quinn a second to get what she was saying, and then he paused for a minute.

At first, he seemed uncertain because it could hurt her, but Kayla reassured him.

"I want this," she breathed. "I told you, I want to try new things."

He hesitated once more, then nodded. "Ok."

The moment was slow, tentative, and new. There was resistance at first, but she guided him through it. It had been years since she had last explored this, and she had almost forgotten the intensity of it. The mix of discomfort and pleasure, the way it built into something deeper.

Quinn moved carefully, his hands firm but gentle as he learned her reactions. And then, finally, he was fully inside her.

A sharp gasp escaped Kayla's lips, her fingers tightening in the sheets.

"Are you ok?" Quinn asked, his voice strained, his own pleasure barely restrained.

Kayla took a shaky breath, then exhaled. "Yes. Don't stop!"

What started as slow, exploratory movements quickly became something more. Something raw, something consuming. Every sensation was heightened, every touch electric.

And in that moment, they weren't thinking about the others they had been with. They weren't thinking about what was coming next.

It was just them.

By the time Quinn collapsed on her, breathless and spent, Kayla realized something important. Swinging had opened up their marriage, but it had also reignited something between them. Something just as thrilling.

As Quinn pressed a final kiss to her shoulder, she smiled.

She had no regrets.

47

The next morning, Kayla and Quinn were practically glowing. There was an ease between them that hadn't been there in years. Every time they passed each other in the kitchen, they stopped to share a kiss, soft but lingering. When Kayla reached for the coffee mugs, Quinn pressed up behind her, his hand grazing her waist. She leaned into him, letting out a small giggle.

"You're in a good mood," she teased, pouring his coffee.

Quinn smirked, wrapping an arm around her waist and pulling her closer. "Can you blame me?"

She turned in his arms, kissing him again, slow and deep. The connection between them felt different — stronger, more intimate. They had always been best friends, but now there was something else between them, something that had been missing for years. Kayla felt truly desired. Finally.

"Don't be late for work," she murmured against his lips.

"I won't," he assured her. "But I'm already looking forward to getting home."

She bit her lip, grinning as he grabbed his bag and headed out the door.

Traffic was worse than usual that morning, and Quinn drummed his fingers against the steering wheel, growing impatient. His mind kept drifting back to the night before — how Kayla had surprised him, how willing he had been to try something new. It had been thrilling in a way he hadn't expected.

His phone dinged from the center console, but he ignored it, keeping his hands on the wheel. When he finally pulled into the parking garage at work, he checked his notifications. His stomach flipped when he saw the name on his screen.

Simone.

He hesitated before opening the message. It wasn't just a text — there was another image attached. When he clicked on it, his breath caught in his throat. It was a close-up of Simone's bare breasts, her skin smooth and glowing in the dim light.

Beneath the image, a message: *Friday night?*

Quinn swallowed hard, his heart pounding in his chest. Seeing her like that again sent a rush of heat through his body.

He hesitated before typing a response.

Quinn: *Friday unfortunately won't work. What about Monday?*

His reasoning was simple. He and Kayla had their night with Erika on Friday. He couldn't exactly bail on that. But Monday? Monday was open.

He sat there for a moment, the guilt creeping in. He knew he should tell Kayla. That was the rule — no side conversations, full transparency. And yet, he hesitated. He again told himself it wasn't a big deal. He and Simone had already slept together, so this wasn't something new. It was just… revisiting an experience.

His phone vibrated again. Another text.

Simone: *Monday works. Can't wait.* 😉

He exhaled slowly, staring at the screen. The anticipation was undeniable. The thought of having Simone all to himself, without Kayla or anyone else, made his pulse race.

Then came the real problem. How was he going to explain being out late on Monday?

His mind worked quickly. A late work meeting? A case that needed extra hours? Maybe a dinner with a colleague? He hated lying to Kayla, but the truth felt too risky. She wouldn't understand.

Like the previous time, he deleted the conversation but saved the picture in a hidden folder.

For the first time since they started swinging, he had officially crossed the line.

48

Kayla had barely stepped into the office when Erika's presence made itself known. It wasn't overt — not in a way that anyone else would notice — but the tension between them was unmistakable.

Throughout the morning, Erika found small excuses to touch Kayla, each instance more deliberate than the last. A light brush of fingers as she handed Kayla a document. A subtle press of her knee against Kayla's beneath the table during a meeting. Even a passing touch along the small of her back as they crossed paths in the hallway. Each time, she would give Kayla a subtle, but devilish grin.

Kayla knew what Erika was doing. And she liked it.

Late that morning, Erika appeared at Kayla's desk with a coy smile. "Come to lunch with me?"

Kayla looked up from her computer. "Where?"

"There's a new spot I want to try," Erika said casually, though her tone suggested there was more to it. "My treat."

Kayla hesitated only for a second before nodding. "Alright."

Erika's grin widened. "Good. Let's go."

Kayla wasn't entirely surprised when Erika insisted on driving. She always liked to take the lead when she could. The ride was filled with light conversation, easy and familiar, but there was an undeniable charge in the air between them.

When they arrived at the restaurant, Erika chose a cozy booth in the back, away from the main crowd. Their legs brushed as they settled in, neither of them moving away. The conversation flowed effortlessly, bouncing between funny work stories and teasing observations.

Halfway through the meal, Erika leaned in slightly. "So," she said, her voice low, "excited for Friday?"

Kayla swallowed her bite of food, heat creeping into her cheeks. "I'd be lying if I said I wasn't."

Erika smirked. "Good."

Kayla took a sip of her drink, trying to steady herself. The flirtation between them had been fun, but the reality of what was coming was starting to set in. And she was hoping she was ready for it.

By the time they finished eating and got back to the car, Kayla was expecting to head straight back into the office. But when Erika pulled into the office parking lot, she parked toward the back, far from the other cars.

Kayla noticed. "Why all the way back here? There were open spots up front."

Erika shrugged, shutting off the engine. "I felt like stretching my legs."

Kayla rolled her eyes and reached for the door handle, but before she could open it, Erika's hand caught her wrist. Kayla turned to look at her, and before she could say anything, Erika leaned in and kissed her.

It was slow at first, soft and testing, but when Kayla didn't pull away, Erika deepened it. Kayla felt herself melt into the kiss, letting it consume her.

Then Erika really surprised her.

With a swift but smooth movement, Erika unbuttoned one of the buttons on Kayla's blouse and slid her hand inside, cupping her breast underneath her bra. Kayla gasped against Erika's lips, her breath hitching as a jolt of pleasure ran through her.

Erika pulled down the lace fabric slightly, teasing Kayla's nipple between her fingers. It was bold. It was reckless. And Kayla let it happen.

When Erika pulled back, she studied Kayla's face, her lips curling into a sly smile. "Did you like that?" she asked, her voice barely above a whisper.

Kayla took a shaky breath and nodded. "Yes. Very much."

Erika's hand drifted lower, sliding between Kayla's legs, and began rubbing on Kayla's pussy over her pants. Kayla exhaled a shuddering breath, her legs straightening and her head falling back against the seat as she surrendered to the sensation.

Just as quickly as it started, Erika pulled away, leaving Kayla breathless.

Kayla sighed. "Pure evil."

"We should get back," Erika murmured, her fingers trailing one last time along Kayla's thigh before she reached for the keys.

Kayla took a moment to compose herself before stepping out of the car. As they walked back into the office, she realized something with certainty.

Their friendship had changed forever, and there was no going back.

49

Friday had finally arrived. That night, they were going over to Erika's apartment for their highly anticipated date. Kayla hadn't told Quinn about the encounter in the car earlier that week, remembering how he reacted when he first heard of their kiss in the bathroom, and she didn't want to sour him on the idea of the night ahead.

As they were getting ready, Quinn sat on the edge of the bed, tying his shoes when he noticed Kayla slipping into a brand-new set of lingerie. His gaze lingered as he took in the sight — something out of a Victoria's Secret runway. It was sheer, lacy, and hugged every perfect curve of her body, accentuating her toned legs, the delicate arch of her back, and the firm roundness of her ass.

His throat went dry.

"You bought that just for tonight, didn't you?" he said, standing up behind her.

Kayla met his gaze in the mirror and smirked. "Maybe."

He knew what that meant. She wanted to impress Erika. The realization stirred something complicated inside him, equal parts excitement and jealousy. He didn't say anything about it, though. Instead, he let his hands graze over her hips before stepping back and finishing getting dressed.

They arrived at Erika's apartment a little after eight, knocking on the door. When it swung open, Quinn's breath escaped him.

Erika stood before them in a tight blue dress that looked as if it had been tailored for her body alone. The deep hue made her piercing blue eyes stand out even more. The fabric clung to her curves, hugging her chest, waist, and hips in a way that made it impossible not to stare.

And Quinn wasn't the only one staring.

Kayla took in the sight of Erika, and for the first time, felt a pang of nerves. She had always thought Erika was beautiful, but now, standing this close, knowing what they were about to do — she felt something deeper. An undeniable attraction.

"Come in," Erika said, stepping aside with a knowing smile.

Inside, a large tray of snacks was laid out on the kitchen island — artisan sourdough bread, orange marmalade, and fancy cheeses. Erika motioned for them to help themselves as she took their drink orders. Kayla opted for a glass of red wine while Quinn chose whiskey, neat.

They sat in the living room, the conversation flowing effortlessly. Laughter echoed in the space, the mood light and natural despite the anticipation simmering beneath the surface.

After a while, Erika set down her glass and leaned forward slightly. "So," she said, her voice sultry yet playful. "Are we still down for this?"

Kayla met her gaze, intense and unwavering. "One hundred percent."

Erika smiled, standing up. Without hesitation, she reached for both of their hands and led them toward the bedroom.

The moment they reached the bed, Erika turned toward Kayla, her hands grazing over her arms before slipping lower. Slowly, methodically, she began undressing her. Kayla's breath hitched as the fabric slid down her shoulders, pooling onto the floor. Now, she stood there in nothing but her lingerie, her toned body fully on display.

Quinn watched intently, noting the way Erika's lips parted as she took in the sight. It was clear that she had expected Kayla to have a great body, but now, seeing her like this — she was captivated. Kayla smiled at Erika's reaction, pleased by the admiration in her eyes.

Then, Kayla took her turn, reaching for Erika's dress. She peeled it down, exposing smooth skin, soft curves, and a stunning figure. Erika's bra and panties matched, a delicate white lace set that made Quinn's pulse quicken.

He hadn't expected this level of intensity, but now that he was here, watching them, it was one of the most arousing things he had ever witnessed.

Kayla turned toward Quinn with a teasing smile. "Your turn."

Quinn exhaled sharply, pulling off his shirt and stepping out of his pants. He barely had time to react before both women sank to their knees in front of him. His pulse skyrocketed as they took turns pleasuring him, pausing only to share heated kisses with each other in between. The sight of them together — Kayla and Erika, so seamlessly in sync — was overwhelming.

The girls then stood, slipping off their remaining clothes before lying back on the bed. Erika settled herself against the pillows, her knees bent, legs open, a silent invitation. Kayla knelt between them, locking eyes with her before leaning in.

It was strange at first. Kayla had only recently done this with other women and never with a close friend before. But the moment her lips touched Erika's skin, all hesitation melted away. The taste of her, the way she responded — it was intoxicating.

Quinn could hardly contain himself. He had never seen Kayla like this, never seen her with another woman in such an intimate way. It was beyond anything he had imagined.

Erika lifted her head slightly, locking eyes with Quinn. A slow smirk played on her lips as she reached out and beckoned him forward. "Join us?"

Kayla turned her head slightly, giving Quinn a playful look over her shoulder. "You heard her."

Quinn moved behind Kayla, his hands gliding down her back before gripping her waist. As he pressed against her, she moaned softly, already lost in the moment. The combination of sensations — Quinn behind her, Erika beneath her — sent her into an overwhelming state of pleasure.

For the next hour, they moved together, alternating between each other, exploring and experiencing everything they had once only imagined. There was no awkwardness, no hesitation. Just raw connection, pleasure, and trust.

But as the night went on, Quinn started to notice something. The more Kayla and Erika connected, the less they seemed aware of his presence. Their touches became solely for each other, their kisses deeper, their hands exploring only each other's bodies. At first, it was arousing — watching them so lost in one another — but then he felt himself slipping into the background, more of an observer rather than a participant.

By the time they collapsed onto the bed, tangled in each other's limbs, breathless and spent, Kayla turned her head, meeting Erika's gaze. A slow, knowing smile spread across both of their lips.

Quinn lay beside them, staring at the ceiling, a realization creeping in.

For the first time since they started swinging, he felt like an afterthought.

50

The rest of the weekend flew by, tied up in sporting events for Zeke and getting ready for the week ahead. Midday Saturday, Quinn casually mentioned that his work group was going to get together for a happy hour Monday night and that he'd be home late. It wasn't unusual. These outings happened every so often so Kayla didn't question it.

But what she didn't know was that Quinn had made other plans.

Whenever he could slip away, Quinn snuck glances at his phone, texting Simone in secret. Their messages were brief but charged with electricity. Each one carried an unspoken promise, an anticipation that grew with every exchange.

Then, after a particularly flirtatious exchange, Simone surprised him by sending another picture.

This time, there was no pretense of subtlety. It was a full view of her body, bare, confident, exuding desire.

Quinn's breath hitched as he stared at the image. His pulse pounded, his body reacting instantly. He had been with Simone before, but there was something about the secrecy of this encounter — knowing it would be just the two of them this time — that sent a thrill through him.

Driven by that feeling, he took a moment to compose himself before snapping a picture of his own, his arousal on full display. He sent it without hesitation, his heartbeat hammering as he awaited her response.

It came quickly.

Simone: *Damn. I've missed that. Monday still?*

Quinn hesitated for only a moment before replying.

Quinn: *Yep, Monday still works. Get the room — don't want it on my card.*

As soon as he sent it, his stomach twisted. He had justified meeting Simone again in his head, but deep down, he knew the truth.

This wasn't swinging.

This was cheating.

Monday evening arrived, and Quinn found himself sitting at his desk long after most of his colleagues had left. His work was open in front of him, but his focus was elsewhere.

Kayla had texted him earlier in the day, reminding him to have fun at happy hour. She sent a kiss emoji at the end of the message, blissfully unaware of where he was actually going.

Quinn sighed, rubbing a hand over his face.

Should he really do this?

There was a part of him that wanted to turn his phone off, go home, and pretend this was never even a possibility. That part whispered to him that Kayla had never broken the rules, had never gone behind his back. That part reminded him that they had always done this together.

But then there was the other part.

The part that burned with need, that craved the way Simone made him feel. He unlocked his phone and tapped on his hidden photo folder.

Her images stared back at him, tempting, undeniable.

He exhaled, long and slow, before closing the folder and standing up.

Decision made.

He was going.

51

Quinn walked into the dimly lit hotel bar, his pulse racing. He scanned the room, searching for Simone. After a moment, he spotted her sitting at a high-top near the back.

She was absolutely stunning, taking Quinn's breath away.

Her long, dark hair cascaded over her shoulders in soft waves. Her makeup was flawless — smoky eyes that smoldered under the low lighting, full lips painted a deep red. She wore tight black leather pants that hugged every curve and a fitted crop top that revealed just a hint of her toned stomach. She looked like something out of a fantasy, too perfect to be real.

As Quinn approached, Simone rose from her seat, a sultry smile spreading across her lips. Without hesitation, she wrapped her arms around his neck and pressed her body into his, planting a deep, lingering kiss on his lips. Quinn felt his face flush with warmth.

They sat at the bar, ordering drinks — whiskey for him, a white wine for her. The conversation was playful, teasing, filled with innuendo. Every glance, every casual touch, sent electricity through Quinn's veins.

After their drinks, Simone took his hand. "Let's go," she whispered, leading him toward the elevator.

The moment the doors closed behind them, Quinn turned to her, unable to hold back any longer. He pressed her against the wall, kissing her hungrily, hands exploring her curves. Simone let out a soft moan, wrapping her leg around his, pulling him closer.

The elevator dinged as they reached their floor, but they barely noticed, only pulling apart when the doors opened. Hand in hand, they hurried down the hall, laughter escaping between their breathless kisses.

As soon as they stepped into the room, the tension erupted into something primal. They tore at each other's clothes, tossing them aside as they stumbled toward the bed. Their bodies crashed together, lips, hands, skin — urgent, desperate, ravenous.

For the next two hours, they lost themselves in each other, exploring every inch, indulging in every desire.

Simone was unlike anyone Quinn had ever been with. She was uninhibited, demanding, taking exactly what she wanted while giving just as much in return. He had never felt this way before — completely consumed, lost in a haze of lust and adrenaline.

Finally, exhausted and breathless, they collapsed onto the bed, tangled in the sheets.

Quinn glanced at the clock and panic set in. It was late. Much later than he had thought. He scrambled for his clothes, muttering, "I have to go."

Simone stretched lazily, watching him with a satisfied smirk. "Leaving so soon?"

Quinn apologized and got dressed. He headed to the door to leave, turning back towards Simone to see her one last time.

He opened the door, and standing in the doorway was a tall, broad-shouldered man with a face twisted in fury.

Simone's husband.

Quinn barely had time to react before a fist connected with his jaw, sending him stumbling backward. Pain exploded through his skull as he hit the floor. The man was on him in an instant, throwing punch after punch, rage pouring out with every strike.

Simone screamed, trying to pull him off, but he was relentless. Blood filled Quinn's mouth, his vision blurred. Then, suddenly, the weight was gone. Simone had pulled him off.

Seizing the moment, Quinn scrambled to his feet and bolted for the door. He didn't stop running — not until he was safely in his car, gripping the steering wheel, panting.

His face throbbed. His body ached. But worst of all was the realization crashing down on him.

Simone had lied about her husband being ok with them having sex again, and he had just destroyed everything.

52

Quinn pulled into a vacant parking lot a few blocks from home, gripping the steering wheel so tightly that his knuckles turned white. His breath was uneven, ragged, his pulse still hammering from the events of the past hour. His face throbbed in pain, and he could already feel the swelling from where David's fists had connected. Blood stained his shirt collar, the coppery taste still fresh in his mouth.

He was panicking.

He wiped at his face with trembling hands, staring at his reflection in the rearview mirror. His left eye was nearly swollen shut, his lip split. His cheeks were bruised, his jaw aching. He looked like hell.

How the fuck was he going to explain this to Kayla?

A dozen scenarios ran through his mind, each more ridiculous than the last. He could say he was mugged. No, that would only make her worried and ask questions. He thought about other options, but none of them were believable.

After a few deep breaths, he settled on his story.

He would tell her that some drunk guy at happy hour got aggressive, and when Quinn tried to walk away, the guy threw the first punch. It was simple, easy to remember. If he downplayed it, Kayla would eventually let it go. But would she buy it?

He wiped his face again, trying to make himself look somewhat presentable before driving home.

As he stepped through the front door, he was relieved to find the house quiet. Zeke was already in bed, and Kayla was likely in their room. Maybe if he could just slip into the shower, she wouldn't even see him.

He was halfway down the hall when he heard her voice. "Quinn?"

He turned toward the bedroom. Kayla was lying on the bed, scrolling through her phone, but the moment her eyes landed on him, she sat up straight.

"What happened to you?"

Quinn let out a forced chuckle, hoping to play it off. "Ran into some drunk guy outside the bar," he said, stepping into the room. "Tried to defuse the situation, but he swung at me."

Kayla frowned, her eyes narrowing as she took in the bruises. "You got in a fight?"

"It wasn't really a fight," Quinn lied. "I didn't even hit him back. Just tried to get out of there."

She just watched him. He waited for her to scold him, to say something about how reckless it was. But she didn't.

Instead, she tossed her phone onto the bed and looked him square in the eyes.

"David called me," she said, flatly. He now saw that her eyes were full of tears.

Quinn's stomach dropped.

The room fell into complete silence, thick with unspoken words. His mouth went dry, his mind scrambling for an escape. But there was none.

Kayla's expression was unreadable, but her eyes burned into him with a sharp intensity.

"Want to try again?" she asked.

Quinn swallowed hard. He had nowhere to run. No lie to spin.

He had been caught.

53

Quinn dropped to his knees, his entire body trembling. His hands reached for Kayla's waist, his fingers gripping the fabric of her pajamas as if holding onto her would somehow keep her from slipping away. His chest rose and fell with each desperate, broken sob, his head pressed against her stomach.

"Kayla, please," he choked out, his voice raw. "Please, just... just let me explain."

Tears streamed down his face as he held onto her tightly. He had completely lost control of himself. He wasn't just crying — he was unraveling, breaking apart before her eyes.

His fingers clutched her waist as if she were the last thing tethering him to reality. "It didn't mean anything. I wasn't thinking. I was stupid, Kayla. I was so, so stupid."

Kayla stood frozen, unresponsive, her arms limp at her sides. She wasn't pulling away, but she also wasn't reciprocating the touch. She was utterly still, like a statue, her face blank.

Quinn kept rambling, searching for any combination of words that could fix this. "I—It was just a mistake! I don't love her. I love you. It was a weak moment. A terrible moment. Please, Kayla, I need you."

His voice cracked, and his grip on her tightened. He kept repeating her name over and over again, like a prayer. Like a plea for mercy.

But Kayla remained unmoved.

He lifted his head, trying to meet her gaze, searching for any sign of sympathy. Instead, her face was eerily calm, her expression unreadable. And then, finally, she spoke.

"You need to go stay at your parents' house tonight."

Her voice was cold. Devoid of emotion. The finality of it sliced through Quinn like a blade. He blinked up at her, disoriented, like he had just been struck. "Kayla—"

"Get the fuck out of this house," she said again, her voice firm, her gaze steady.

She didn't yell. She didn't cry. And somehow, that made it even worse.

Quinn slowly let go of her, his fingers slipping from the fabric of her clothes as he sat back on his heels. He wiped his face with his sleeve, his entire body trembling. He wanted to keep pleading, to keep groveling at her feet if it meant she wouldn't turn away from him. But he could see it in her eyes.

She was already gone.

With slow, defeated movements, he pushed himself up from the floor. His legs felt like lead as he moved toward the closet, grabbing an overnight bag and stuffing a few things into it. His mind screamed at him to say something, to do something to fix this. But there was nothing left to say.

When he finally turned back toward her, she was still standing in the same spot, arms crossed, her expression unchanged.

He swallowed hard, gripping the bag strap so tightly his knuckles turned white. "I'll—I'll call you in the morning."

Kayla didn't respond.

Quinn lingered for a second longer before finally stepping out of the room, his heart hammering in his chest. When he reached the front door, he turned back one last time, hoping, praying, that she would come after him.

But she didn't.

The door clicked shut behind him, and Quinn realized, for the first time in his life, that he might have lost her for good.

54

Quinn ended up choosing to stay at a hotel that night. He had considered going to his parents', but shame kept him from doing so. How could he explain why he had been kicked out of his own home? His hands trembled as he checked in at the front desk, barely able to sign his name on the receipt. The room was nothing special, just a generic hotel bed, a small desk, and a window overlooking the parking lot. It felt cold and isolating.

He sat on the edge of the bed, his hands gripping his thighs as the weight of what he had done came crashing down on him. He had destroyed everything. He had betrayed Kayla, lied to her, gone behind her back. And now… he was alone.

The realization made his chest tighten, and before he could stop it, the tears came. He buried his face in his hands, his body convulsing as sobs wracked through him. He cried until his throat was raw, until his body was too exhausted to do anything else. Even then, he couldn't sleep. Every time he closed his eyes, he saw Kayla's face — her cold, emotionless expression as she told him to leave.

When the morning light streamed through the curtains, he checked his phone. No messages. Nothing from Kayla. He stared at the screen, willing it to change, but it never did.

At work, he couldn't concentrate. He kept checking his phone, his pulse quickening every time the screen lit up, only to be met with disappointment. The silence was agonizing. He wanted to reach out to her, but he didn't know what to say. Would she even want to hear from him?

Kayla, meanwhile, went through the motions of her morning. She got Zeke ready for school, packed his lunch, and kissed him on the forehead before sending him off. It was all mechanical, robotic. Her mind was numb, her body moving on autopilot.

She had spent most of the night staring at the ceiling, unable to sleep. Her thoughts raced in circles, replaying every moment leading up to Quinn's betrayal. The lies. The deception. The choice he made to be with Simone when he could have easily chosen otherwise.

And yet, there was something gnawing at her — a small, painful realization that she wasn't entirely innocent, either. Her mind drifted to Erika, to that moment in the car when she had let herself be swept away. She never told Quinn about it, had chosen to keep it a secret. It hadn't felt like a betrayal then, but now? Now she wasn't so sure.

She shook the thought away. This wasn't about her. It was about Quinn. He had lied to her. He had planned the whole thing, knowing it was wrong.

She refused to justify it.

Late that night, her phone buzzed. She glanced at the screen. It was a message from Quinn.

Quinn: *Kayla, please. Can we talk?*

She stared at the message, her thumb hovering over the screen. She could see that he was watching, waiting for a response. She could feel his desperation through the silence. But she didn't type anything. She let him wait.

Ten minutes passed. Her phone buzzed again.

Quinn is calling...

She answered, her voice devoid of emotion. "Hello."

"Kayla," he breathed, as if just hearing her voice was a relief. "Please, I just — I need to talk to you."

There was a long pause.

"I don't know," she said finally.

His heart clenched at the coldness in her tone. "Please. I'll come to you. Anywhere. Anytime. Just give me a chance to explain."

Her silence stretched again, and then she simply said, "I'll think about it."

The line went dead before he could respond.

The next morning, Quinn woke up to a notification. His heart leapt in his chest when he saw Kayla's name.

Kayla: *Meet me at Dr. Simmons' office at 4:30.*

His stomach twisted. Their therapist.

She was willing to talk — but not alone.

55

Quinn arrived at the therapist's office a few minutes early, his stomach twisting into knots. He had barely slept the night before, haunted by what had happened. Today, thoughts of what Kayla might say, of whether there was anything left to salvage, scared him. He had a sick feeling that whatever was about to happen in this session would determine the course of the rest of his life.

When he stepped into the waiting room, Kayla was already there in the therapy room, sitting stiffly in one of the chairs. She barely acknowledged him, her eyes locked on the floor. It was obvious she had been talking to Dr. Simmons before he arrived.

"Come in," Dr. Simmons said, offering them both a measured smile. "Let's talk." Quinn swallowed hard and took the seat next to her, his presence met with a cold silence.

Quinn could already feel the weight of the session pressing down on him. He braced himself as Dr. Simmons turned to Kayla.

"Kayla," she said gently. "Would you like to start?"

Kayla exhaled sharply and nodded. She turned to Quinn, and for the first time in days, she truly looked at him. But there was no warmth there. No love. Only hurt.

"I don't even know where to begin," she said, her voice steady but hollow. "I thought we were in this together, Quinn. That no matter what, we were honest with each other. That was the entire point of what we were doing — to explore together, to push our boundaries as a couple. But you… you went behind my back. You planned it and then you lied about it."

Quinn dropped his gaze, shame washing over him like a wave. Hearing it put so plainly made his stomach turn.

"I know," he murmured. "I—I have no excuse."

Kayla let out a humorless laugh. "No excuse? That's all you have to say?" She shook her head, her hands gripping the edge of the couch tightly. "Do you have any idea what it felt like to hear from *David* of all people? To have *him* tell me that my husband was sneaking around with his wife?"

Quinn's jaw clenched. He wanted to tell her how much he hated himself, how much regret and guilt were suffocating him, but he knew that wasn't what she needed to hear right now.

Dr. Simmons cleared her throat. "Quinn, let's talk about that. You knew the boundaries you both set. Why did you choose to cross them?"

He exhaled slowly, rubbing a hand down his face. "I—I don't know," he admitted. "At first, I told myself it wasn't a big deal. That we'd already been with Simone and David before, so what difference did it make?" He paused, shaking his head. "But deep down, I knew it wasn't the same. I knew what I was doing was wrong."

Kayla stared at him, her lips pressed into a tight line. "Then why did you do it?"

Quinn hesitated, struggling to put the mess of emotions inside him into words. "Because I was selfish. Because I wanted to know what it would be like with just her. Because I got caught up in something that made me feel powerful, wanted, desired in a way that scared me."

Kayla inhaled sharply, and Quinn saw the way her hands trembled. "And I didn't make you feel that way?"

His heart shattered at the pain in her voice. "Kayla, that's not—" He reached for her hand, but she pulled away. "You do. You always have. I was an idiot. I had something amazing, and I was too stupid to see that I didn't need more."

Dr. Simmons observed them carefully before speaking. "Kayla, I know you've had very little time to sit with this, but how do you feel about what Quinn is saying?"

Kayla let out a slow, measured breath. "I don't know. Part of me wants to believe him. Part of me wants to forgive him because I love him. But another part of me..." She trailed off, shaking her head. "Another part of me thinks I might never be able to trust him again."

Dr. Simmons leaned forward. "Kayla, do you want to try? Do you want to work through this, or are you already done?"

Kayla hesitated, looking down at her hands. Then, after a long moment, Dr. Simmons asked, "Take a second to think about that. Before we go any further though, do either of you have any other secrets that need to come to light?"

Quinn immediately shook his head. "No. There's nothing else."

Silence.

Kayla didn't respond. She sat there, looking down at her lap, her fingers twisting in the fabric of her dress.

"Kayla?" Dr. Simmons prompted gently.

A lump formed in Kayla's throat. She could feel both of them staring at her, waiting. Her fingers tightened.

Then, in a voice barely above a whisper, she admitted, "There's something I haven't told you."

Quinn stiffened. "What?"

Kayla swallowed hard, forcing herself to look at him. "I kissed Erika."

Quinn's face went blank. "I know. I was there with you."

Kayla's voice wavered. "Not then. It happened in her car... a few days before we met her for the threesome. I didn't tell you because... because I was scared."

The words hung in the air like a bomb ready to explode.

56

The silence after Kayla's confession was deafening. Neither she nor Quinn spoke, both unable to meet the other's gaze. The weight of everything that had been said filled the room, thick and suffocating. Quinn shifted uncomfortably on the couch, while Kayla stared down at her hands, fingers twisting in her lap. Finally, Dr. Simmons cleared her throat, breaking the tension.

"Kayla," she said gently, "can you tell us more about what happened in the car?"

Kayla exhaled slowly and lifted her eyes to meet the therapist's. "It wasn't planned," she said. "We had gone out for lunch, and I had been confiding in Erika about everything. She was being so supportive, and I guess I felt safe with her. When we got back to the office parking lot, we were just sitting there, and then she leaned in and kissed me."

Quinn clenched his jaw, his fingers digging into his thighs. "And you kissed her back."

Kayla lowered her head and nodded. "I did."

Quinn took a second to collect his breath, and then asked, "Is that all that happened?"

Kayla paused, looking at the floor as if she were burrowing a hole to escape in. "She also reached in my shirt and played with my tit, and then rubbed me over my clothing."

"Seriously? When did this happen?" Quinn's voice was quiet but sharp, cutting through the room.

Kayla hesitated, choosing her words carefully. "It was a couple days before our date with her, and I hate to say it but I did it because it felt good. Because, for a moment, I wasn't thinking about all the complications of our marriage or what we were going through. I was just... in the moment."

Quinn let out a breath through his nose, shaking his head slightly. "And you didn't think I deserved to know?"

"I wanted to tell you," she admitted, "but after everything we had already done — after Lacey, Simone, and everyone else — I didn't think it was that big of a deal."

Dr. Simmons raised an eyebrow. "And yet, you kept it a secret."

Kayla nodded again, shame flickering in her expression. "I knew it was wrong. I knew that if I told Quinn, he'd be upset. And honestly... I think part of me didn't want to admit how much I enjoyed it."

Another heavy silence. Quinn shook his head and leaned forward, elbows on his knees. "I don't know what to say," he muttered. "I know I don't have the right to be upset, but I didn't realize we were keeping so many secrets from each other."

Dr. Simmons steepled her fingers. "Let's take a step back," she said. "I want you both to think about the journey that led you here. The choices you've made, the agreements you entered into when you decided to explore this lifestyle."

Kayla and Quinn both looked at her, waiting for her to continue.

"Your relationship has undergone an intense transformation," she continued. "You were once a monogamous couple, deeply in love, and then you began experimenting with something completely new. You explored together, but in doing so, you blurred the lines of what was acceptable and what wasn't. Swinging can be exhilarating, but it can also be destabilizing, especially if the foundation of the relationship isn't secure."

Kayla crossed her arms, glaring back at the therapist. "Are you saying that swinging caused Quinn to cheat?"

"I'm saying it likely played a role in both of your actions," Dr. Simmons said carefully. "You've both been operating on adrenaline, caught up in the excitement of something new. But that kind of rush can lead to reckless decisions — like the ones you both made."

Quinn exhaled. "So what do we do now?"

Dr. Simmons looked at them both, her expression serious. "I want you to take the night to think about it. Really think about how you got here, about what you want, and about whether this marriage is something you're willing to fight for."

Kayla swallowed, her throat dry. "And then what?"

"Then you come back tomorrow, and we talk about your future."

The next day, Quinn walked into Dr. Simmons' office feeling a little lighter, but still unsure. He had spent the night replaying their conversation, reflecting on his own guilt, his own desires. He wasn't sure where this was going, but he knew he wasn't ready to let Kayla go.

Kayla was already sitting in the waiting room when he arrived, and they shared a brief glance before walking into the session together.

Dr. Simmons waved them in and wasted no time. "Have you both given this some thought?"

They nodded.

Quinn spoke first. "I can't think about anything else. I don't want to lose my marriage. I don't want to lose my best friend," he said. "But I also know that I broke something and I don't know how to fix it."

Kayla took a deep breath. "I don't know if I can ever trust him the way I used to," she admitted. "But I also don't know if I'm ready to walk away."

Dr. Simmons leaned forward. "That's something, at least. Now, let's talk about a plan."

She paused before continuing. "Over this next month, I want you to go on three dates."

Kayla and Quinn exchanged looks.

Dr. Simmons smiled slightly. "You need to remind yourselves of who you were before all of this. Quinn, I want you to plan meaningful dates — something that makes Kayla feel special, like she's someone you're pursuing again. Kayla, I want you to allow yourself to be open to that."

Quinn nodded quickly. "I can do that."

Kayla hesitated, then nodded as well.

Dr. Simmons continued. "During these dates, there are rules. No talking about your marriage, no talking about the betrayals, and no talking about Zeke. You are simply two people getting to know each other again. Understood?"

They nodded again.

"Good," Dr. Simmons said. "And at the end of the month, we'll meet again. We'll discuss how you feel and whether you see a future together."

Quinn's heart pounded. It wasn't a guarantee. But it was a chance. And he was willing to take it.

57

Quinn had been looking forward to this night all week. Staying at the hotel had been miserable, and while he knew he deserved it, the separation from both Kayla and Zeke had weighed on him like an unbearable weight. He needed tonight to go well. He needed to prove to Kayla that he could be the man she once fell in love with.

He made a reservation at her favorite restaurant, thinking it would be a romantic touch. It had always been their go-to for birthdays and anniversaries, and he was sure it would bring back good memories.

When he arrived at the house to pick her up, Zeke was the first one to greet him when he walked in. "Daddy!" Zeke shouted, launching himself into Quinn's arms. The weight of his little body against him made Quinn's chest tighten. He missed him so much.

"Hey, buddy! How was school?" Quinn asked, squeezing him tightly.

Zeke immediately started rambling about his day, but Quinn's eyes drifted toward Kayla, who had just stepped out of the kitchen. She looked beautiful, as always, but something was different. Unlike the extravagant outfits she had worn for their double dates with other couples, this time she had put in minimal effort. It stung.

"Hey," he said, offering her a small smile.

"Hey," she responded, not meeting his eyes.

They said their goodbyes to Zeke and the babysitter, and as they walked to the car, Quinn instinctively reached for Kayla's hand, but she pulled it away.

"I can't do that right now," she said quietly.

Quinn swallowed hard and nodded. "Ok."

When they got into the car, Kayla crossed her arms. "Also, you need to knock when you come over. You can't just walk in like you're still living there."

That statement knocked the wind out of him. "I pay half the mortgage," he muttered before he could stop himself.

Kayla shot him a deadly glare. "If you want even a sliver of a chance of getting back together, or to even have the rest of these dates Dr. Simmons told us to go on, you'll honor my wishes."

He sighed, gripping the wheel. "Understood."

The drive to the restaurant was filled with small talk, though Quinn felt like he was pulling teeth to get more than a few-word response from Kayla. He hated this distance between them. He had hoped that tonight would be a turning point, but so far, it felt like they were moving backward.

When they arrived at the restaurant, he expected her to smile in appreciation. Instead, she simply gave him a blank look. "I knew you'd pick this place," she said.

He blinked. "What?"

"This is where you always take me when you think you're being romantic," she said, stepping out of the car before he could respond.

Quinn felt deflated. He had thought this was a safe choice — something familiar, something that would make her happy. But instead, it just felt… predictable to her.

During dinner, the tension between them remained thick. Quinn tried keeping the conversation light, but Kayla's answers were clipped, her eyes constantly drifting around the restaurant rather than focusing on him.

Finally, after a long, heavy silence, Quinn set down his fork and sighed. "I'm sorry, Kayla. For everything. I know I messed up, and I—"

Kayla immediately held up a hand, her expression sharp. "We're not supposed to talk about our marriage."

"I know," he said quickly. "But I just—"

"If you don't stop, I'll take an Uber home," she said firmly.

That shut him up.

The rest of dinner was quiet, with Kayla turning down dessert and saying she was ready to leave. Quinn opened the car door for her, but she still seemed distant, her expression unreadable.

The drive back home was even worse. The air between them was thick with unspoken words, and Quinn couldn't take it anymore.

"Why did you even agree to this if you clearly don't want to be here?" he asked, gripping the wheel tighter than necessary.

Kayla let out a humorless laugh. "Are you serious?"

"Yes," he said, frustration creeping into his voice. "You've been acting like this is some obligation."

She shook her head, letting out a long breath. "Quinn, you didn't act like you wanted to be here either."

His brows furrowed. "What are you talking about?"

Kayla turned her body slightly to face him, her expression firm. "That's not a date, Quinn. That's muscle memory. That's what you do when you don't want to think. A real date is spontaneous. It's fun. It's exciting. A real date is about showing someone how much you like them." She shook her head. "This… this wasn't a date."

Her words hit him hard, and for the first time in a long time, he realized just how much he had taken her for granted. She had a point. He had gotten comfortable — lazy, even — assuming that doing the bare minimum would be enough.

When they pulled into the driveway, Kayla didn't even say goodbye. She simply got out of the car, shut the door, and walked inside without a second glance.

Quinn sat there for a long moment, staring at the closed door. His heart sank. He was losing her. And for the first time, he truly understood what that meant.

58

The next morning, Kayla was pouring herself a cup of coffee in the break room when she heard footsteps approaching. She turned to see Erika entering, her eyes immediately locking onto Kayla's face. Without hesitation, Erika walked straight toward her.

"How was the date?" she asked, leaning against the counter.

Kayla opened her mouth, but instead of answering, she felt her throat tighten. A lump formed, and before she could stop herself, she lowered her head, her shoulders shaking slightly.

"Hey, hey," Erika said softly, immediately stepping forward and wrapping an arm around Kayla's shoulder. "Come with me."

Erika guided Kayla into her office, closing the door behind them. She gestured for Kayla to sit on the couch against the wall while she pulled up a chair across from her.

"Ok," Erika said, her voice softer now. "Talk to me."

Kayla took a deep breath, struggling to collect her thoughts. "It was awful," she admitted finally. "I wanted to enjoy it. I wanted to be excited for it. But I just… couldn't."

Erika tilted her head. "Why not?"

Kayla let out a frustrated sigh. "I don't know. I mean, I do know. It's the anger. It's still there, and I can't let it go. I thought maybe, if I just gave it a chance, I'd be able to move past it, but it's like this giant wall between us."

Erika nodded slowly. "You're allowed to feel that, Kayla. You're still healing."

"I don't even know if I can heal," Kayla admitted. "I mean, I agreed to the dates, right? So I should be trying. But I just sat there last night, completely disconnected. I couldn't even pretend to be excited."

Erika reached over and squeezed her hand. "It's ok. You're not on some timeline. Healing doesn't happen just because you schedule a date. And you don't have to go through it alone."

Kayla looked at Erika, her expression vulnerable. After a moment, Erika smiled gently. "Come over tonight. Have some drinks with me. No distractions, no kiddo running around. Just us talking, and you getting everything off your chest."

Kayla hesitated, then slowly nodded. "Yeah… I think I'd like that."

59

That afternoon, Quinn sat in his office, staring at his computer screen but not truly seeing it. His mind was replaying the disastrous date from the night before. No matter how hard he tried, he couldn't shake the feeling that he had just driven another wedge between him and Kayla.

He regretted bringing up their marriage issues at dinner. He wished he had just kept quiet, followed their therapist's advice, and let the night unfold naturally.

He also regretted choosing that restaurant. He thought it would spark some nostalgic feelings in Kayla, but instead, she said he was predictable and unimaginative.

The more he thought about it though, the more he realized she was right. When they had first started dating, he would go out of his way to plan fun, creative dates. He had worked to impress her, to make her smile, to make her feel special. When had that stopped? When had he become so predictable? So... boring?

Quinn ran his hands across his face, exhaling deeply. He didn't want to just go through the motions with Kayla. He wanted to reignite what they had lost. If he had any chance of salvaging their relationship, he needed to show her that he could still be the man she fell in love with.

Determined, he grabbed his phone and pulled up their text thread.

Instead of assuming she would agree to the second date, he decided to do things differently this time.

Quinn: *Hey, Kay. I know last night didn't go well, but I'd still really like to take you out again. This time, I want to do something different. Would you please go on another date with me?*

He stared at the message for a moment before hitting send. Then, he sat back and waited, hoping — praying — that she would give him another chance.

60

Kayla saw Quinn's text message as she was leaving work. She just stared at it, not knowing what to say. She honestly wasn't sure whether she wanted to go on the date or not. She decided to kick that can down the road, choosing to think about that later.

That night, she showed up at Erika's apartment. She was still in her work clothes but saw that Erika had changed into a pair of yoga pants and a sports bra. It showed off everything that was gorgeous about Erika — her curves, her tight ass, her toned stomach, and her inviting cleavage. Kayla found herself staring longer than she should have. It was undeniable. Erika was beautiful.

"Hey, come in. I made drinks," Erika said, smiling warmly, sensing the weight Kayla was carrying.

Kayla stepped inside, inhaling the scent of vanilla and something citrusy. Erika's signature scent. She kicked off her heels and followed Erika into the kitchen, where a tray of snacks sat beside two glasses of what looked like Manhattans.

"I figured you might need something strong tonight," Erika said, handing her a glass.

Kayla took it gratefully and let out a light laugh. "You figured right."

They moved to the couch, sinking into the cushions as Kayla finally let out a deep sigh. Erika tucked her legs underneath her, her body angled toward Kayla. "Alright, spill it. Tell me about the date."

Kayla let out a humorless laugh and rubbed her face. "I told you. It was awful."

"Was it really that bad?" Erika raised an eyebrow.

Kayla took a sip of her drink before answering. "Worse. I couldn't even pretend to be happy to be there. I wanted to — God, I wanted to. I thought maybe once we were sitting across from each other, I'd feel something again. But I just... couldn't. I felt blocked, like I was going through the motions just to check a box."

Erika nodded, listening. "Did he try to make it special?"

Kayla hesitated. "Yeah. I mean, kind of. He took me to my favorite restaurant, but that's just it. He didn't plan anything new or exciting. He just defaulted to what he thought would work."

Erika smirked. "Quinn's always been a little... routine-oriented."

Kayla scoffed. "That's a nice way of putting it. He did the bare minimum and expected some grand emotional reaction from me, but all I could think about was how predictable he's become. How predictable we had become."

Erika sipped her drink, watching Kayla closely. "And how did it end?"

Kayla exhaled heavily. "In silence. We barely spoke. When we got back to the house, he asked why I agreed to go if I wasn't going to try. And I told him that it wasn't a date — it was a muscle-memory routine. It wasn't special, and I needed special."

Erika tilted her head. "And what do you need for it to be special?"

Kayla stared into her drink, swirling the liquid. "I don't know," she admitted. "I want to feel something again. I want to be excited again."

Erika reached for her hand, squeezing it. "You will. Maybe with Quinn, but maybe not. Maybe not now. But you will."

Something about Erika's confidence and the warmth of her hand comforted Kayla in a way she hadn't expected. She looked up, her eyes filled with tears, and before she could stop herself, she broke down.

Erika immediately set her drink down and pulled Kayla into her arms. "Hey, hey. It's ok. Let it out."

Kayla sobbed into her shoulder, her entire body shaking as she released everything she had been holding in. The anger, the betrayal, the confusion — it all poured out of her like a dam had broken.

"I hate him," Kayla choked out. "I hate what he did to me. To us."

Erika ran a hand through Kayla's hair, her touch gentle. "I know, baby. I know."

The term of endearment sent a strange warmth through Kayla's chest. She didn't pull away. Instead, she sank into Erika's embrace, letting herself be held.

After what felt like forever, Kayla lifted her head. Their faces were inches apart. Erika reached up, brushing a stray tear from Kayla's cheek. "Better?"

Kayla didn't answer. She didn't think. She just leaned in and kissed her.

Erika froze for half a second, shocked, before surrendering into the kiss. It was slow at first, careful, but then something inside Kayla snapped. She deepened the kiss, gripping Erika's waist and pulling her closer.

Erika let out a small gasp as Kayla pushed her back against the couch, climbing onto her lap. "Kay," Erika breathed against her lips. "Are you sure?"

Kayla nodded, her breath heavy. "I don't want to think. I just want to feel something real."

Erika didn't need any more convincing. Her fingers slipped beneath Kayla's blouse, tugging it down her arms until it pooled on the floor. Kayla's hands were steadier this time, practiced, as she pulled Erika's sports bra over her head, revealing the strong lines of her torso and the soft swell of her breasts. She already knew the taste of Erika's skin, the way she sighed when kissed along her collarbone, but the hunger between them tonight was fiercer — less tentative, more urgent.

Their mouths crashed together, teeth grazing, tongues tangling. Kayla pushed Erika back against the couch, straddling her with a certainty that came from familiarity. She knew what she wanted. What neither of them expected was where their bodies would take them.

Erika shifted beneath her, tilting her hips and guiding Kayla lower. Their legs tangled, skin sliding against skin until suddenly — there it was. The press of heat against heat, slickness meeting slickness. Kayla gasped, her whole body jolting at the startling intimacy of it. She had been with women before, but not like this.

Never like this.

Erika's grip tightened on her waist, holding her there, rolling her hips until their centers aligned more firmly. The friction was immediate, raw, electric. Kayla's breath caught, her thighs trembling as the sensation pulsed through her. "Oh my god..." she whispered, almost to herself.

"Yeah," Erika panted, her voice ragged. "Just like that."

Kayla's hips began to move instinctively, grinding against Erika's in a rhythm that felt both foreign and natural at once. The pleasure was sharper, more consuming than she had expected, each stroke sending a flood of heat through her body. She could feel every twitch of Erika's muscles, every slick, desperate slide as they moved in sync.

It wasn't just physical. It was intimate in a way that startled her. Their bodies were so closely entwined, every nerve ending exposed, every gasp and moan echoing between them. Kayla's head tipped back, her hair spilling over her shoulders, her hands clutching at Erika's arms for balance as she lost herself in the raw rhythm.

She had touched women, tasted them, been touched in return. But this — this joining — was different. It was almost too much, the closeness unbearable in its intensity, and yet she couldn't stop. Didn't want to stop.

Erika's legs locked tighter around hers, pulling her down, pushing her harder into the grind. Their cries mingled, ragged and needy, filling the room. Kayla felt herself spiraling, every thrust sending her closer to a precipice she hadn't expected to reach so quickly. God, this is what I was missing, she thought, shuddering with the realization.

And as her hips moved faster, more urgently, Kayla knew this was a memory she would never be able to shake.

Their movements slowed, their kisses becoming softer, more languid. Kayla rested her forehead against Erika's, both of them catching their breath.

After a long silence, Erika spoke. "Kay... what does this mean?"

Kayla closed her eyes, her fingers tracing slow circles on Erika's arm. "I don't know," she admitted. "But I don't regret it."

Erika smiled softly. "Good."

They stayed like that for a while, tangled in each other, before Kayla finally sat up, running a hand through her hair. Reality was creeping back in, but she wasn't ready to face it yet.

"I should go," she said reluctantly.

Erika nodded, though there was disappointment in her eyes. "You know can stay if you want, right? No expectations. Just... stay."

Kayla hesitated, her heart torn in two directions. But for once, she let herself choose what felt right. She leaned down, pressing one last lingering kiss to Erika's lips before whispering, "Ok, I'll stay."

And just like that, the line between friendship and something more blurred beyond recognition.

61

As Quinn was getting ready for work, he was constantly checking his phone. He had yet to hear back from Kayla on the date, which was weird because usually she was a very quick responder. His stomach twisted as he tried to come up with reasons. Was she still thinking about it? Was she just ignoring him? Or worse, had she already decided but couldn't bring herself to tell him?

As he buttoned his shirt, he sighed and tossed his phone onto the bed. The waiting was killing him.

Later that day, while at work, he sat at his desk, his mind kept wandering, so he pulled up a browser and started searching for unique date ideas. He needed something different, something that would take them out of the routine they had fallen into. He considered taking her dancing, but he wasn't sure she'd enjoy that without feeling forced. A comedy show at the improv? Maybe, but it felt too impersonal. A play at the theatre? That might be nice, but did it show any real effort?

Then he stumbled upon something interesting — hot springs in a cave, with drinks and snacks served while they soaked in the naturally heated water. It sounded different, exciting, and a little bit intimate. It had a kind of raw, earthy romance to it, something that could break down walls instead of building them up. He could already picture it — the steam rising, the soft glow of lanterns reflecting off the stone walls, just the two of them with no distractions.

He immediately texted Kayla: *I came up with a great date idea. Bring your bathing suit.*

And then he waited. Again.

An hour passed, and still, no response.

He tried to push down the anxiety gnawing at him. Maybe she was busy. Maybe she needed time to think. Or maybe... she just didn't care anymore.

Quinn ran a hand through his hair and leaned back in his chair, staring at the ceiling. He wasn't ready to give up. He had messed up — badly — but he had to believe that some part of her still wanted to make this work.

His thoughts drifted back to their past, to when they were dating. Back then, he would put so much effort into making every date memorable. He would plan scavenger hunts around the city, surprise her with rooftop picnics, and book last-minute road trips just because. He had chased after her like she was the best thing that had ever happened to him. Because she was.

So when had he stopped trying? When had he become complacent?

He exhaled heavily and looked at his phone again. Still nothing.

His mind went to a darker place. What if she had already moved on? Was she seeing someone? Was she out with someone right now?

The thought made his stomach churn.

He tried to shake it off. He had no proof of anything like that. And even if she was interested in someone else, it was his fault for pushing her away.

Determined, he decided that if Kayla didn't answer by the evening, he'd call her. He wouldn't just sit here waiting for an answer that might never come.

He had to fight for her. Even if she wasn't sure yet, he had to show her that he was.

62

Kayla woke up the next morning in a daze, her body wrapped in warmth that wasn't her own. As her mind adjusted to wakefulness, she slowly opened her eyes and, for a moment, didn't recognize where she was. The soft glow of sunlight filtered through unfamiliar curtains. The sheets smelled different. She turned her head slightly and realized why. This wasn't her room. She was in Erika's bed.

Panic shot through her, a sharp and immediate burst of adrenaline.

"Fuck. Fuck. Fuck!" The words repeated in her mind like a warning siren. What had she done?

She shifted slightly, careful not to disturb Erika, who was still sound asleep beside her. Kayla's heart pounded as she took in the sight of Erika's peaceful face, her long lashes resting against her cheek, her lips slightly parted. Even in sleep, she was breathtaking.

Kayla squeezed her eyes shut, willing herself to think. She had crossed a line — again. Sleeping with Erika once was one thing, but last night had felt different. More intense. More deliberate. It wasn't just passion. There was emotion tied to it.

She knew she had feelings for Erika, but she also knew she had to try to fix things with Quinn. He was her husband and they had a child. A family. And they had a history. Could she really justify her anger toward him when she was doing the exact same thing, if not worse?

Trying to untangle herself from the sheets without waking Erika, Kayla moved cautiously. But as she did, Erika stirred, her blue eyes blinking open slowly. A lazy, satisfied smile spread across her face.

"Morning, gorgeous," Erika murmured, her voice thick with sleep.

Before Kayla could respond, Erika pulled her back down onto the bed, resting her head against Kayla's bare chest. Kayla inhaled sharply at the warmth of Erika's skin against hers. The contrast between her own internal turmoil and Erika's tranquility was jarring.

For a moment, Kayla wanted to forget everything. To let herself get lost in this moment, to give in to the urge to kiss Erika again, to run her hands over her soft curves. She wanted to wake Erika up in the best way possible.

But she couldn't.

With effort, Kayla gently untangled herself and sat up. "I should go," she whispered.

Erika propped herself up on her elbow, looking at Kayla with an expression that was both understanding and disappointed. "You sure?"

Kayla nodded, swallowing hard. "Yeah. I need to think."

Erika sighed and let her hand trail down Kayla's arm before finally pulling away. "Alright. But just so you know… I really like you, Kay."

Kayla's breath hitched. She forced a small smile but didn't trust herself to respond. She grabbed her clothes and dressed quickly, feeling Erika's gaze on her the whole time. She didn't look back as she left the apartment.

At work, Kayla stayed mostly in her office, keeping her door closed as much as possible. Her mind was spinning.

She glanced at her phone for the hundredth time, still seeing Quinn's text message: *I came up with a great date idea. Bring your bathing suit.*

Why would she need a bathing suit?

She wanted to reply, but every time she started typing, she deleted it. What could she even say?

Erika had been acting normal around the office, but Kayla knew she had noticed the shift. They weren't exchanging secret smiles. Erika wasn't brushing against her when they passed in the hallway. The flirtation had been dialed back, and that absence felt heavier than Kayla expected.

She had to figure out what she really wanted. But how?

She sighed and leaned back in her chair, staring at the ceiling, lost in thought. She wasn't sure how much longer she could keep living in this in-between.

63

Quinn sat on the edge of the hotel bed, gripping his phone so tightly his knuckles turned white. He took the day off from work, knowing he would be unable to focus. A basketball game from the previous night was replaying, flickering unnoticed in the background, a meaningless distraction from his real focus —Kayla's silence.

She still hadn't responded.

Not to his first message. Not to his follow-up. Not to the one where he told her about bringing a swimsuit, promising that this date would be different. She'd read them — he could see that — but she hadn't replied.

His stomach twisted into knots as he imagined every possible reason why. Maybe she was still upset about their last date. Maybe she just needed space. Or maybe... maybe she was with someone.

That thought made his jaw clench. His mind immediately went to Erika.

Was she with *her*?

His fingers hovered over the screen. Should he call her? Would that make him look desperate?

He inhaled sharply and locked his phone, placing it onto the nightstand. He wasn't going to beg. Not yet.

A few minutes later though, he grabbed his phone again and typed out another message.

Quinn: *I promise this one won't be boring. Just say yes.*

He hit send, placed his phone back on the nightstand, and waited.

Minutes passed. Then an hour.

Nothing.

His chest tightened. Was she *done*?

Kayla sat at her desk at work, staring at her phone, Quinn's messages staring back at her. She could feel the weight of each unread text, pressing against her chest.

I promise this one won't be boring. Just say yes.
Bring your bathing suit.

She wanted to respond. She really did. But something in her stopped her every time she started typing.

Her body still ached from the night before — from Erika.

Her lips tingled with the memory of Erika's mouth on hers. Her skin burned where Erika's hands had explored. And yet, the guilt churned inside her stomach like poison.

What the hell am I doing?

She was supposed to be fixing things with Quinn. She was supposed to be figuring out if their marriage could be saved.

But instead, she had woken up in another woman's bed.

And the worst part?

She had liked it.

No — she had loved it.

Kayla swallowed hard and locked her phone, placing it face down on the desk. She needed to focus.

A soft knock at her office door made her jump.

"Hey," Erika's voice was soft, but there was something else there — hesitation.

Kayla looked up, forcing a smile. "Hey."

Erika stepped inside and closed the door behind her. "You've been avoiding me all day."

Kayla exhaled, rubbing her temples. "I just... I have a lot on my mind."

Erika studied her for a moment before speaking. "About last night?"

Kayla hesitated before nodding. "Yeah."

Erika took a cautious step closer. "Are you regretting it?"

Kayla closed her eyes, shaking her head. "No. That's the problem."

Erika's lips parted slightly, her blue eyes searching Kayla's face. "Then what's wrong?"

Kayla opened her mouth to respond, but the words caught in her throat.

How was she supposed to explain the war raging inside her? How was she supposed to say that she was falling for her, but that she also still needed to see if she could make things work with Quinn?

Erika sighed. "Kay, talk to me. Please."

Kayla swallowed hard. "I'm married."

"I know."

"I'm trying to fix things with Quinn."

"I know that, too."

Kayla met Erika's gaze, her voice barely above a whisper. "But I want this, too."

Erika's breath hitched.

The silence between them stretched, thick with tension and unspoken words.

After a long moment, Erika spoke. "Do you still love him?"

Kayla's stomach twisted. Did she?

She thought so.

She *hoped* so.

But why did saying it out loud feel so hard?

"I don't know," she admitted, her voice breaking.

Erika reached for her hand, lacing their fingers together. "Then maybe that's what you need to figure out first."

Kayla squeezed Erika's hand, then slowly pulled away. "I think I need a little space."

Erika nodded, though disappointment flickered across her face. "I get it."

Kayla forced a small smile, stepping toward the door. "I need to go."

Erika didn't stop her.

That evening, Quinn sat alone in his hotel room, staring at his phone.

Still. No. Response.

His jaw tightened.

Was she testing him? Was she done?

Or was she with someone else?

He stood abruptly, pacing the room, his hands on his hips. He couldn't keep doing this.

Without thinking, he grabbed his phone and called her.

It rang. And rang.

Finally, she answered.

"Hey," Kayla's voice was soft but distant.

Quinn exhaled sharply. "Hey. Did you get my texts?"

A pause. "Yeah."

His heart pounded. "And?"

Another pause.

Then, finally — "Can we talk tomorrow?"

His stomach dropped.

"Kayla," he said, his voice tight, "just tell me — are we still trying? Or am I wasting my time?"

She hesitated.

"I don't know," she whispered.

Quinn squeezed his eyes shut.

His hands clenched into fists, but his voice was calm when he spoke. "Then meet me at the therapist's office tomorrow. I'll call in the morning and get us an appointment."

Silence.

Then — "Ok."

The line went dead.

Quinn stared at the phone, his pulse hammering in his ears.

This was it.

Tomorrow, he would either fight for his marriage... or finally accept that it was already over.

64

Quinn stepped out of his car and into the intense heat of the afternoon air, his breath coming out in sharp, uneven bursts. He wasn't sure if it was from the heat or from the nerves tightening his chest like a vice. He checked his phone again. No new messages from Kayla.

He walked toward the glass doors of the therapist's office, his stomach twisting in knots. He'd barely slept the night before, his mind racing with worst-case scenarios, so Dr. Simmons seeing them on such short notice was a godsend.

Was this it? Was today the day she told him she was done?

As he reached the elevator, he saw her.

Kayla stood a few feet away, arms wrapped around herself, staring at the closed elevator doors.

She looked… exhausted. Her face was pale, her eyes red-rimmed. She had been crying.

Quinn's heart clenched.

"Hey," he said softly, hoping for something — anything — some sign that she wasn't shutting down completely.

She didn't respond.

She didn't even look at him.

His throat tightened, but he forced himself to stay quiet. Pushing her right now would do no good.

The elevator dinged, and the doors slid open. They stepped inside, standing side by side, but the space between them felt like a canyon.

Neither spoke.

The ride to the therapist's floor felt endless.

Once they were seated in Dr. Simmons' office, Quinn felt an unbearable tension settling over them like a thick fog.

The therapist glanced between them with a knowing, measured look before speaking. "Kayla, Quinn, I know this has been a very difficult week. Why don't we start by talking about how you're both feeling coming into this session today?"

Before Kayla could speak, Quinn leaned forward, his voice urgent.

"Listen, I just — I need to say something first," he said quickly, glancing at Kayla, then back at Dr. Simmons. "I know I messed up. Seeing Simone was the dumbest, most selfish thing I have ever done in my life. I can't even explain how much I regret it. If I could take it back, I would in a heartbeat. But I can't, so all I can do is tell you how sorry I am. I was 100% in the wrong."

Kayla still wasn't looking at him.

He swallowed, trying to push through the tightness in his throat. "I know I hurt you. And I know I can't just erase that. But Kayla, I swear, I will never do anything like that again. Ever. If you give me another chance, I'll spend every day for the rest of my life making it up to you and rebuilding your trust."

His voice cracked on the last few words, but he didn't care.

Kayla still didn't respond.

Dr. Simmons held up a hand. "Quinn, I appreciate you being honest about your emotions, but I need you to take a deep breath and pause for a moment. You're speaking from a place of desperation, and that's understandable. But right now, I think Kayla has something she needs to say."

Quinn frowned, his stomach twisting.

"Kayla?" Dr. Simmons prompted gently.

Kayla took a deep breath, still staring down at her lap. Her fingers twisted together, knuckles going white. Her body was trembling, as though the words she needed to say were clawing their way out of her.

Finally, she spoke.

"I slept with Erika again."

The words dropped into the silence like a nuclear bomb.

Quinn went completely still.

His brain took a few seconds to process what she had just said.

Kayla's hands curled into fists in her lap, her breath shaky. "It happened two nights ago."

Quinn felt his body lock up. His jaw clenched, his nails digging into his palms.

She had cheated on him. Again. And again, with Erika.

His first instinct was anger. How could she? How could she act so cold to him these past few days while she was doing the same thing?

But then, almost as quickly, a realization of hypocrisy crashed over him.

How could he judge her for this? He had cheated too. And worse — he had lied about it. She at least is volunteering the news.

His mind reeled.

"You… You're serious?" His voice was rough, unsteady.

Kayla nodded.

Quinn exhaled sharply, rubbing his face. "Jesus, Kayla!"

Dr. Simmons intervened. "Quinn, take a breath."

He tried but failed. He tried again.

After a long silence, he spoke again, his voice quieter this time. "Are you in love with her?"

Kayla flinched slightly. "I… I don't know."

Quinn stared at her, searching her face. "Do you want to keep seeing her?"

She hesitated. "Yes."

His stomach churned.

"But I also want to fix things with you," she added quickly, finally looking him in the eyes. "I *need* to know if we can fix this."

He wanted to believe her.

God, he wanted to believe her.

Dr. Simmons leaned forward, folding her hands. "It's clear that both of you are experiencing a lot of complex emotions. You're navigating pain, betrayal, and new realizations about yourselves and your relationship. It's understandable to feel lost."

Quinn let out a shaky breath. "So what now?"

Dr. Simmons gave them both a measured look. "That's up to you two. But let me ask you both this — do you still want to try?"

Quinn turned to Kayla. "Do you?"

Kayla swallowed hard. "I think so. I just… I don't know how."

Dr. Simmons nodded. "Then let's take this one step at a time."

The conversation continued, Dr. Simmons helping them navigate their emotions, fears, and next steps.

Toward the end of the session, Quinn turned to Kayla, his voice hesitant.

"Can I ask you something?"

She nodded.

"Will you please go on another date with me?"

Kayla's lips parted slightly in surprise. She looked at him for a long moment, as if trying to decipher something in his expression.

Then, in a soft voice, she said, "Should I wear my red or black bathing suit?"

Quinn let out a breath he hadn't realized he'd been holding.

Hope.

It was small, but it was there.

<h1 style="text-align:center">65</h1>

Quinn was standing in his hotel room, gripping a bouquet of deep red roses tightly in his hands. His heart pounded against his ribs, and his stomach churned with nervous energy. He had to make sure this date was perfect. No. Check that — *beyond perfect.*

He knew this could very well be his last chance.

The last date they had was a disaster. No, *he* had been a disaster. He had chosen the wrong place, said the wrong things, and worst of all, he had failed to make Kayla feel special. She had walked away that night colder than when she arrived. He could not — would not — let that happen again.

This time, he needed to remind her of something real. He needed her to *feel* something when she was with him.

As he got ready, he took extra care in his appearance. He wore fitted dark jeans, a pressed black polo shirt, and a sleek navy-blue suit jacket. His usually scuffed sneakers were replaced with a brand-new pair of polished white shoes. He even trimmed his beard and styled his hair, making sure every detail was right.

Quinn had to look the part. He had to show her that he was willing to put in the effort again. Most of all though, he needed her to be attracted to him again.

He took one last look in the mirror and let out a deep breath. It was time.

Kayla heard the knock at the door and frowned slightly.

It felt odd.

She knew she had made the request on their last date that Quinn should knock instead of just walking in, but it felt... weird.

For eight years, he had come and gone through that door like he belonged there. But now, standing in the doorway like a man asking permission to enter, it was as if he understood that things had changed.

She hesitated for a second before pulling the door open.

Her breath caught in her throat.

Quinn stood there, his posture straight, his expression nervous but confident. His suit jacket hugged his broad frame, his crisp polo shirt highlighting his familiar physique. He looked good. Really good.

He had clearly put some thought into his appearance tonight.

And then, from behind his back, he pulled out a bouquet of deep red roses and held them out to her.

Kayla blinked, startled.

She slowly reached for them, her fingers grazing the soft petals. *Roses.*

He had never given her flowers outside of their anniversary and Valentine's Day. Never.

Well, except for once.

The first time he ever took her out.

The realization hit her like a wave, and suddenly, her mind was flooded with memories.

It had been their very first date. She had met Quinn while at a bar the week before, both of them there with mutual acquaintances. He introduced himself when he arrived but then spent the next hour chatting up one of her friends. She remembered thinking he was cute, but he hadn't seemed interested in her.

As the night progressed, the deejay began playing some slower, more relaxed music. Music that you can enjoy a drink to with some great conversation.

The Frank Sinatra song, *Strangers in the Night*, began playing over the speakers. She subconsciously began swaying to the music, her eyes closed while she listened to Ol' Blue Eyes crooning. Then she heard a whisper near her ear. It was Quinn. "I love this song. Can I have this dance?"

She looked over to respond but he had already grabbed her hand and was leading her out to an open space between tables. That bar didn't have a dance floor, but they made one for that song. Quinn quickly tucked some chairs to the side and turned towards Kayla, holding his hand out. She grabbed it, and he pulled her tight, pressing her body up against his. All she could remember was that he smelled really good, a mixture of cedar and coffee scents.

They danced, and even though most of the bar's eyes were on them, they got lost in the music and each other's eyes. They ended up going straight through two more songs, moving from making small talk to Kayla cuddling into Quinn's shoulder.

They returned to the bar and began really talking, not small talk but deep topics. They discussed their lives and passions, including what kept them up at night and what really excited them. It was like they were alone in the bar, and suddenly, looking down at her phone, Kayla saw that they had been talking for almost three hours. She had to get up early for work the next morning, so she decided to call it.

She turned to him and thanked him for a good time, indicating that she had a great time. She then asked to see his phone, which he hesitantly handed over. She then put her phone number in his contacts and told him to call her sometime.

She then began walking away before he called her name, startling her. He had a look of longing in his eyes, afraid to let a moment slip by. "Are you busy Friday night?"

She blushed. "I'm not sure. I don't know what my weekend looks like yet."

He then flashed her a boyish grin with a sly wink of his eyes. "Cool. Then we have a date. I'll call you tomorrow to get your address."

His confidence. It was exhilarating.

That Friday night, she was sitting on her tiny apartment couch, nervously smoothing down the skirt of her dress, checking the time on her phone every thirty seconds. When a knock finally came at the door, she jumped to her feet, inhaled deeply, and opened it.

And there he was.

Quinn, looking effortlessly handsome in dark jeans and a button-up shirt, holding a bouquet of fresh flowers. And not just any flowers — roses. Deep red ones.

Her heart leapt.

No one had ever brought her flowers before, let alone ones that seemed to symbolize something as heavy as romance.

"Wow," she had breathed out, staring at them like they magically appeared.

"You like them?" he asked, looking both nervous and pleased.

She smiled, tucking her hair behind her ear. "I love them."

That night, Quinn was perfect.

He had taken her to an outdoor festival, a surprise location that kept them moving, laughing, and providing endless things to talk about. She remembered the way he held her hand when they weaved through the crowd, the way he bought her a drink without asking what she wanted and yet somehow picked exactly what she would have chosen.

It had been effortless. Fun.

And then, he took her to one of the most exclusive Italian restaurants in the city. It was the kind of place that required a reservation a full month in advance.

When they walked up to the hostess stand, Quinn confidently gave their name, but the hostess frowned and said there was no reservation under it.

"I'm sorry, sir," she had said. "But we're completely booked for the evening."

Kayla had felt the momentary disappointment rolling off Quinn.

He sighed, rubbing the back of his neck. "I was really hoping to impress you," he admitted.

She had smiled, touched by the sentiment. "It's ok. The festival was amazing. We can find another place—"

But then Quinn grabbed her hand and led her around the side of the building, determination flashing in his eyes.

She was so confused.

Then he knocked on the back door of the restaurant.

A few seconds later, a young man in a dishwashing apron answered, looking puzzled.

Quinn gave him a handshake — one that included a few folded bills tucked in his palm — and whispered something to him. The guy nodded, glanced around quickly, then waved them inside.

Kayla followed, her heart pounding.

They walked past steaming plates of pasta, trays of tiramisu, and servers rushing in and out of the kitchen. The dish boy approached an older waiter, whispered something in his ear, and the man nodded knowingly, motioning to Kayla and Quinn to follow him through the kitchen door and into the seating area.

He walked over and grabbed an empty table that was connected to another one someone was eating at, and pulled it over to an open space. Two other waiters then came out of the back with chairs while the older waiter put new linens, table settings, and a lit candle on the table. A young lady then brought a chiller full of ice and a bottle of wine, and the waiter poured them some drinks.

Kayla was speechless.

"Are we… allowed to be here?" she had whispered, half-laughing, half-in awe.

Quinn smirked, taking her hand across the table. "I have connections."

It wasn't until months later that she learned the truth.

The entire thing had been staged.

The hostess, the dishwasher, the waiter.

Months later, when they were out with some friends, Quinn's best friend slipped up. Quinn's uncle owned that restaurant and had let him come in earlier that night to set the whole thing up.

She had loved the date when she thought it had been spontaneous. But after learning just how much effort Quinn had put into it, she fell in love with him all over again.

That night, she proposed to him.

Kayla stared at the roses in her hands, lost in the memory of the

Quinn she had once known — the man who went out of his way to woo her.

The man who used look at her as if she was his only desire.

Had they really lost all of that?

She lifted her gaze to Quinn. His expression was uncertain, waiting for her reaction. Something about the way he looked at her — hopeful, vulnerable, afraid — sent an unexpected warmth through her chest.

"Thank you," she finally said, her voice quieter than she intended.

She didn't know what else to say.

Quinn gave her a small smile. "Ready to go?"

Kayla nodded. "Yeah. Let me put these in water first."

She stepped away, placing the roses carefully in a vase.

She didn't know if this was the beginning of something new or the last time she would ever accept flowers from Quinn.

But for the first time in a long time, she wanted to find out.

She turned back to him.

"Ok," she said. "Let's go."

66

The drive to the hot springs was quiet but not uncomfortable. Kayla sat in the passenger seat, stealing glances at Quinn now and then. He had clearly put in the effort. He smelled amazing, like his expensive cologne that she hadn't smelled on him in a long time. His jawline was sharp, his beard freshly shaved, and there was a calm confidence about him tonight that she hadn't seen in years.

She still wasn't sure where her heart was, but she knew one thing for certain — she was looking forward to this date.

They pulled into a secluded parking lot at the edge of a winding path. There was a small sign that read *Private Reservation: Follow the Path to Your Destination.* Quinn shut off the engine and turned to Kayla with a grin.

"It's about a ten-minute walk," he said, stepping out of the car.

Kayla followed, her heels clicking against the stone path before she switched into a more comfortable stride. The walk was peaceful, lined with trees that stretched high into the sky. The night was cool, but not cold, and the fresh scent of pine lingered in the air. The path was dimly lit by small lanterns, giving it a dreamlike quality.

As they walked, their conversation naturally flowed.

"How was work?" Quinn asked.

Kayla sighed, rolling her eyes. "It was the usual. A client insisted they never received my email, even though I had a read receipt. It caused a small fire alarm but I took care of it."

Quinn chuckled. "Classic. What'd you do?"

"Resent it with a 'Just following up on my last email' message, knowing full well they had already read it," she said with a smirk.

He laughed. "Passive-aggressive, I like it."

"What about you?" she asked.

"Not much. Just a lot of paperwork today. But—" He paused for dramatic effect. "I did win an argument with my boss about a client's legal loophole, so I'm feeling pretty smug."

Kayla smiled. "Good to know you still enjoy proving people wrong."

"Oh, I live for it," he teased.

By the time they reached the cave entrance, Kayla was already feeling lighter, more relaxed. But nothing could have prepared her for what she saw when they ducked down to enter.

The cave was breathtaking.

Dark red rocks surrounded them, creating a dome-like structure. At the center was a large hot spring, the steam rising in delicate waves. But what truly took her breath away was the light — iridescent blues, purples, and greens dancing across the cavern walls, shifting and blending together like the northern lights.

It was mesmerizing.

She stood in awe, eyes wide. "Quinn… this is unreal."

He grinned, pleased by her reaction.

A man, dressed in a sleek uniform, greeted them with a warm smile. "Welcome to your private hot spring experience. You have three hours reserved and drinks and snacks will be served periodically. If you need anything, there's a call button by the entrance."

He took Quinn's jacket and gestured them toward a small enclave with fold-up blinds. "You can change in there."

Kayla went first, stepping inside the small space. She slipped out of her dress and into her black bathing suit — one of her most revealing. It lifted her breasts perfectly, emphasized her curves, and the thong bottom accentuated her toned figure in a way she knew Quinn would notice.

She hadn't dressed this way for Quinn — or at least, that's what she told herself. But a part of her wanted to feel seen again. To see if she could still stir something in him.

When she stepped out, she caught Quinn's expression immediately.

His eyes widened slightly before he quickly composed himself, but it was too late — she saw it. The way his gaze lingered. The way his throat bobbed as he swallowed.

Good.

Kayla smirked and slowly climbed into the hot spring. The water was perfect, warm and soothing against her skin.

"Your turn," she told him.

Quinn hesitated for a second, as if shaking himself from a trance, then stepped into the changing area. When he emerged a minute later, he was wearing blue swim trunks, his toned chest and arms on full display. Kayla hadn't really looked at him like this in a long time, but *damn.*

He climbed into the water, sitting across from her, the steam curling around them.

A soft jazz melody filled the cave, barely loud enough to break the silence but adding a sensual touch to the atmosphere.

Then the host returned, carrying two glasses of wine. "Would you like to order food now?"

They listened as he listed the offerings — nigiri sushi, tartes, and salmon dip with crackers.

Kayla ordered a pear and shallot tarte tatin with whipped goat cheese, along with some nigiri. Quinn opted for the chips with dip and some additional sushi.

As the host left, Kayla exhaled, taking in her surroundings once more.

"This is… beautiful," she admitted, her voice softer. "I can't believe you found this place."

Quinn smiled. "I wanted this to be different. I wanted this to feel like an actual date."

Kayla looked at him. For the first time in a long time, really looked at him.

He seemed different tonight. Not just in how he looked, but in his energy. There was a sincerity to him, a rawness she hadn't seen in years.

And then, out of nowhere, Quinn spoke again.

"Kayla, I am so sorry."

She blinked. "For what?"

"For everything," he said, his voice thick with emotion. "For our last date. For all the dates before that where I stopped trying. For making you feel like I wasn't paying attention. For making you feel like you weren't the most important person in my life." He sighed. "I don't know when it happened, but somewhere along the way, I stopped showing you how much you mean to me. And that's 100% on me."

Tears welled in Kayla's eyes before she could stop them.

Hearing him say those words hurt.

Because he was right.

She had felt like she was losing him for years, like she was fading into the background while they fell into the rhythm of co-parenting and day-to-day responsibilities. And she had ached for him to notice before it was too late.

Now, finally, he was seeing it.

Her voice wavered. "I've missed this version of you."

Quinn swallowed hard. "I never stopped loving you, Kayla. I just... forgot how to show it."

Kayla let out a shaky breath. She couldn't hold back anymore.

She reached for him.

Quinn immediately pulled her into a tight hug, his arms wrapping around her tightly. She buried her face in his chest, crying softly, releasing emotions she had been holding onto for too long.

He didn't rush her.

He didn't speak.

He just held her, rubbing slow circles on her back with the palm of his hand, pressing a kiss to the top of her head.

When she finally pulled away, she wiped her eyes and laughed softly. "Now I look like a mess."

Quinn smirked. "You've never looked more beautiful."

She rolled her eyes but smiled.

For the rest of the evening, they talked.

Not about the past — not about their mistakes — but about everything else. Politics. Funny work stories. The time Quinn had walked into the wrong wedding and almost gave a speech before realizing he didn't know the bride or groom. The time Kayla had mistaken a stranger for her boss at a holiday party and almost asked him for a raise.

They laughed. A lot.

When Quinn pulled into the driveway, Kayla exhaled, turning to him.

"Thank you for tonight," she said sincerely.

Quinn gave her a small smile. "You're welcome."

She hesitated for only a second before leaning over and kissing his cheek.

Quinn froze, his breath catching.

And then, before stepping out of the car, she poked her head back in and smiled.

"Now that. That was a real date."

And then she was gone.

67

That night, both Quinn and Kayla slept soundly, something neither of them had done in a long time.

Kayla stirred once in the middle of the night, her body moving on instinct. Half-asleep, she reached across the bed, her hand searching for the warmth of Quinn's body, something she used to do every night for years.

But all she found was an empty space.

Reality set in, and she opened her eyes, blinking into the darkness. She sighed softly, staring at the ceiling for a moment before rolling over and pulling the blanket tighter around herself.

She wasn't sure who she had wished to be in that bed with her.

The next morning, Kayla arrived at work earlier than usual. She felt… lighter. As if a weight had lifted off her chest. The date with Quinn had been great, better than she could have expected. She wasn't sure what it meant yet, but for the first time in a long time, she felt something real between them again.

She was staring at her computer screen, trying to focus, when Erika knocked on her doorframe.

"Hey, gorgeous," Erika said, walking in without waiting for an invitation. She held two coffees in her hands, extending one toward

Kayla. "I figured you might need this."

Kayla took it with a smile. "You're a lifesaver."

Erika plopped down in the chair across from Kayla's desk, crossing her legs. "So..." she started, her tone teasing, but her eyes searching. "How did it go last night?"

Kayla blushed, looking down at her coffee. "It was... actually really nice."

Erika raised an eyebrow. This was a much better reaction than the previous date.

"Oh?" Erika asked, feigning casual curiosity. "Tell me everything."

Kayla leaned back in her chair, smiling as she recalled the evening. She told Erika about the walk through the lantern-lit path, the stunning cave, the hot spring's glowing walls, the gentle jazz playing in the background. She talked about the wine, the amazing food, and the way Quinn had genuinely *tried*.

The way he had looked at her. The way he had made her feel special. Erika listened, nodding and reacting in all the right places, but inside, she was struggling.

She wanted Kayla to be happy.

She had been so mad at Quinn for hurting Kayla, for making her doubt her worth, for making her feel alone in a marriage where she should have been cherished. Erika had been there to pick up the pieces, and in the process...

She had fallen in love.

At first, it was just an attraction — a fantasy she had suppressed for years. Kayla was her best friend, and straight, or at least Erika had thought she was. But everything changed once she kissed Kayla for the first time.

Then it changed again when they spent the night together that first time.

And again when Kayla had melted into her arms, crying after the disastrous first date with Quinn.

Somewhere along the way, Kayla stopped being just a crush. She wasn't just an unattainable fantasy anymore. She was everything Erika wanted.

She tried telling herself that Kayla was just exploring — just curious — but it didn't feel like that. Not when Kayla looked at her the way she did. Not when Kayla kissed her with such intensity. Not when Kayla's fingers traced every inch of her body like she was memorizing it.

Not when Erika felt like she belonged to her.

But now… where did that leave her?

Because from the way Kayla was talking about Quinn, something was shifting. And Erika wasn't sure she could handle it.

She realized Kayla was still talking, still smiling, and Erika forced herself to stay present.

"That sounds really nice," Erika said, keeping her tone neutral. "He really went all out, huh?"

Kayla nodded, stirring her coffee absentmindedly. "Yeah. He did."

Erika took a slow sip of her own coffee, needing the distraction. "So… what does this mean? Are you guys back together?"

Kayla hesitated.

"I don't know," she admitted. "It's complicated."

Erika felt a flicker of hope at that answer.

Complicated. That meant there was still uncertainty. That meant Kayla wasn't gone yet.

And if she wasn't sure… then maybe there was still a chance.

"I just…" Kayla sighed. "I want to take things slow. I want to be sure I'm making the right choice and not falling back into something just because it's familiar."

Erika's stomach twisted at that.

She wanted to tell Kayla to choose her, to take a chance on something new instead of trying to fix something that was already broken. Because she wanted to be the right choice.

But she couldn't.

She knew Kayla wasn't ready to hear that yet.

Instead, Erika forced herself to smile, even though it felt like her chest was caving in. "That makes sense," she said, keeping her voice light. "You deserve to take your time."

Kayla smiled, reaching across the desk and squeezing Erika's hand. "Thank you. For always being here for me."

Erika felt the warmth of Kayla's touch, the softness of her skin. It took everything in her not to pull Kayla forward and kiss her right then and there.

Instead, she just nodded.

"Always," Erika said softly.

And as she left Kayla's office, she realized this was going to hurt like hell.

Because no matter how much she loved Kayla, she wasn't sure if Kayla would ever be hers.

68

The moment Quinn and Kayla stepped into their therapist's office, Dr. Simmons noticed a difference.

There was a subtle shift between them, an almost imperceptible lightness in the air. The heaviness that once loomed over their sessions — the awkward tension, the resentment, the heartbreak — was still there, but diluted.

They didn't sit with a canyon of space between them like they had before.

And they were making eye contact.

Dr. Simmons clasped her hands together, leaning slightly forward in her chair. "You both look... different today," she observed, a small knowing smile forming on her lips. "Tell me, what's changed?"

Quinn and Kayla exchanged a glance.

Kayla let out a soft chuckle, tilting her head slightly. "I guess we actually had a... good date?" she said, as if testing the words out.

Quinn nodded, grinning. "Yes. A really good one."

Dr. Simmons's eyebrows lifted. "That's great. Why don't you walk me through it?"

Quinn and Kayla began telling the story together, each adding little details and commentary, overlapping at times like they were reliving it together.

Quinn started, leaning forward. "So, I really wanted to do

something different this time. Something that wasn't predictable."

Kayla nodded. "Which, honestly, was refreshing," she admitted with a teasing smirk. "He told me to bring my swimsuit, and I had no idea what to expect."

Quinn laughed. "Yeah, I could tell you were suspicious. But when we got there and walked through the lantern-lit path, I could see it on your face — you were actually excited."

Kayla's expression softened, remembering the moment. "I was. I mean, the cave itself was just... breathtaking. The way the light bounced off the water, the colors constantly shifting — it felt almost magical."

Quinn smiled, looking at her, his chest tightening at how beautiful she looked when she talked about it. "And then we got into the hot spring. The host brought us wine, and we ordered some food — small bites, things we could share."

Dr. Simmons took a note. "How did that feel? Sharing that experience together?"

Kayla took a breath, thinking. "It felt... nice," she admitted. "Like, for the first time in a long time, we weren't just co-existing. We were actually just... there. Together. No pressure, no expectations."

Quinn added, "And we talked. Like, really talked. Not about Zeke, or work, or our problems. Just... life. It felt like when we first started dating."

Kayla nodded, looking down at her hands. "I think that's what got to me the most. It reminded me of... us."

Dr. Simmons smiled warmly. "That's wonderful to hear. It sounds like you both reconnected in a meaningful way. Quinn, it seems like you really put effort into this."

Quinn nodded, glancing at Kayla. "I realized Kayla was right – I had gotten too comfortable. I stopped trying to make her feel special, and that was a huge mistake. She deserves to feel like she's being pursued, not just settled for."

Kayla's lips parted slightly, as if surprised by his words.

She looked away, blinking back unexpected emotion.

Dr. Simmons sat back. "Quinn, that's an important realization. And Kayla, how does it feel hearing him say that?"

Kayla hesitated, then softly smiled. "It... means a lot."

* * *

Dr. Simmons let a beat of silence pass before shifting the conversation.

"Now, while I think this is wonderful progress, I do want to remind you both not to rush into conclusions about what this means for your future just yet," she cautioned.

Quinn and Kayla both nodded.

"I also think it's important we address the other major factor in this dynamic - your relationship with Erika."

Kayla stiffened slightly.

Dr. Simmons gave her an encouraging look. "Kayla, I know this is complicated for you. Can you tell me where your head is with that right now?"

Kayla let out a slow breath, choosing her words carefully. "There… hasn't been anything else between us since the last time. No more physical things."

Dr. Simmons nodded. "But emotionally?"

Kayla shifted in her seat. "That's… harder to answer."

Quinn, who had been sitting quietly, observing, noted something. Every time Kayla spoke about Erika, she lit up in a way that she didn't even realize. Her fingers subconsciously traced over her wrist, a small smile playing at the corner of her lips.

He had spent years watching Kayla, learning her body language, the way she reacted to certain things. And now, for the first time, he saw something undeniable.

Erika wasn't just a fling to Kayla.

She wasn't just a friend.

She was something more.

Something important.

Something that could very well change everything.

He swallowed, forcing himself to stay calm. He wasn't sure what he wanted to feel. Jealousy? Anger? Or relief?

Because if Kayla loved Erika — truly, deeply — then maybe… maybe he wasn't the one she needed.

And as much as that thought terrified him, he also wanted Kayla to be happy. Even if it wasn't with him.

Dr. Simmons, sensing the shift in energy, looked between them. "Quinn, how are you feeling hearing all of this?"

He was quiet for a long moment. Then, finally, he exhaled.

"I don't know," he admitted, looking down. "I don't want to lose her. But... I also don't want to stand in the way of whatever makes her happy."

Kayla turned toward him, startled by his response. She had expected anger, maybe even an argument. But instead... Quinn was considering the possibility.

That scared her, because if he let her go too easily... Did that mean he had already given up on them?

Dr. Simmons, sensing the weight of the moment, spoke carefully. "I think this is a crossroads for both of you. Kayla, you're exploring who you are in a way that maybe you hadn't before. And Quinn, you're showing remarkable maturity by wanting Kayla's happiness even if it comes at the cost of your own."

She folded her hands. "But I urge you both not to make any final decisions right now. Take this time to keep learning, keep growing."

Kayla bit her lip, nodding. "That's what I want too. I don't have answers yet. I just... need to figure it out."

Quinn nodded as well, though a part of him felt like time was slipping through his fingers.

Towards the end of the session, Dr. Simmons redirected them.

"So, let's talk about the next date."

Kayla and Quinn exchanged a look.

"I think we should do something completely different," Quinn said. "Something where we have fun, let loose."

Kayla considered this. "Like what?"

Quinn smirked. "What about... rock climbing?"

Kayla blinked, surprised by the suggestion. "Rock climbing?"

"Yeah," he said. "Something we've never done together before. Something where we can just be in the moment, laughing, pushing ourselves. No pressure, just... fun."

Kayla smiled genuinely for the first time in the session. "You know what? I actually love that idea."

Dr. Simmons nodded approvingly. "That sounds like a great plan."

She folded her hands together. "I want you both to go on that date, experience it, and then come back next session ready to discuss your future. No holding back."

They both nodded.

As the session wrapped up, Quinn and Kayla walked out together, both lost in their own thoughts.

Kayla was still torn between Quinn and Erika.

And Quinn… he was preparing for the possibility that he might have to let Kayla go.

69

The past week had been torture for Kayla.

Every morning, she woke up with the same ache in her chest — the same unanswered question looping in her head.

What do I want?

She had been so sure that she wanted to repair things with Quinn. That she needed to fix her family, to restore the life they had before everything spiraled.

But the problem was... she wasn't the same person anymore.

And neither was Quinn.

Their time apart, their swinging experiences, the betrayals, the awakening of new desires — everything had changed them.

And then... there was Erika.

Kayla didn't expect to fall for her, not really. At first, their intimacy had been new, thrilling, a way to explore a part of herself she never fully acknowledged. But now? Now it was so much more than that.

Erika made her feel light. Made her feel like herself again. There was no weight of a failing marriage, no pressure, no expectations — just happiness.

But how could she walk away from Quinn? From Zeke? From the life they had built together?

She had spent so much time blaming Quinn for his infidelity, for straying from their marriage, for losing sight of them. But hadn't she done the same thing? Hadn't she let her feelings for Erika cloud her judgment? Hadn't she, too, made a decision to betray him?

How could she expect Quinn to forgive her when she still didn't even know if she wanted to be with him?

The thought haunted her.

She was drowning in the weight of indecision, feeling like she was trapped in a purgatory between two lives — one with Quinn, and one with Erika.

Ever since Kayla had told Erika about the hot springs date, things had been different between them.

At first, she had brushed it off, thinking maybe Erika was just busy. But as the days passed, the change in her became impossible to ignore.

The playful banter? Gone.

The lingering touches? Gone.

The flirting that had once felt like second nature between them? Completely absent.

Every time Kayla asked Erika to grab drinks, she made an excuse. Every time they passed each other at work, Erika barely looked at her. It was like she was pulling away, brick by brick, walling herself off. And Kayla hated it.

She hated how much she missed her. How much she ached for their closeness again.

Maybe it wasn't fair to Erika. Maybe she had put her in an impossible situation, asking her to wait in the shadows while Kayla tried to figure out what she wanted.

But that didn't mean it wasn't hurting Kayla too.

And it wasn't just about the sex, or the passion, or the thrill of being wanted.

It was about Erika, the person.

Her best friend. The one who always made her feel safe. The one who could read her emotions without her saying a word. The one who made her laugh until she cried.

Kayla had never needed anyone the way she needed Erika. Not in the same way.

And now?

She was losing her.

By the end of the week, Kayla couldn't take it anymore.

She waited until she saw Erika step into her office, watching as she settled behind her desk. Then, without hesitation, Kayla followed her in and shut the door firmly behind her.

Erika glanced up from her computer, her expression neutral, unreadable. "Hey."

Kayla's heart squeezed. That simple, distant greeting felt like a knife to the gut.

"Hey," Kayla said softly, but there was a determination in her voice. She folded her arms, taking a slow breath. "Are you gonna tell me what's going on?"

Erika's fingers froze over her keyboard. "What do you mean?"

Kayla let out a sharp laugh, shaking her head. "Are you serious? You've been acting like a complete stranger all week, Erika."

"I've been busy," Erika muttered, focusing on her screen.

Kayla stepped closer, her voice rising slightly. "Bullshit. You're not avoiding me because you're busy. You're avoiding me because of Quinn."

At the mention of his name, Erika's jaw tightened.

Kayla sighed, softer now. "Erika… I get it. I know this hasn't been fair to you. I know I haven't been fair to you."

Erika kept her eyes fixed on the screen.

Kayla swallowed the lump in her throat. "But can you at least talk to me? I feel like I'm losing you, and I… I can't stand that."

Finally, Erika exhaled, pushing herself away from the desk and standing up. She turned toward the window, her back facing Kayla.

"Kayla… what do you want me to say?" she said quietly.

Kayla took another step forward, her throat tightening. "I want you to tell me why you're shutting me out."

Erika turned, her eyes flashing with frustration. "Because this hurts, Kayla."

Kayla's breath hitched.

Erika shook her head. "Do you have any idea what it's like to sit here and listen to you talk about trying to fix things with Quinn while I'm over here feeling like an afterthought?"

Kayla's lips parted, but Erika kept going.

"I am in love with you, Kayla."

The words hit like a bomb, sucking all the air out of the room.

Kayla froze, her pulse roaring in her ears.

Erika shook her head, letting out a shaky laugh. "God, I promised myself I wasn't gonna say that. I was gonna wait. But screw it — I love you."

Kayla's eyes stung. She felt lightheaded, like the floor beneath her had suddenly vanished.

Erika ran a hand through her hair, looking exhausted. "And the worst part? I don't even know if it matters to you. Because you're still trying to piece things together with Quinn, and I'm just — what? Some experiment? A phase?"

Kayla felt tears swell in her eyes. "You're not a phase."

Erika's voice was hoarse. "Then what am I?"

Kayla swallowed thickly, her hands clenching into fists at her sides. "I don't know."

Erika let out a bitter laugh, shaking her head. "That's the problem, Kay. You don't know. And I can't keep sitting here waiting for you to figure it out."

Kayla felt a tear slip down her cheek, her whole body trembling.

She took a step closer, her voice breaking. "Please don't do this. Please don't push me away."

Erika closed her eyes, her shoulders rising and falling with a shaky breath.

When she opened them again, there was something softer there — something broken.

After a long pause, she sighed.

"...you can come over tonight. We can talk," she whispered.

Kayla's breath caught.

Erika swallowed hard, looking her in the eyes. "If we're gonna talk about this... really talk about this... I need to do it somewhere that isn't here."

Kayla blinked back the burning behind her eyes, nodding. "Ok."

Erika gave her a final, unreadable look before moving past her and opening the door.

Kayla hesitated, turning back one last time.

Erika's voice was quiet. "Tonight."

Kayla nodded before slipping out the door, her heart racing.

She had no idea what tonight would bring.

But she knew one thing for certain — she wasn't ready to lose Erika.

By the time Kayla left work, her nerves were shredded.

She sat in her car for a solid five minutes, gripping the steering wheel, trying to force herself to breathe.

It was ridiculous. She had been to Erika's dozens of times before. But this time... this time felt different.

Because this time, she wasn't just going to talk to her best friend.

She was going to have to face her feelings. She was going to have to figure out the truth. And she had no idea what that truth was going to be.

With a deep, shaky breath, she turned the key in the ignition and pulled out of the parking lot.

The entire drive to Erika's was a blur. Her mind was racing, her emotions twisting in ways she couldn't even name.

She kept glancing at her phone, half-expecting a text from Quinn. He had been so hopeful after their last date. She knew he was still holding onto the idea of fixing their marriage. But how could she fix something when she wasn't even sure she wanted to?

Her stomach twisted.

She didn't want to hurt him, but she also didn't want to lie to herself.

By the time she pulled up to Erika's apartment, her hands were shaking.

She turned off the car and sat there for a moment, staring at the building, her heart pounding so hard she could feel it in her throat.

Then, before she could twist herself into a spiral, she grabbed her purse, got out of the car, and walked inside.

Erika opened the door before Kayla even knocked.

Her eyes were tired, her expression guarded.

For the first time since they had met, Kayla realized that Erika was afraid of her.

Afraid of what she was going to say.

Afraid of being rejected.

Afraid of getting hurt.

The sight of it made Kayla's chest ache.

"Come in," Erika said softly, stepping aside.

Kayla swallowed hard and walked inside, her stomach in knots.

The apartment smelled like lavender and chamomile, a soft, soothing scent that had always made Kayla feel at home.

But tonight? Tonight, it felt different. More intimate. More dangerous.

Erika led her to the couch, then sat down, tucking her legs beneath her. Kayla hesitated for a moment before sinking down beside her. A heavy silence stretched between them.

Erika was the first to break it.

"You came," she said quietly.

Kayla nodded. "Of course I did."

Erika gave a soft, humorless laugh. "I wasn't sure if you would."

Kayla bit her lip, her throat tight.

"I'm sorry," she whispered.

Erika's eyes flickered. "For what?"

Kayla exhaled, feeling the weight of everything pressing down on her.

"For all of this," she admitted. "For dragging you into something so messy. For making you feel like you were… waiting around for me to figure myself out."

Erika shook her head. "You didn't make me feel that way, Kay. I just… I let myself hope for something I didn't even know I could have."

Kayla's heart twisted. "And now?"

Erika took a deep breath, then looked her right in the eyes.

"Now, I need to know where we stand," she said. "Because I love you, Kayla. But I can't keep being something you hide in the background while you try to fix things with Quinn."

Kayla's eyes burned.

"I don't want to hide you," she whispered.

Erika searched her face. "Then what do you want?"

Kayla's breath hitched.

She didn't know. She wanted Quinn. She wanted Erika. She wanted her family. She wanted her freedom. She wanted everything.

And she couldn't have it all.

Tears slipped down her cheeks. "I don't know," she admitted, her voice barely more than a breath.

Erika's face fell.

Kayla let out a shaky laugh, wiping at her eyes. "I wish I did. I wish it were simple. But it's not. It's so not."

Erika nodded, her own expression pained. "Then let's make it simple," she said.

Kayla looked at her, confused. "What do you mean?"

Erika swallowed hard, then reached out — softly, hesitantly — cupping Kayla's cheek.

Kayla's breath stuttered.

"If you don't know what you want," Erika whispered, "then let me help you figure it out."

Then, before Kayla could overthink, before she could pull away, before she could talk herself out of it — Erika kissed her.

And Kayla? Kayla let her. She melted into it, gripping Erika's waist, pulling her closer, letting herself feel instead of think.

The moment their lips met, the uncertainty faded.

For the first time in weeks, Kayla wasn't drowning in confusion.

Because in that moment, in Erika's arms, everything felt right.

Erika pulled her closer, whispering, "What do you feel for me?"

Kayla, breathless, heart pounding, finally knew.

She looked into Erika's eyes and whispered, "I'm so madly in love with you."

70

Quinn sat on the edge of the chair in his hotel room, hands clasped together, staring at the floor. The room around him felt too quiet, too impersonal. It wasn't home.

Home was Kayla. Home was Zeke. Home was the life he had broken apart with his own hands.

He let out a slow breath, rubbing his palms against his jeans. It had been a little over a week since the hot springs date, and for the first time in what felt like a long time, he felt something he hadn't dared to allow himself to feel before — hope.

Kayla had smiled at him that night. A real smile. She had leaned in for a kiss, even if it was just on his cheek. She had told him that it was a real date, that she had felt something again, even if she hadn't explicitly said the words.

For the first time in a long time, he felt like he had a chance.

But that chance came with fear. The kind that gnawed at the edges of his confidence, the kind that kept him up at night staring at the ceiling.

Because there was one thing he couldn't ignore.

Erika.

Every time Kayla talked about her, something changed in her eyes. She tried to sound neutral, like she was still figuring things out, but Quinn could see through it.

Kayla wasn't just confused. She was in love with Erika.

And that scared the hell out of him.

Cheating on Kayla had been the biggest mistake of Quinn's life.

And now, standing at the edge of losing her, he was starting to truly understand why he had done it in the first place.

It wasn't just about temptation.

It wasn't just about Simone's beauty.

It wasn't just about thrill-seeking.

It was about insecurity.

Kayla was his world, but for so long, he had felt like he was losing her. And instead of doing the hard work of fixing things, he ran to another woman.

He had tried to feel powerful again. Desired. Wanted.

And in doing so, he had destroyed the one person who had truly made him feel like he was enough.

And now?

Now, the tables had turned. Now, he was the one watching Kayla slip away. Now, he was the one who felt powerless.

Because this wasn't just about another man.

If Kayla had been sleeping with some guy, Quinn could have rationalized it, could have tried to compete.

But this was Erika.

A woman.

Someone who could give Kayla something he never could. And that terrified him.

What if Kayla was starting to realize that she didn't just want a life with Quinn? What if she was starting to see that a future with Erika made more sense? What if, despite all of his efforts to win her back, it was already too late?

That fear had driven Quinn to make changes.

Real ones.

For the past three weeks, he had been hitting the gym every morning before work, pushing his body in ways he hadn't in years.

When he and Kayla had first gotten together, he had been fit, active, strong.

Then life had settled in — marriage, fatherhood, work stress — and he let himself slip.

He stopped trying, not just in their marriage, but everything. But now? Now he was pushing himself. Lifting heavier. Running farther. Sweating out his demons. He had lost five pounds since moving into the hotel. He felt sharper. More focused. For both Kayla and himself.

Because the truth was, he hadn't liked who he had become either.

And if he had any hope of fixing things with Kayla, he couldn't just talk about change.

He had to become the man she deserved.

Quinn exhaled deeply and reached for his phone.

It was time to plan their next date.

This was the one.

If the last date had been about reconnecting, this one had to be about proving something.

Kayla had told him that their last date was perfect because he had tried so hard to make it that way. He needed to do that again.

He needed something exciting. Rock climbing was bold. It was different. And, if he was honest, it was a little terrifying. He had never been great with heights, but that didn't matter because this was about showing Kayla that he wasn't afraid to take risks for her.

That he was willing to push past his fears — for her.

That he was still the man who could make her heart race.

He typed out the text.

Hey. I have our next date planned. Wear something comfortable. Sneakers, not heels. Remember, we're going rock climbing. You'll thank me later.

He hesitated for a second before hitting send.

Then he exhaled, leaned back on the bed, and stared at the ceiling.

This was it.

This was make or break.

As Quinn lay in bed that night, his mind wandered to what came next.

What if this date was amazing? What if she laughed, smiled, looked at him the way she used to? What if she chose him?

Could he really just forget about Erika? Could he really erase the way Kayla's eyes lit up when she talked about her? Would he ever feel like enough if Kayla's heart was split in two?

He hated the idea of sharing her and he hated the idea of knowing that some part of her would never fully be his again.

But… maybe that was the price of forgiveness.

Maybe that was the cost of the life he had broken.

And maybe — just maybe — if he was strong enough to accept it, he could finally be the man she needed him to be.

Even if it meant learning to live with her loving someone else.

His phone buzzed beside him. He grabbed it, heart pounding.

Kayla: *"You still want to go rock climbing? Seriously? Are you trying to kill me?"*

Quinn chuckled, shaking his head.

Then another message came through.

Kayla: *"Fine. But if I break something, I'm making you pay my medical bills."*

A grin spread across Quinn's face. This was his chance and he wasn't going to waste it.

71

Quinn had been up since dawn, his stomach a tangled mess of nerves.

It wasn't about the date itself. He was excited to see Kayla again, to keep building on what they had started at the hot springs.

No, the nerves came from the fact that he was terrified of heights.

And today, he had decided that their date would be rock climbing.

Brilliant choice, Quinn, he thought to himself sarcastically as he pulled on a pair of athletic shorts and a moisture-wicking t-shirt. He laced up his sneakers and grabbed his keys, hoping Kayla wouldn't sense how much he was secretly dreading this.

The date had to be perfect, and if that meant pushing through his fear of plummeting to his death in a controlled indoor setting, then so be it.

When Quinn knocked on the door, he could hear Kayla calling out, "Hold on, hold on! I swear, I hate shoelaces."

A moment later, the door swung open, and Kayla stood there in black leggings, a fitted tank top, and sneakers. Her hair was up in a ponytail, her face fresh and natural.

He was stunned for a second.

It had been so long since he had seen her like this — casual, effortless, yet still breathtaking.

"You look..." he started, then smirked. "Like a woman about to be humiliated in a rock-climbing competition."

Kayla scoffed and crossed her arms. "Oh, please. I am going to destroy you."

Quinn chuckled, stepping aside as she grabbed her bag and locked the door.

On the drive to the climbing gym, they bantered back and forth.

"So, what made you pick rock climbing?" Kayla asked, stretching her legs out in the car.

"I thought it would be fun. Something different."

"You mean something dangerous?"

"It's only dangerous if you let go," Quinn said with a grin.

Kayla rolled her eyes. "That's literally the definition of dangerous."

He shrugged. "I figured if you did fall, at least I have life insurance on you."

Kayla gasped dramatically, slapping his arm. "Oh my God! You're terrible. You need help."

Quinn laughed, enjoying the way she smiled — a real, genuine smile.

It was moments like this that reminded him what he was fighting for.

When they arrived, the climbing gym was massive. Tall walls covered in colorful holds stretched up toward the ceiling, some with easier routes, others looking like they required superhuman strength.

Kayla looked around, eyebrows raised. "Ok, I was picturing a cute little wall, not a freaking indoor Mount Everest."

Quinn chuckled. "What, scared already?"

"No," she said quickly. "I just... might fake an injury before we start."

"Nice try."

A young instructor led them to the orientation area, where they were fitted with harnesses and given a brief safety lesson.

"Alright, so the most important thing," the instructor said, "is to always check your harness before you climb. If you don't, well… gravity takes over."

Kayla leaned toward Quinn. "He really sucks at making this sound fun."

Quinn smirked. "Yeah, I think I preferred not knowing the actual risk."

After going over proper hand placements and belay commands, the instructor clapped his hands together. "Alright, you're ready to climb!"

Quinn shot Kayla a grin. "Shall we?"

Kayla sighed. "If I die, haunt Simone first, then come back and check on me."

Quinn laughed hard, shaking his head. "Deal."

They stood in front of their respective climbing walls, harnessed in, chalk dust floating around them.

"Alright," Kayla said, tightening her grip. "First one to the top wins."

"Damn. That's a lot of pressure."

"Afraid?"

Quinn scoffed. "Please. You're the one who almost backed out at the door."

"Shut up and climb."

They both grabbed onto the first holds, and Quinn instantly realized something important — this was WAY harder than it looked.

Kayla, surprisingly, was moving quickly. She had natural balance and flexibility, stretching her legs and reaching holds with ease.

Quinn, on the other hand, felt like a dysfunctional, drunk spider, gripping onto holds for dear life.

"Oh my God," Kayla laughed from a few feet above him. "You look like a baby deer."

Quinn gritted his teeth. "I am strategizing, thank you very much."

Kayla grinned and pulled herself up higher. "You better hurry up, old man."

"I am literally one year older than you!"

Kayla smirked. "A lot can happen in a year."

Quinn, after finally figuring out this climbing thing, was nearly to the top, arms burning but determined to win.

Kayla was slightly behind him, but not by much.

Then, suddenly —

A blood-curling scream.

A loud, panicked yelp echoed through the gym, making Quinn's heart plunge into his stomach.

His head snapped downward. "Kayla?!"

In that instant, his grip slipped. Before he could process what was happening, his foot lost its hold, and — WHOOSH. He fell.

Not far, thanks to the safety ropes, but enough to send a wave of panic through his body as he dangled mid-air.

Then he heard Kayla's laughter.

Quinn blinked, looking down to see her still firmly on the wall, grinning ear to ear.

"You… you tricked me?!" he asked, still hanging in his harness.

Kayla burst into more laughter. "Oh my God, I can't believe that worked!"

Quinn groaned, rubbing his face. "You are evil."

Kayla smirked. "No, I am victorious."

She climbed the last few feet and rang the small bell at the top.

Quinn shook his head, still hanging, still processing the betrayal.

"I'm filing for a rematch," he muttered.

Kayla grinned down at him. "That's loser talk."

Quinn chuckled, shaking his head. "You are ridiculous."

"And you are hanging there like a sad little bat."

"I am re-evaluating all my life choices."

Kayla smirked. "Should I come down and help you?"

Quinn sighed dramatically. "I'll find my own way, thank you."

Once they were both safely back on the ground, Quinn pulled off his harness and turned to Kayla and said, "That was a dirty trick."

Kayla shrugged innocently. "I don't know what you're talking about."

"You screamed."

"You fell."

Quinn narrowed his eyes playfully. "I hope you know this means war."

Kayla arched a brow. "Oh? What's next, a thumb war? Maybe an overly dramatic staring contest?"

Quinn smirked. "Nope. Because this date isn't over."

Kayla raised an eyebrow.

Quinn nodded. "There's one more stop before I take you home."

Kayla crossed her arms. "You planned a two-part date?"

Quinn shrugged. "Gotta keep you on your toes."

Kayla smiled, shaking her head. "Fine. But if this next part involves skydiving, I'm out."

Quinn chuckled. "Nope. Trust me."

She exhaled. "Fine. I'll trust you. For now."

Quinn grinned. "Then let's go."

And with that, they walked out together, smiling, laughing — just like they used to. It wasn't just a date. It was progress.

72

Kayla had almost canceled their third date.

She could have said she was sick. She could have said work was overwhelming. Hell, she could have simply said, *I don't think I can do this anymore.*

But she didn't. Because despite everything, she still owed him this much. She owed him one last date, one last attempt to reconnect. For their family.

She had made up her mind before she even stepped out of the house, though. This was just an obligation, a way to make sure there wasn't anything left between them, before she walked away for good.

Because deep down, she was starting to believe that her future wasn't with Quinn.

It was with Erika.

From the second she opened the door and saw Quinn standing there — dressed nicely, holding another bouquet of deep red roses, smiling that old familiar smile — her resolve wavered.

It wasn't the flowers, though those were a nice touch.

It was the effort. The fact that he was trying again, in a way he hadn't in years. That alone was worth something, wasn't it?

She let him in, accepted the flowers with a small, polite smile, and told herself she just had to get through the night.

But then, he made her laugh.

And for the first time in a long time, it wasn't forced.

As soon as they arrived at the climbing gym, Kayla was thrown off balance.

Not because of the actual climbing — though that was intimidating enough — but because Quinn seemed so comfortable, so effortlessly charming.

It was like stepping back into a different version of their relationship, one where they were still young, still playful, still *them*.

"Well, well, well," Quinn said as they looked up at the towering rock wall. "I hope you're ready for a humiliating defeat."

Kayla snorted. "Humiliating? Honey, you'll be lucky to make it halfway up before your arms give out."

Quinn clutched his chest dramatically. "Wow. Disrespectful."

She smirked, crossing her arms. "I call it realistic."

He stepped closer, his voice dropping. "Just so you know, when I beat you, I expect an official apology. In writing."

He then leaned in slightly. "But… if *you* somehow win? I'll do whatever you want for a full day. No questions asked."

Kayla's lips twitched. "You're really gonna regret saying that."

Kayla had expected to tolerate the date. She hadn't expected to have this much fun.

The climbing was challenging, sure, but it was the teasing, the competition, the lightheartedness that made her forget everything else.

Every time Quinn struggled to reach a hold, she mocked him. Every time Kayla hesitated, he egged her on mercilessly.

At one point, she paused, catching her breath, and Quinn smirked.

"What's wrong? Getting tired?"

Kayla scoffed. "Tired? No. Bored? Absolutely."

Quinn chuckled. "Uh-huh. You just rest up while I take first place."

Kayla narrowed her eyes. "First place? Oh, it's on now."

She surged ahead, pushing herself to beat him.

And she did.

But not before tricking him into falling off the wall.

His expression — pure betrayal — as he dangled mid-air made her laugh so hard she almost fell herself.

"You… you tricked me?!" Quinn sputtered.

Kayla grinned, gripping the last hold. "I prefer the term outsmarted."

Quinn groaned. "You are evil."

Kayla rang the bell at the top. "You say that, but I just won."

Quinn sighed dramatically. "This is why we need marriage counseling."

Kayla burst into laughter, shaking her head. "Oh my God, shut up."

It was fun.

And that was the problem.

Because she hadn't had this kind of fun with Quinn in years.

Somewhere along the way, their relationship had turned into something comfortable but stagnant. They had love, sure. They had history. But they had lost the spark.

Tonight, though?

Tonight, she felt it again.

As she stood at the top of the climbing wall, looking down at Quinn hanging in the air — his grinning, breathless, competitive expression — a feeling hit her out of nowhere.

She wanted him, and not just in a physical way, though that was part of it.

She wanted this version of him. The one who laughed with her, who teased her, who pushed her to be competitive and spontaneous. She wanted the Quinn she had fallen in love with. The Quinn who had once chased after her like she was the most important thing in his world.

When had that stopped?

And when had she stopped chasing him back?

Memories hit her like a wave.

Their first date.

His carefully planned, *yet somehow effortless* way of making her feel special — convincing the restaurant staff to give them the last-minute table, laughing as he pulled her through a back entrance like a secret agent.

It had all been for her. Even if it was staged.

He had always put in the effort.

Until he didn't.

Until life got busy. Until they had Zeke. Until the routine settled in.

Somewhere along the way, their love had stopped being intentional. And maybe that was the real problem.

By the time they were driving to their next destination, Kayla was more confused than ever.

She had walked into this date thinking she knew exactly what she wanted. *Who* she wanted.

And now?

Now she wasn't sure of anything.

Quinn glanced at her as he drove. "You ok?"

Kayla blinked. "What? Yeah. Just tired."

Quinn smiled. "Tired from winning unfairly, you mean?"

Kayla huffed. "It was a strategy."

Quinn grinned. "A strategy to distract me and make me fall."

Kayla smirked. "And it worked."

He shook his head, chuckling. "Pure evil."

Kayla laughed, but inside, she was a mess.

She is in love with Erika.

But tonight, she had felt something real with Quinn again. And she didn't know what to do with that.

When they reached the next destination for their date, Quinn smirked and asked, "Since I lost, I'm assuming you're going to cash in that no-questions-asked favor?"

Kayla narrowed her eyes. "Oh, absolutely."

Quinn grinned. "I'm afraid to ask."

Kayla smirked. "You should be."

For the first time in months, it felt easy between them again.

As she stepped out of the car and turned to leave, she hesitated. Then, she leaned in and kissed his cheek, brushing the top of his hand with hers.

"Thanks, Quinn," she whispered.

Then, before he could respond, she got out and shut the car door.

She didn't have answers yet. But tonight had given her something to think about. And maybe… just maybe… that was enough.

73

Kayla followed Quinn down the dimly lit street, still trying to figure out where the hell he was taking her.

The climbing had been fun — way more fun than she had expected — and a part of her had almost hoped the date would end there. It was easier to leave things on a good note, to let the fun linger without getting too close.

But Quinn had other plans.

And now, here they were, walking toward a nondescript building with no sign, no windows — just a single unmarked door.

Kayla frowned, stopping in her tracks. "Ok, seriously, where are we?"

Quinn just smirked, pulling open the door. "You'll see."

The second they stepped inside, the first thing that hit her were the smells — warm vanilla, fresh-cut herbs, hints of citrus and musk blending together in a symphony of scent.

Then, the colors. Shelves stacked high with glass jars of wax, dried flowers, bits of herbs, and amber-colored oils in tiny bottles.

It wasn't a storefront. It was a workshop.

Kayla blinked, realization dawning.

They were in a candle-making studio.

A tall man in a worn leather apron approached, a bit of wax still clinging to his fingers. He looked like he belonged here — hands rough with work, an easy smile on his face.

"You must be Quinn," the man said, shaking his hand. "I'm Marco. Welcome."

Quinn nodded. "Yeah, thanks for having us. This is Kayla."

Marco turned to her, his eyes twinkling. "Kayla, huh? You ever make a candle before?"

Kayla smirked. "Nope. But I do buy a lot of them. Does that count?"

Marco chuckled. "It does. It means you have good taste. But tonight, you're going to learn how to make one from scratch — one that's unique to you."

Kayla arched a brow at Quinn. "So let me get this straight... we're making candles?"

Quinn grinned. "You love candles. I thought it'd be fun."

Kayla crossed her arms. "You hate candles."

Quinn shrugged. "Yeah, well, I'm making an exception."

She stared at him, trying to find any sign of sarcasm or teasing, but there was none.

This was real effort. And damn it, that meant something.

Marco led them to a large wooden table where different materials were spread out — wax blocks, dried herbs, small bowls of essential oils.

"So," Marco began, rolling up his sleeves. "The first step is to choose your base scent. You'll do this by picking three different elements — one floral, one herbal, and one deep wood or spice note."

Quinn looked lost immediately.

Kayla grinned. "Need help?"

Quinn scoffed. "No, I got this." He then grabbed the first three things his hands landed on — a bundle of lavender, a small bowl of sage, and a deep red cinnamon stick.

Marco examined his choices. "Interesting combo. Earthy, but with a hint of warmth."

Kayla looked at Quinn with mock suspicion. "You just picked the first things you saw, didn't you?"

Quinn smirked. "Absolutely."

Kayla laughed — a genuine, belly-deep laugh that surprised even herself.

She turned back to the table, running her fingers over the selection of ingredients.

Her fingers hovered over rose petals, then over vanilla bean shavings, and finally, she picked up cedarwood chips.

"Classic," Marco said approvingly. "Romantic, warm, and just a little grounded. I like it."

Kayla glanced at Quinn. "See? Mine actually makes sense."

Quinn rolled his eyes. "Teacher's pet."

They moved on to melting the wax, stirring it in small metal pitchers over gentle flames.

Quinn, naturally, made a mess within minutes.

"Quinn, you're spilling wax everywhere!" Kayla scolded, trying to suppress a laugh.

"It's part of my process," he shot back.

Marco watched them bicker with amusement. "You two must've been married a long time."

Kayla hesitated for half a second before answering. "Yeah… eight years."

Marco didn't pry. Instead, he just grinned. "That explains the bickering."

Quinn shot her a smug look. "See? It's charming."

Kayla snorted. "It's something."

As the wax melted, they mixed in their essential oils and dried elements, watching their candles take shape.

Kayla leaned close to Quinn's pot, sniffing the mixture. "Not bad. Smells like… a forest witch's secret recipe."

Quinn smirked. "Better than yours, which smells like a sexy lumberjack."

Kayla's face heated. "You say that like it's a bad thing."

Quinn's voice dropped just slightly. "Didn't say it was."

For half a second, something in the air shifted.

But before she could think about it, Marco clapped his hands together. "Alright, final step — pouring the wax into the jars."

They carefully poured their mixtures into small glass containers, each with a wick standing tall in the center. Marco labeled them with their initials. "Now, they need to sit overnight to cure. You'll be able to pick them up tomorrow."

Kayla looked at her candle, then at Quinn's. "So... we just made fire hazards together?"

Quinn grinned. "Romantic, right?"

Kayla laughed — because it was.

God help her, it actually was.

The night ended too soon.

Quinn drove her home, both of them quieter than before, lost in their own thoughts.

When they pulled up in front of her house, Kayla reached for the door handle of the car, ready to say a simple goodnight. But Quinn got out first. And before she could argue, he walked around and opened her door for her. She hesitated, then stepped out. They walked up the stone pathway and reached the front door.

She reached for a hug — something casual, easy.

But then, as their arms wrapped around each other, neither one pulled away.

Their faces were close. Too close.

Kayla could feel his breath, see the uncertainty in his eyes, feel the warmth of his hands against her back. Neither of them moved. Neither of them spoke. And then —

He kissed her.

Not a hesitant kiss. Not a mistake. A kiss that was deep, full of years of history, full of longing and regret and need.

Kayla melted into it, her hands gripping his jacket, her lips parting under his. This wasn't like before. It wasn't routine. It was like finding something they had lost.

When they finally broke apart, breathless, Kayla stared at him, her heart pounding.

Then, wordlessly, she turned and walked inside.

She closed the door, leaned against it, her hands shaking. Her head spun. Her body burned.

And all she could think was —

FUCK FUCK FUCK!

74

Kayla sat in her car miles away from home, parked at a scenic overlook, her phone face-down on the seat beside her.

She couldn't go.

She couldn't face Quinn.

She couldn't say it out loud. Because the second she did, it would be real. And she still didn't know if she was making the right decision.

Her hands gripped the steering wheel, knuckles white.

Her heart felt like it was ripping in half.

But in the end… she had made her choice.

Quinn had barely made it out of the therapist's office before pulling out his phone again.

His hands were shaking, but he wasn't sure if it was from anger, panic, or heartbreak. Maybe all three.

He didn't even wait to get to his car before he called Kayla again. Voicemail.

Jaw tightening, he tried one more time. Nothing.

By the time he sat down in the driver's seat, his emotions boiled over. He tossed his phone onto the passenger seat and slammed his palms against the steering wheel.

"Damn it, Kayla," he muttered under his breath, fighting back

251

tears of panic.

Why would she do this? Why would she make him believe there was hope, let him put everything he had into this, only to not show up?

Finally, after several long minutes of staring at the dashboard, he grabbed his phone and sent a text.

Quinn: *I deserve to know why you didn't show up.*

He sat there, staring at the screen, waiting.

A full minute passed. Then two. Then five.

Just when he was about to throw his phone out of the car window in frustration, it lit up with an incoming call.

Kayla.

He answered before the first ring finished.

"Kayla," he said, his voice sharp but controlled.

There was a long silence on the other end. He could hear her breathing, but she wasn't saying anything.

Finally, he exhaled and tried again, forcing his voice to soften. "Why, Kay? Why didn't you show up?"

More silence.

Then, in a voice so soft he almost didn't hear it, she said, "I couldn't do it."

Quinn's grip on the steering wheel tightened.

"Couldn't do what?" he pressed.

She hesitated. "I couldn't — I just —"

She sighed, and when she spoke again, her voice cracked. "I can't make that kind of life decision yet," she admitted.

Quinn closed his eyes, resting his forehead against the steering wheel. She wasn't ending things, but she wasn't choosing him either.

"Kayla," he said slowly, "I need to know what's going on inside your head. I need to know if—"

"I need time," she cut in. "And I need you to be ok with that."

Quinn swallowed hard.

She was asking for more time. More waiting. More uncertainty. But what choice did he have?

"Ok," he finally said, even though it wasn't ok at all.

Kayla exhaled in relief. "Thank you."

Quinn didn't respond.

There was nothing left to say.

After hanging up with Quinn, Kayla needed to breathe.

She needed to think.

Now, she sat in her car, parked at the scenic overlook, staring at the world stretching out in front of her. And she still didn't have a damn clue what to do.

Quinn was the safe choice. He was her husband, the father of her child. The man she had built a life with. The man she had once been so madly in love with that she had proposed to him first.

But Erika…

Erika was passion.

She made Kayla feel alive. Light. Free.

Being with Erika wasn't just about attraction. It was about how effortless everything felt. How she made her feel alive again.

Kayla could laugh with her for hours. Could talk to her about anything.

And when Erika touched her? It felt like lightning igniting every nerve in her body.

So how the hell was she supposed to choose?

How could she give up the life she built with Quinn? But how could she walk away from Erika when her heart ached for her every second?

Her thoughts spiraled, her stomach twisting into knots. Then, as if her body acted on its own, she picked up her phone and texted Erika.

Kayla: *Can I see you?*

A full minute passed before the dots appeared, and then—

Erika: *You know where I am.*

Kayla immediately turned the key in the ignition.

She knew exactly where she needed to be right now.

Meanwhile, Quinn sat in his car, gripping the steering wheel, replaying the conversation over and over again.

She needed time. But time for what?

She was still conflicted. And he knew why.

He had seen the way she lit up when she talked about Erika in therapy. He had seen how she hesitated every time he asked where they stood.

Kayla was in love with Erika. Maybe she hadn't admitted it to herself yet. Maybe she had. But Quinn knew the truth now.

It wasn't just about his mistake with Simone. It wasn't just about how distant they had become. Kayla hadn't just fallen out of love with him and had fallen for someone else. And maybe, just maybe, that was something he could never compete with.

For the first time since all of this started, Quinn felt something more terrifying than anger, more painful than jealousy, more crushing than regret. He felt defeated.

And for the first time…

He considered that maybe he needed to let Kayla go.

Even if it killed him.

When Kayla arrived at Erika's apartment, she didn't even hesitate before knocking.

The second Erika opened the door, Kayla was hit with a wave of emotion so intense it almost knocked her back.

Erika was, as always, beautiful, standing there in a loose sweatshirt and shorts, her blue eyes full of emotions that Kayla wasn't sure she was ready to face.

They stared at each other for a long moment. Then Erika sighed heavily, stepping back to let her in.

"You're running, aren't you?" Erika said softly, closing the door behind her.

Kayla swallowed hard. "I don't know what I'm doing."

Erika nodded slowly. "Do you love him?"

Kayla opened her mouth. Then closed it.

Did she love Quinn? Yes. Did she love him enough? She didn't know.

Erika exhaled through her nose. "Kayla, I told you, I love you."

Kayla's heart stopped. Her breath caught. Her entire body shivered.

And then, before she could talk herself out of it, Kayla whispered:

"I know, and I love you, too."

Erika stilled, searching her face. "Are you saying that because it's true? Or because you don't want to lose me?"

Kayla felt her stomach twist. Because the answer was both. And she didn't know what to do with that.

So instead of answering, she grabbed Erika's face and kissed her like she would never get the chance to again.

And maybe, just maybe, she wouldn't.

75

Kayla woke up to the sound of rain pattering softly against her bedroom window.

For a moment, she forgot everything – the turmoil, the weight of the decision she had to make.

She forgot about Quinn, about Erika, about the way her heart was being pulled in two opposite directions. But the second she opened her eyes, reality crashed back in like a tidal wave.

She groaned, pulling the blanket over her head, willing herself to disappear beneath it. She had never felt so exhausted. Her mind had been running in circles for days, endlessly dissecting every feeling, every moment, every possibility.

And she was no closer to an answer. She wanted Quinn. But… she also wanted Erika.

She wanted to have it all, but she knew she couldn't.

At some point, someone was going to get hurt and she was the one who had to decide who that would be.

For the next three days, Kayla disappeared.

She called in sick to work, making up an excuse about a stomach bug.

She ignored every single message and call from Quinn.

She ignored every single message and call from Erika.

She even kept her conversations with Zeke short, just enough to make sure he was fed, dressed, and taken care of. But she had no energy to engage, to be present.

She just… existed.

She spent most of those three days lying in bed, staring at the ceiling, trying to make a decision that refused to be made.

Her phone sat on the nightstand, buzzing every so often, but she couldn't bring herself to look. She knew that every unanswered text was another question she didn't have the answer to.

Quinn: *Hey, Kay, I just want to know if you're ok.*

Erika: *Kayla, I'm getting really worried. Just let me know you're alive.*

The more she ignored them, the guiltier she felt.

But she wasn't ready to talk. Because talking meant she had to decide. And deciding meant breaking someone's heart.

By the third day, Kayla had reached her breaking point.

She sat on the floor of her bedroom, her back against the bed frame, silent tears running down her face.

She had spent hours — days — trying to convince herself that there was a right answer.

That there was some perfect choice where nobody got hurt. But the truth was, there wasn't. She was going to lose someone. And she had to be ok with that.

For the first time in three days, she picked up her phone.

She scrolled through all the unread messages, her stomach twisting with each one.

Then she took a deep breath.

And finally…

She made a decision.

Her hands were shaking as she typed the text.

She read it over three times before pressing send.

It was simple. Straight to the point. But it carried the weight of everything.

Come to the house tomorrow night at 7.

She put her phone down, exhaling sharply.

The decision was made. Now there was no turning back.

76

Quinn stood at the front door to the house, his stomach churning like a storm brewing in the distance.

He couldn't shake the feeling that this was it. This was when everything would come crashing down. He had been preparing himself for the worst all day, running through every possible scenario in his mind. Would Kayla tell him it was over? Would she tell him she had chosen Erika? Or would she still be caught in the middle, unable to choose?

He didn't know, and that terrified him.

Taking a deep breath, he knocked.

A few seconds later, the door opened.

And there she was. Kayla. His wife. The love of his life. And she was smiling at him. A warm, genuine smile. His heart leapt with a sudden, irrational hope.

"Hey," she said softly.

"Hey," he responded, his voice barely above a whisper.

She stepped aside, motioning for him to come in.

As he followed her inside, he tried to read her body language — was she nervous? Excited? Relieved? He couldn't tell.

"I was gonna stop in the kitchen, maybe grab a glass of wine," he said, trying to keep things light.

Kayla shook her head. "I already have a bottle open in the living room."

Something in her tone made Quinn's stomach drop. Whatever was about to happen, it wasn't casual.

It was deliberate.

When he turned the corner into the living room, he froze. Sitting on the couch, looking just as startled as he felt, was Erika. His entire body went rigid.

"What…?" He swallowed, his throat suddenly dry. "What's going on?"

He looked at Kayla, then back at Erika. Erika's brows were furrowed, her hands clasped tightly in her lap. "I have no idea," she admitted.

Kayla exhaled slowly, asked Quinn to sit on the couch with Erika, and then walked over and sat down in the chair across from them. She laced her fingers together, resting them in her lap.

The silence in the room was heavy, stretching unbearably between them. Neither Quinn nor Erika spoke. They were waiting. Waiting for Kayla to find the words.

And for a moment, it seemed like she couldn't.

She opened her mouth. Closed it. Took a deep breath. Tried a few more times. Finally, her voice came out in a whisper.

"I don't know how to say this."

Quinn leaned forward, his elbows on his knees, hands clasped. "Just say it, Kayla."

Kayla swallowed, staring down at her lap.

"When this all started," she began, "I thought it was just about us finding excitement again. I thought it was about fixing something that had come to feel… stagnant."

Quinn's jaw tightened. He had thought the same thing.

She continued.

"But somewhere along the way… it became so much more than that."

She glanced at Erika, her expression pained.

"I didn't expect this to happen. I didn't expect to feel the way I do now. And I know I've been avoiding the truth, hiding from it because I didn't want to face what it meant."

Quinn's pulse pounded in his ears. Kayla looked back at him.

"I love you, Quinn."

His breath hitched.

"But…"

And there it was. The word that cut through everything.

"But I love Erika, too."

Quinn blinked, trying to process the words. He had suspected it, had seen it in the way Kayla lit up when she talked about Erika. But hearing it out loud? It felt like a knife to the gut.

Erika sat frozen beside him, her face pale, her lips slightly parted. "Kayla…"

Kayla shook her head, her voice stronger now. "I love you both. And I don't know what to do about it."

Silence. Long, unbearable silence.

Then Quinn cleared his throat, his voice rough.

"Well, you have to make a choice."

Kayla's eyes snapped up to his. "Do I?" she whispered.

His brows furrowed. "What?"

She exhaled deeply, looking at both of them.

"What if I don't want to choose?"

Erika stiffened. Quinn's jaw clenched.

Kayla pressed on.

"What if there's another way?"

Quinn felt a pit form in his stomach. "Kayla, what are you saying?"

Kayla hesitated.

Then, slowly, she looked at Erika.

Then at Quinn.

And then she dropped the bombshell.

"I want you two to fuck."

The words hung in the air like a grenade with the pin just pulled.

Quinn felt his entire body lock up. Erika's eyes widened, her lips parting in shock.

"What?" Erika breathed.

Kayla didn't flinch. "I want you two to have sex."

Quinn let out a dry laugh, shaking his head. "Kayla, what the actual fuck?"

Erika was staring at Kayla like she had grown a second head. "You're joking, right?"

Kayla's gaze was steady. "I'm not."

Quinn leaned back, running his hands over his face. "This is insane," he muttered.

Kayla leaned forward. "No, what's insane is pretending that we haven't all been wrapped up in this impossible situation for months. What's insane is thinking that we can go back to the way things were without confronting what's right in front of us."

Quinn stared at her, still trying to process.

Kayla continued.

"I love you, Quinn. And I love you, Erika. But if there's even a chance of this working… if there's even a possibility of me not having to choose… then I need to see something."

Quinn's heart pounded. "See what?"

Kayla took a deep breath.

"I need to see if you two have any chemistry."

Erika exhaled sharply, shaking her head. "Kayla, I might be bisexual, but this—" She stopped herself, struggling to find the words. "I don't even know how to process this."

Kayla's voice was gentle now. "I'm not asking you to fall in love. I'm asking you to explore it. To see if this… this thing between the three of us… could actually work."

Quinn's stomach flipped. Could it work? Could he really share Kayla with Erika? And more than that… Could he really be intimate with Erika?

The thought sent conflicting waves through him.

She was undeniably beautiful. But she had always been Kayla's.

He looked at Erika, saw the conflict in her eyes. He saw the way she was processing, calculating, analyzing.

Then, slowly, Erika looked at him.

Then back at Kayla.

Then back at him.

77

Kayla sat on the edge of her seat, her heart pounding as she took in the stunned expressions on both Erika's and Quinn's faces. Silence stretched between them, thick with tension and uncertainty. She could see the disbelief in their eyes, their hesitancy, the unspoken questions they were struggling to put into words.

This was a pivotal moment, and she knew it. It was the moment where she would either lose them both or open a door to a future none of them had ever imagined.

She took a deep breath. "I know this is unexpected," she started, her voice softer now, less demanding than before. "But I need you both to understand why I'm asking this."

Quinn rubbed the back of his neck, shifting uncomfortably on the couch. "Kayla... what exactly are you asking for?" His voice was tight, cautious.

Erika, arms crossed, exhaled slowly, eyes darting between Kayla and Quinn. "Yeah, Kay, I... I don't understand."

Kayla swallowed hard. This was it. She had to lay it all out there. "I love you both," she admitted, her voice thick with emotion. "And I can't — I won't — choose between you."

Quinn blinked, stunned.

Erika's lips parted slightly, her breath catching. "Kayla..."

Kayla pressed forward before she lost her nerve. "You two give me different kinds of love, but they're both real, and they're both necessary. Losing either of you would break me." She clenched her hands together, tears forming in her eyes. "So I need to know if this can work. If we can be something together."

Quinn ran a hand over his face. "You're asking us to be in a relationship together?" His voice carried disbelief, but there was something else there too — a flicker of curiosity.

Erika's brows furrowed. "How would that even be possible?"

Kayla nodded. "I don't know. But I know we won't know unless we try. And before we even have that conversation, I need to see if you two have something between you. If there's chemistry."

Quinn shook his head, exhaling sharply. "Kayla, this isn't a science experiment."

"No," she agreed, her voice gentle now. "It's not. But you and Erika have never… crossed that line before. I need to know if you can. If there's something there, then maybe this — we — have a chance. If there's nothing… then we'll know."

The weight of her request settled over them again, and Quinn let out a slow breath. He looked at Erika, his eyes filled with uncertainty. "What are you thinking?"

Erika let out a nervous laugh, shaking her head. "I'm thinking this is insane." But then her expression softened as she looked at Kayla. "But… I trust you. And if this is truly what you need, then I'm willing to at least try."

Quinn hesitated, his jaw tightening. Then, after a long pause, he nodded. "Alright. Let's try."

They both stood and headed to the bedroom, but Kayla stopped them.

Kayla bit her lip. "I need to see it for myself."

Erika looked at Quinn, then back at Kayla, her fingers pressing into her thighs. "You want to watch?"

Kayla let out a breath she hadn't realized she was holding, relief washing over her. But now came the moment of truth. "Here," she whispered, motioning to the couch. "I want it to happen here."

Quinn and Erika exchanged glances. Then, with slow, measured movements, Erika turned toward Quinn. She reached out, fingers tracing along his jawline, testing the waters. Quinn inhaled sharply but didn't pull away. He tilted his head slightly, leaning into her touch.

Then, cautiously, Erika leaned in, pressing her lips to his.

At first, it was hesitant, unsure. Kayla could see their awkwardness, the uncertainty of newness between them. But as seconds passed, she saw the shift, saw the tension fade as instinct took over. The kiss deepened, slow and exploratory, and something inside Kayla twisted.

She watched as Quinn's hands found Erika's waist, pulling her closer, as Erika's fingers threaded through his hair. It was strange and surreal, watching this moment unfold, but it wasn't jealousy she felt. It was validation.

She leaned forward slightly, her breath catching when Quinn lifted Erika onto his lap, his hands splaying across her back. The intensity between them built, the initial awkwardness dissolving into something more organic, more fluid. More passionate.

Kayla's heart pounded. It's working.

They were getting lost in the moment, in each other. And Kayla now knew — knew that they could have something real. Knew that she wasn't crazy for wanting this, for wanting them both.

Erika broke away from Quinn, her gaze found Kayla's, searching. "Is this what you wanted?"

Kayla, breathless, nodded. "Yes."

But before she could say anything more, Quinn and Erika turned back to each other, their eyes now filled with something different. Curiosity had transformed into desire.

Quinn reached up, cupping Erika's face as he kissed her again, this time with more confidence. His hands explored her, learning the curves of her body, while Erika melted into him, matching his energy, letting herself go. Kayla watched, captivated by the way their hesitation morphed into hunger.

Erika slowly unbuttoned Quinn's shirt, sliding it off his shoulders. Kayla noticed the way Quinn's breath hitched, the way his hands tightened on Erika's hips as she ran her palms over his bare chest. He wasn't just responding — he was wanting this now.

Quinn lifted Erika slightly, guiding her onto the couch beside him, their bodies tangling in new ways. Kayla could see the fire in Erika's eyes, the way she gasped softly when Quinn kissed her neck, the way her fingers dug into his arms. It was real, it was electric.

She didn't just have her answer — she had hope.

78

The first month of their new reality was a delicate dance — a mixture of passion, learning, and adapting. Quinn moving back into the house had been a given, but what had truly changed everything was Erika moving in, too. It wasn't something they had planned out in great detail.

It had simply happened. The morning after their first night together as a throuple, Kayla had woken up tangled between the two of them, her head on Erika's chest and her hand curled into Quinn's. It felt right. It felt whole. And so, without much discussion, Erika started staying every night. A few days turned into a week. A week turned into two. And by the end of the month, it had become routine.

Eventually, they would look for a new house, one that was all three of theirs.

Adjusting to Their New Life

Adjusting to their new reality wasn't without its complications. They had to construct a careful narrative for Zeke and the outside world. They agreed early on that Erika's presence in the home couldn't seem unusual or out of place. The cover story was simple: Erika had recently ended the lease on her apartment and was staying with them temporarily until she figured out her next steps. Zeke, young and trusting, accepted this explanation without much question. To him, it was just more time with his favorite "Aunt Erika." They would explain their relationship to him over time.

But inside the walls of their home, the three of them were building something different, something intimate, something undefined but real. They had to set rules and boundaries, not just for Zeke's sake but for their own.

Sleeping Arrangements: Initially, Quinn and Kayla maintained their usual bedroom routine, and Erika would retreat to the guest room. But as days passed, the three of them found themselves longing for each other at night. So they developed a system. Quinn and Kayla's room became *the* bedroom — the space where they all retreated together after Zeke had gone to sleep. Erika's "room" remained just for appearances. If Zeke ever asked, she could truthfully say she had her own space. But in reality, once the house was quiet and the world outside had faded away, they would slip under the same sheets, Kayla sandwiched between the two people she loved.

Affection in the Home: They quickly realized though that they had to adjust their natural affection for each other when Zeke was around. While hugging and casual touches were normal in the house before, the kind of lingering gazes, stolen kisses, and whispered promises they now shared had to be carefully concealed. Instead, they poured their affection into small moments — gentle touches in passing, long glances over dinner, fingers brushing against each other as they passed plates or folded laundry.

Space and Balance: Living with two partners meant learning how to share space in new ways. Quinn had always had his routine — morning coffee, an early run, evenings spent reading or watching the news. Erika, however, brought an energy that disrupted that quiet. She played music while she cooked, sang in the shower, and moved through the house with an effortless presence that drew both Quinn and Kayla in. At first, it was a challenge — Quinn had to learn to make room for Erika's presence, and Erika had to learn when to pull back. But they eventually found that balance.

Jealousy and Reassurance: There were of course moments of tension, moments when one of them felt unsure or insecure. Quinn struggled at first, watching Kayla and Erika together. He had always known their chemistry was undeniable, but now, in this new context, he sometimes felt like an observer rather than an equal participant. Kayla sensed it before he could put it into words. One night, as they lay in bed, Quinn stared at the ceiling, deep in thought. Kayla rolled over and rested a hand on his chest. "You're not losing me," she whispered. "We're gaining something together."

The Passion That Held Them Together

If there was one thing that flourished in their first months together, it was passion. It wasn't just about sex, though the intimacy they shared was exhilarating. It was the connection — the newness, the intensity, the depth of exploration.

The nights they spent together were unlike anything they had ever known. Quinn had been hesitant at first, unsure of where he fit in when it came to the bond between Erika and Kayla, but, as time passed, the rhythm between them became seamless. There was no longer an imbalance; they flowed together effortlessly.

One night, after an evening of wine and laughter on the back patio, Kayla found herself pulled between them, Erika kissing her neck while Quinn traced slow circles on her bare thigh. It was moments like this — slow, deliberate, intoxicating — that reminded her why she had chosen this path. She needed them both, in different ways. And they needed her.

The passion wasn't just confined to the bedroom, either. It was in the way they moved through life together, in the shared glances across the room, the teasing exchanges over breakfast, the way Quinn and Erika took turns making Kayla feel like the most cherished woman in the world.

Challenges and Triumphs

There were hurdles, of course. The first time Erika had to go out of town for work, Kayla found herself feeling unexpectedly empty without her there. Quinn noticed the way she kept glancing at her phone, waiting for a message. He didn't say anything, but later that night, as Kayla curled into his chest, she finally admitted, "I miss her when she's not here."

Quinn had his own struggles. He sometimes wondered what people would say if they knew. He worried about how long they could maintain the facade, whether Zeke would start to pick up on things. But every doubt was soothed when he watched Kayla's happiness bloom in a way he hadn't seen in years. She was radiant, full of life in a way she hadn't been in a long time. That made every challenge worth it.

One of their biggest triumphs came unexpectedly. One evening, Zeke was struggling with homework, frustrated beyond reason. Erika sat down with him, her patience infinite, walking him through each problem until he understood. Kayla stood in the doorway watching, her heart swelling. Later that night, when the three of them curled up in bed, she whispered, "I can't imagine doing life without you."

A Love Rewritten

For the first time in a long time, Kayla felt whole. This wasn't the life she had ever imagined for herself, but it was the life that made sense. She had spent so long trying to choose between the two people she loved, only to realize she didn't have to.

As they settled into this new chapter, Kayla knew there would still be challenges ahead. But for now, in this moment, with Quinn's arm around her and Erika's hand resting in hers, she felt like she had everything she ever needed.

Afterword

Afterword

At its heart, The Space Between isn't about sex, but about love — the kind that challenges us, scares us, and sometimes demands we rewrite the rules we thought were fixed.

Kayla and Quinn's journey may be fictional, but the questions they face are universal: What are we willing to risk for truth? For passion? For the chance to feel fully alive?

If this story stirred something in you, I hope you'll carry that curiosity into your own life, and see where it leads.

Author Bio

About the Author

Jordan Marlowe writes contemporary fiction that explores love, desire, and the spaces where convention and longing collide. Fascinated by the complexity of human relationships, Jordan creates stories that blend emotional intimacy with bold explorations of passion.

When not writing, they can be found either writing in an out-of-the-way independent bookstore or taking their dog on a long hike to their favorite winery.

This is Jordan Marlowe's debut novel.

www.ingramcontent.com/pod-product-compliance
Lightning Source LLC
Chambersburg PA
CBHW071501110726
47908CB00003B/685